A Plan
of the Isle of
PORTLAND
— and —
parts adjacent
1710.

W E S T

The Fleet

Beach of Pebbles

B A Y

The

The Passage Houses

Wyke

THE MARE

Small Mouth

The Road

THE COMMON

P O R T L A N D

A

A

The Com...

Flag

D

The Castle

Weymouth Castle

to Weymouth

A

R O A D

AA. *Cliffs 40 or 50 feet perpendicular Hight from whence*
the Ground slopes steeply to the water side cover'd with rocks.
BB. *The Crane & Pier; above which are the rolls of Earth*
occasioned by the sliding down of the Rubbish from CC 1695 & 1708.

here the Island is 430 feet above
Water & at the Beell. 20 or 30 feet.

ISLAND OF STONE

ISLAND OF STONE

CLAIRE HUNTER

THE LONGSTONE PRESS

First published in Great Britain 1981 by
The Longstone Press Ltd
The Old Brewery, Tisbury, Wiltshire
Telephone No. (0747) 870747

Distributed by
Element Books Ltd
The Old Brewery, Tisbury, Wiltshire

Printed in Great Britain by
Eastern Counties Printers Limited
Ely, Cambridgeshire

ISBN 0 9507526 0 6

iv

FOR MY FAMILY

ACKNOWLEDGEMENTS

I wish to thank Miss Margaret Holmes, the Dorset County Archivist, and her staff at the Dorset Record Office, Mr G. West, Curator of the Weymouth and Portland Museum, and Miss M. Boddy of the Weymouth Library, for their invaluable assistance and unfailing interest in the project; and I am especially grateful to Miss Holmes for reading the original script. Also to Dr W. Hassall, formerly of the Department of Western Manuscripts at the Bodleian Library for making papers available to me there.

I must thank the Honourable David Erskine for allowing me to use material from his *Augustus Hervey's Journal*, and I am deeply indebted to Mr Dudley Pope for allowing me to use material from his excellent study of the trial of Admiral Byng and the events which led up to it, *At 12 Mr Byng was Shot*.

I must also thank Mr Eric Ricketts, R.I.B.A., for his help in describing the old buildings of Weymouth and identifying them on the plan; my editor, Mrs Miriam Hodgson, for her guidance, encouragement and unfailing patience; and Skylark Durston and his wife for their help, hospitality and friendship, which has made my research upon the Island a time of deep delight for me.

AUTHOR'S NOTE

The story of John Dainton and his family is fictitious, but in portraying the Islanders I have used the old Portland family names, and hope that I have brought to light the sterling characteristics of this splendid race of people.

In the eighteenth century the Island was a self-sufficient, closed community; strangers, referred to as "kimberlins", were unwelcome, and any who tried to flout the traditional customs were hounded out.

John Dainton's defence of his commander, in the face of the powerful opposition of the Establishment, together with his wife's connections with the stone trade, would have made the Islanders basically sympathetic towards his coming amongst them. The story makes clear how his subsequent actions established his position of trust on the Island.

With the exception of the imaginary Fleece House, placed on the present site of the new blocks of flats at Mutton Cove, all buildings and places, flora, fauna and customs are described as accurately as three and a half years' research has allowed. Many of the buildings and places may be seen today, and will I hope be of interest to the many thousands of visitors who come to the Island each year.

Throughout the book I have used many of the delightful Dorset expressions heard in my childhood, but I have not written them in the Dorset dialect, as to do so would only bewilder anyone unacquainted with its peculiar grammatical form.

CLAIRE HUNTER

Extract from a letter from the Honourable Horace Walpole to Sir Horace Mann.

Arlington Street, March 3, 1757.

I have deferred writing to you till I could tell you something certain of the fate of Admiral Byng; no history was ever so extraordinary, or produced such a variety of surprising turns. . . . . I never knew poor Byng enough to bow to; but the great doubtfulness of his crime and the extraordinariness of his sentence, the persecution of his enemies, who sacrifice him for their own guilt and the rage of a blinded nation, have called forth all my pity for him. His enemies triumph; but who can envy the triumph of murder?

Chapter 1

The library at Wanworth Priory was a pleasant room with long windows looking out on an ornamental knot garden that was famous throughout the neighbourhood and a centre of attraction for visitors on Public Days. Its fame was a source of great pride to Henry Dainton, seventh Baron Wanworth, the owner of the estate, but for his tall, fair-haired, younger brother, John, the knot garden represented something very different. Its intricate patterns of shaped flower beds and gravel paths, and the scents of the great variety of herbs permeated all his memories of childhood and the home that he loved. The home that was no longer his — that he might never see again. He stared angrily out of the library window, his hands clenched behind his back, and tried not to listen to the comprehensive homily being delivered by his elder brother. Suddenly the words "the Government needed a scapegoat" caught his attention, for they were the same words that had been spoken by another man — a man who had befriended him throughout his boyhood at sea, a man whom he had served under with the utmost loyalty, a man who had died before a firing squad that very morning.

The words evoked for John the scene that had taken place eight months ago in the Admiral's cabin of the *Ramillies*. He had been standing at the window there, staring angrily at the sunlit waters of the Mediterranean, their brightness in startling contrast to the shadowed coolness of the panelled cabin. Seated at the long oak table was the Honourable John Byng, Admiral of the Blue, Commander-in-Chief in the Mediterranean. At least he had been so until the previous evening, when the 50-gun *Antelope* had sailed into Gibraltar bearing shattering news. The Admiral had been ignominiously relieved of his command, condemned on the evidence of a single enemy dispatch, by a Government which had not even waited to read

1

his own account of the indecisive naval engagement fought off Minorca on 20 May 1756, in which, although not outnumbered in ships, he had been heavily outgunned.

Admittedly the Admiral's plan of action had somewhat miscarried, because Captain Andrews of the *Defiance*, the leading ship, had misunderstood his signals, and the early dismasting of the *Intrepid*, bringing her to a standstill, had caused havoc in the line. The French fleet was faster-moving, and as soon as the heavy guns of each ship had raked its immediate opponent, they drew off to leeward out of range, refusing further action.

The Admiral had felt in no position to pursue them, for as well as the helpless *Intrepid*, the *Defiance* and *Portland* were also badly damaged. Neither was the Admiral satisfied with the conduct of three of his officers, who had failed to go to the support of the damaged ships. Forty-five men had been killed, including Captain Andrews, whose misinterpretation of the signals had started the train of misfortune, although his subsequent gallantry in action was not in question, for the *Defiance* had inflicted severe damage on the heavier-gunned *Orphée* which had soon dropped to leeward. A hundred and sixty-two men had been wounded and a further 411 were sick, so the squadron was now lacking another 617 seamen, for they had been 500 short when they sailed from Gibraltar.

In fact the Admiral had found himself in an extremely vulnerable position, and so had decided to retire to cover Gibraltar, to land his wounded men there and to refit his ships, a decision unanimously supported by a Council of War.

On 25 May, the Admiral had sent off his dispatch to London, giving a lucid and detailed account of the action and making his future intentions clear: "I hope indeed we shall find stores to refit us at Gibraltar; and if I have any reinforcement, will not lose a moment's time to seek the enemy again, and once more give them battle."

But the Government had not waited to hear the Admiral's account of the action, or to discover his future intentions. They had hoped that a great naval victory might have momentarily assuaged their unpopularity, and in a despicable attempt

2

to divert public opinion away from their palpable shortcomings, they had sought a scapegoat in the Admiral.

It was the injustice of this dishonourable action that made Captain John Dainton seethe with fury, and he gave vent to his feelings in a spirited condemnation of the Government's conduct. The diatribe lightened the older man's heart and brought a smile to his drawn countenance: "I agree with all you say. It is a disgraceful business, but the Government need a scapegoat, and I, it seems, am to be it."

"Then you will need your friends to speak for you."

"I could not ask it of you — it would put your future promotion at risk."

"Since my present promotion is entirely due to your good offices, I shall not let that weigh with me. Besides, my ship will not be ready to put to sea for another month — if then — when you consider the appalling lack of dockyard spares here. I shall resign my command, and accompany you back to England."

"You are a good friend John, and I shall be glad of your company in Berkeley Square — the house seems so empty since Susannah died."

"Then that is settled, sir. I suppose I shall have to offer my resignation to Sir Edward Hawke, but if there is any difficulty perhaps you would backdate it."

The brisk words masked the deep sympathy John felt for his superior officer, for his ignominious dismissal was the last of a series of misfortunes that Admiral Byng had suffered of late. A lonely bachelor of fifty-two, he was not an easy man to be on intimate terms with, for his precise and rather pompous manner tended to keep people at a distance. John, who, at the age of thirteen, had been sent to sea under his command, knew that this intimidating manner was only a defence mechanism; but, unfortunately, outside the Admiral's family circle, few others realised this. The death of his mistress, Mrs Susannah Hickson, the widow of a respectable tradesman, in the winter of 1755, had been a great blow to the Admiral, for her comfortable companionship had given him the only real happiness he had known.

Sir Edward Hawke, anxious to do all in his power to alleviate the awkwardness of his mission, acceded to John's request without demur.

"But there is no need for you to resign your command, Captain Dainton. I have orders that all the officers serving in the *Ramillies* are to return to England, and as you were on board her at the time of the action I can rightly include your name with the others." He paused, and then said deliberately: "I find the Government's action over-hasty to say the least, but I must warn you that public feeling against the Admiral is being whipped up in the most disgraceful fashion, and he may not find it easy to clear his name."

"But surely, sir, when the Admiral's own dispatch is published in the *London Gazette*, people will understand that his actions were fully justified."

"Indeed I hope so," replied Sir Edward gloomily. "But I cannot say that I feel sanguine about such an outcome."

The interview did nothing to alleviate John's burning sense of injustice, and he had himself rowed over to the *Defiance* to talk the matter over with the one person in the Squadron whose sentiments matched his own.

Captain the Honourable Augustus Hervey was in a disgruntled mood, for besides the shocking news brought by the *Antelope*, he had troubles of his own. On the death of Captain Andrews, he had been appointed Captain of the 60-gun *Defiance*, but had accepted reluctantly, for he was an energetic character and had been really happy as the Captain of the 20-gun frigate *Phoenix*, for the work of being "the eyes and ears" of the Squadron exactly suited his restless nature, and gave him full scope to use his own initiative.

"I'm delighted to see you, John. This damnable hulk is no exchange for the *Phoenix*, I can tell you, and *that* as you know was in such poor condition that I offered it to the Admiral as a fireship: — Help yourself."

Augustus settled himself in a chair, a cynical expression on his determined countenance: "As for this other business — to send such an inadequate force so late, and then to turn on the

Admiral for not performing miracles with it. The whole thing disgusts me!"

John helped himself to a liberal measure of port, and moved restlessly towards the stern windows. Augustus watched him closely, for they were old friends. John's slim build was always a source of envy to him, for he was inclined to be corpulent, but today John seemed thinner than ever and his restless pacing reminded Augustus of some caged animal.

"For Heaven's sake sit down! It's me that needs exercise, not you — you look like a damned scarecrow already!"

Thus admonished, John laughed and took a chair opposite his companion: "It's this shocking news that makes me so restive. I hate injustice, and will never forgive the Government for their incompetence. You sent word by your brother last autumn didn't you?"

"Yes, sailed over to Leghorn to see Bristol myself. I actually gave him the names of the French ships being built at Toulon, and George Edgcumbe wrote twice in November giving their expected date of sailing."

"So the Government cannot pretend they were not warned of the French intentions. It is iniquitous! . . . They do nothing at all until March, but are now determined to put the whole blame on the Admiral. Sir Edward tells me they have even sunk to stirring up public feeling against him."

"So you have seen our new Commander-in-Chief?"

"Yes. I went to resign my command. I am determined to accompany the Admiral home."

"Resign your command! Did he accept it?"

"No. He was most kind, and has ordered me home with the other officers of the *Ramillies*."

"I am thankful to hear it. It would have been folly to resign when you have just completed such a successful independent command. Your crew will be sorry you are leaving though. The twenty that have been sent to me while your ship is refitting, are first-rate men, and the tales they have been telling in the messes — how did you do it, John? They worship you."

A look of real pleasure lightened John's face at this tribute, for it was true that his had been that rare thing in the eighteenth century navy, a happy ship. "It was quite simple. I treated them like men not animals, and did what I could to alleviate the appalling conditions they lived in. The filth and stench of the lower decks of the *Barchester* was indescribable. The pigs on the upper deck were far better housed! In consequence most of the men were lousy, and as for the food — I ordered the whole lot to be thrown overboard, and reprovisioned her myself out of my prize money." He glanced at his friend and the hint of laughter in his voice was reflected in his eyes: "It might pay you to inspect the holds of this damnable hulk as you call her."

"Thank you, I can imagine the squalor I should find! But your paternalism does not explain your excellent discipline. According to your boatswain, only one flogging was recorded in your log book in six months."

"But it does. I replaced brutality with reward for efficiency, and it was efficiency that enabled us to take prizes — and good luck of course. Well, I must be off, and I heartily wish it were back to my own ship, but somehow this other business must be gone through with."

Augustus rose and accompanied John to the entry-port: "I suppose there will be a Court Martial. Promise me that you will make the Admiral send for me as a witness. Together we may be able to do something for him."

"You may be able to, but apart from my brother Henry, I don't know many political figures — and I have never been one of Anson's favourites, as you know."

"Nor I, but I do know most of the political world. I don't envy you your voyage home in the *Antelope*, crowded in with half the officers of the Squadron and all the senior Army officers. The whole boat-load intent on saving their own skins, if I know anything of the matter."

Augustus was right in his prediction that the *Antelope* would be unpleasantly crowded, but the Admiral, although bitterly hurt at his dismissal, remained confident that he would be able to clear his name as soon as he arrived in London, and busied himself in composing a lengthy memorandum. John was a willing assistant, but found it increasingly difficult to be cheerful. He could not share the Admiral's optimism in the

6

face of Sir Edward's warning, but he had not the heart to tell the older man about the violent public feeling being whipped up against him — it would be time enough for him to discover that when they reached London.

The *Antelope* anchored off Spithead on 26 July to the relief of all aboard. John, watching Vice-Admiral Henry Osborn's barge approaching, felt a sudden lightening of heart, now the Admiral would have the comfort and advice of his own family, for Osborn's brother had been married to John Byng's sister, Sarah. But one look at Henry Osborn's grim demeanour as he asked to speak privately with Admiral Byng, and John's relief faded to be replaced by the blackest forebodings. Half an hour later they were realised, for Henry Osborn had been assigned the unpleasantest task of his career — to place his friend and relative under immediate arrest.

But within seventy-two hours a more shattering disaster occurred. Colonel Edward Byng, the Admiral's loyal but delicate brother had set out from London as soon as he received the news of the *Antelope's* arrival at Portsmouth, bearing the grim news of the vendetta against the Admiral. Worn out with anxiety, he had collapsed on board and died of heart failure the following morning.

It was indeed a terrible homecoming for the Admiral, but even his brother's anxiety and untimely death failed to shake his conviction that he would be able to prove his innocence. Confined as he was, he could not even make the funeral arrangements, so he ordered John to London with a dignified letter to the Admiralty, and confidently awaited his immediate release.

When he had delivered the Admiral's letter, John sought out Joseph Corder, a retired shipwright with whom he had often lodged. Corder was a swarthy man nearing sixty, whose house in Queen Anne's Gate was a popular venue for well-to-do naval officers on leave in London. He made John welcome saying that his most handsome suite of rooms was available, a suggestion John found very acceptable after his stifling quarters in the *Antelope*. Corder, ignorant of the reason for John's return to England, was soon regaling him with the latest anti-Byng gossip, but John cut him short: "Did you not read the

Admiral's own dispatch? Surely it was published in the *Gazette*?"

"I read it," replied Corder, "but it didn't make the matter no better."

John glared at him. "Nonsense! I assisted with the writing of that dispatch myself. It clearly showed that the Admiral's action was the only one possible under the circumstances."

"It may be as you say, Captain Dainton, but I didn't read it like that. I've still got the copy of the *Gazette*, I'll fetch it for you."

A horrifying suspicion presented itself to John, for Corder was a sensible man who had spent his life among ships and seamen. He seized the paper and read it in gathering fury. It was as he feared, the dispatch had been heavily censored, and every word proclaiming the Admiral's innocence had been cut out.

The bedchamber of the suite was furnished with a large, comfortable four-poster bed, but sleep eluded John. The censored dispatch had been the final dastardly act in a series of malignant manoeuvres designed to ruin the Admiral, and it seemed to John that men who would stoop to forgery, (for that was what it really was), would stop at nothing to preserve their own reputations. He felt helpless in the face of such opposition, that whatever he did it would be doomed to failure. And what could he do? At the end of four hours of restless deliberation he decided that there were two courses open to him. First he must seek an interview with Lord Anson, which he knew would do no good because Anson disliked him, but it must be gone through with, and then he must approach his brother Henry, who held an important position in the Home Department.

The knowledge that this second step would also be doomed to failure depressed John beyond measure, because it would be the cause of a serious family quarrel and it would bring into the open his long-felt, but hitherto unacknowledged contempt for his brother. The consequences of such a quarrel were impossible to estimate, but they would be far reaching, for John's children, George and Maria, had been brought up by Henry and his wife since the death of their mother two years earlier. There was only one other course — the course he was sure his brother Henry would recommend — to abandon his championship of the Admiral, and that course John rejected outright.

The interview with Lord Anson, First Lord of the Admiralty, had tried John's temper to the limit. He had been as outspoken as he could without having to resort to offering his resignation. That he had dared not do at the present time, in case he would not be allowed to be called as a witness at the Court Martial if he were no longer in the Service. So when Lord Anson had delicately suggested that to continue in his championship of the Admiral might be prejudicial to a future command, John had gritted his teeth, straightened his shoulders, and in a voice devoid of any emotion, had replied: "I am only interested in the truth and justice. I am sure Your Lordship will agree that these are not unworthy motives." Whereupon he had been summarily dismissed.

A call at the Home Department elicited the information that Lord Wanworth was away; it was believed that he had taken his family to Yorkshire to visit his wife's relations, and he was not expected in London again for at least a month. Frustrated, but somewhat guiltily relieved that the impending scene with his brother must be postponed, John decided that his best course would be to write to Henry setting out all the facts, and to send him a copy of the infamous dispatch marking the glaring omissions. The letter, which turned out to be a lengthy memorandum, took several days to compose, and it was with considerable relief, that he at last deposited it at the Mail Office.

London was unpleasantly hot and the dust and stench of the streets made John long for the fresh green fields of the countryside, so he decided to journey into Sussex on the chance of finding his beloved sister, Elspeth, at Wanworth, but before he could carry out this plan a new development occurred. Instead of being released, Admiral Byng was to be brought to London under strong guard, and be confined at the Royal Naval Hospital at Greenwich.

Another sign of the Government's relentless hostility, John thought bitterly, so he abandoned his plan of visiting Sussex, and took a boat to Greenwich on the morning following the Admiral's arrival there. The Admiral was pathetically glad to see him, for he had been housed in a bare room on the top floor of the Hospital, and had been told by the Governor that if he needed furniture he would have to buy it. John's indignation knew no bounds at this callous petty-mindedness; he hurried back to London and sent Hutchens, the Admiral's valet, down to Greenwich with clothes, furniture and other necessities.

On his next visit to Greenwich John found that the guards had been doubled. A week later he was told that he must leave before dusk, as no visitors were to remain with the Admiral after dark — not even his valet. The following week John arrived to find stonemasons placing bars over the window and chimney — a measure so absurd that the two men at last had something to laugh at.

In spite of all these indignities the Admiral remained calm, and bent his precise and orderly mind to the task of preparing his defence, aided by his devoted relatives and John. They worked unceasingly throughout the daylight hours, for the Admiral had at last come to realise that he was not fighting for his reputation, but his life.

Chapter 2

The Autumn of 1756 was one of increasing misery and disillusionment for John. He longed to be at sea again, but now realised that he was unlikely to be given another command, so what was he to do, and where was he to go? He felt he would no longer be welcome at Wanworth his beloved home to which he had returned whenever he was on leave in England, for Henry, his brother, had behaved exactly as John had feared he would; regardless of the principles involved, he had supported the Government's vendetta against Admiral Byng. There were his children to consider too, for what would the future hold for them if they had to leave the happy nursery they shared with their cousins?

John's wife Emma had died two years previously leaving him with a son and daughter, George and Maria. The children had lived at Wanworth since their mother's death, for Henry Wanworth for all his faults, was passionately fond of children. This fondness, combined with an overwhelming sense of the responsibilities and importance of his position as head of the family, had prompted him to make himself answerable for the upbringing of the motherless pair. George and Maria returned their uncle's affection, in their eyes he could do no wrong, for they were too young to see him in the same light as did their father and his sister, Elspeth.

Henry Augustus Clarence Dainton, seventh Baron Wanworth, was a portly man of medium height in his early forties, with pale protruding eyes and an air of considerable self consequence. At the age of twenty-two he had inherited a handsome fortune and a prosperous estate. These two acquisitions had ensured him a prominent place in local society, and had enabled him to satisfy a youthful ambition for a political career. The advancing years had brought him the reward of public office, for which he had secretly yearned. He discharged his duties with a painstaking thoroughness which earned him the respect, but not the affection, of his staff. Except in his love of children he was not a warm-hearted man, and his many charitable actions were dictated by his desire to be thought correct and worthy of his position.

In the eyes of his younger brother and sister, Henry was dull, pompous and wholly without a sense of humour, and all these unattractive characteristics had been strengthened by his marriage to the daughter of a bishop. Amelia Wanworth was a tiresome, insipid creature, whose life was wholly devoted to furthering her husband's interests. To this end she filled the house with those politicians and public figures she considered to be of the first consequence, most of whom John and Elspeth castigated as dead bores.

John knew that both Henry and Amelia had condemned him for his support of Admiral Byng — in fact Henry had called on him in his lodgings in London after receiving his letter to upbraid him for what he called his "quixotic foolishness", and to warn him against bringing the family name into disrepute. When John had refused to give way even if it meant risking his naval career, Henry had been horrified.

"Risk your career *and* mine for the sake of a man whose action, or should I say *in*action in failing to relieve the island of Minorca has greatly added to the Government's troubles! I must tell you, John, that I find your attitude irresponsible, selfish and wholly lacking in family feeling. You must consider my position — Amelia has had the excellent sense to entertain very influential members of the Government at Wanworth, it would be most undesirable for you to express such opinions there; and what of your children — what will they feel if their father is dismissed the Service?"

"My children are too young to be affected by malicious gossip," John had replied hotly. "Damn it, Henry, it is not as if I was penniless — I have an adequate independence even if I do have to leave the Service."

Not all Henry's arguments, and he put forward many, could persuade John to abandon Admiral Byng, and he left the interview shaking his head over the foolhardiness of a younger brother who refused to obey the dictates of reason and self-interest.

The rift between the two brothers widened during the autumn, and John came to realise that his loyalty would cost him both his career and his home. Various plans for living abroad passed through his mind and were rejected, for although he had revelled in the hot sunshine of the Mediterranean when he had been stationed there, he did not wish to live in such a climate permanently. There were English communities in Paris and the capitals of the Low Countries, but he hated cities, and the thought of being cooped up in one for the rest of his life was unbearable.

John was by nature a countryman, never so happy as when he was wandering gun in hand, through the fields and woods surrounding his Sussex home, but although Wanworth held a special place in his heart because it was the scene of his childhood, the area of England he loved the most was the south-western coastal district bordering the English Channel. The rugged cliffs of Cornwall; the softer red hills of Devon with their deep inlets, tree-lined and secret; the beautiful Torbay; on to Lyme Bay where the magnificent Golden Cap marks the beginning of the great sweep of shingle forming the Chesil Bank; the Island promontory of Portland; Weymouth Bay, and beyond, the chalk cliffs stretching eastwards to St Aldhelm's Head, their whiteness broken by the black outcrop of Kimmeridge shale. This was the area of England where his heart lay — the land he had dreamed of retiring to through those long night watches, as the ships of the line beat their way up or down the Channel — but was there sanctuary for him there now, or was some desert island to be his portion?

The chance phrase lingered in John's brain, but he failed to realise its significance until one afternoon when Mr Rapperley, his attorney, visited him to tell him the exact state of his financial affairs. These at least were a source of satisfaction, for after setting aside generous portions for his children, John had more than enough for his own needs, indeed he had sufficient to command all the luxuries of life. Much of this wealth he had inherited from his father, but his wife had brought him a substantial dowry as well.

"What was the original source of this money?" John asked Mr Rapperley, whom he had not seen since shortly after Emma's death.

"The original sum was obtained from the sale of shares in the Portland stone quarry belonging to the late Mrs Dainton's great-uncle, who was childless," replied the attorney primly.

John stared at him, then rose and searched in a cupboard until he found a roll of maps and charts. Selecting one of the south-western coast, he stared down at it, seeing in his mind's eye the Island promontory of Portland — that bare and wind-swept plateau of limestone standing out into the English Channel, only joined to the mainland by a narrow strip of shingle. For a few minutes he continued to study the chart, then he turned impulsively to the attorney.

"Mr Rapperley, I have a commission for you. I cannot leave London at present, so I want you to go to Portland immediately and find me a house there, — preferably to lease."

It was the attorney's turn to stare.

"Go to Portland to find you a house! But Mr John, you are surely not going to live there! I've not been to the Island myself, but Mr Gadsby, the Weymouth attorney who was in charge of old Mr Gilbert's affairs, said it was a terrible place — nothing but a barren plateau!"

"I certainly *am* going to live there, and it is nonsense to call it a barren plateau, its pastures support thousands of sheep."

"But Mr Gadsby said its only communication with the mainland was by a ferry, and that was often unusable because of the strong currents and terrible gales."

"I *don't want* any communication with the mainland — and as for gales, I have lived through plenty of them at sea." Then seeing that Mr Rapperley was looking really distressed, John added: "Don't try to dissuade me. You can tell me nothing about the Island that I do not already know — I have anchored in Portland Roads a score of times."

Seeing that nothing could recall his client to sanity, Mr Rapperley collected his papers together and said: "Very well,

I will set out for Weymouth tomorrow, but I hope you will not regret this folly."

John smiled disarmingly and patted the older man on the shoulder. "I shall not do so, but find me a house quickly, for I want everything settled before I have to face my brother. Travel post, and take some warm clothing with you, but unless one of Mr Gadsby's gales blows up, you need not sleep on the Island — the Golden Lion in Weymouth is a tolerable hostelry, and of course I will pay all your expenses."

Stunned by the fact that his favourite client was now adding feckless extravagance to folly, Mr Rapperley tottered away, his only consolation being that he felt it was most improbable that he would find a suitable house available.

However, a month later he called again at John's lodgings bringing with him the lease of Girt House, lying between Easton and Wakeham: "It's a Jacobean house," he explained, "very old-fashioned and inconvenient; but the only one available that I thought suitable for a gentleman to reside in. I have brought a water colour of it to show you."

John studied the painting with growing delight. The house was a tall, three-storeyed stone building with a slate roof, high arched gables surmounted by ornamental finials and attractive mullioned windows. Various outbuildings were attached to it, lending solidity and strength, and it stood in an open position in the centre of the Island plateau, and would, John knew, have commanding views over the English Channel. He turned to Mr Rapperley, his face alight with pleasure. "I cannot thank you enough, you have relieved my mind of a great burden. I shall be very happy to live in this house for the present."

"It is a pleasant house," Mr Rapperley conceded. "And I hope I have done right in hiring a couple to prepare it for you, and act as caretakers. It has stood empty for some years, and is sadly in need of refurbishing, but the woman promised to have it scrubbed and polished for you within a month."

"Admirable, and what are the terms of the lease?"

The two men spent some time discussing business, but when Mr Rapperley rose to take his leave, John could not resist

15

asking him with a hint of mischief: "And what did you think of the Island?"

Mr Rapperley pursed his lips and said primly: "It is no fit place for a gentleman of culture to reside in, Mr John, but I will concede that it has a wild beauty of its own." And with that admission he left.

The acquisition of the Girt House was a source of great relief to John, now at least he would have somewhere to go when the sickening business of the Court Martial was over. Somewhere where he could find peace, and where the fatal division in his family would not be the latest *on-dit* being discussed in every drawing room. The thought did cross his mind that the Islanders (well known for their dislike of strangers) might not welcome his presence any more than his brother did, but he dismissed it — he had troubles enough for the moment without dwelling on hypothetical ones.

Only one event lightened the November gloom. John, returning from Greenwich one fog-bound evening, was met by Corder with the news that a visitor had called and was waiting to see him. "A Captain Hervey, sir," said Corder, taking John's dripping greatcoat.

John's face lit up with pleasure and he went swiftly into the drawing room: "Augustus! I cannot say how delighted I am to see you! Corder has looked after you I hope."

"Yes indeed, you would seem to be most comfortable here." He looked narrowly at the younger man's drawn face: "But don't you eat anything? You are thinner than ever. Have you been ill?"

"No, I am perfectly all right. It was cold coming up the river tonight, that's all." John moved towards the blazing fire, and spread out his hands to warm them.

"Then it's this damnable business of the Court Martial that has reduced you to a skeleton I suppose," said Augustus, settling his well-covered limbs in a comfortable chair.

"Yes — I feel I am hitting my head against a stone wall," confessed John, helping himself to brandy from a side-table and refilling Augustus's glass.

"Don't tell me the new Administration are as bad as the last lot?"

"Well they don't seem to be any better. I had hoped that when Newcastle resigned at the end of last month and Temple replaced Anson at the Admiralty, that the Admiral's confinement might be made less rigorous. But no! Even now when the days are so short all visitors have to leave at dusk."

"Scandalous! How does he take it?"

"With his usual unimpaired calm, but he feels it very deeply. He will be delighted to see you, Augustus, and there is so much to be done preparing his defence, all these witnesses to be questioned. Besides you may be more successful than me at rallying help for him."

"Of course I will do all I can, but when I went to St James's this morning, the King did not bother to speak to me, although I was the only officer there just returned from the Mediterranean. You didn't get much help from your brother Henry, I gather."

"My brother Henry," said John, in tones vibrant with contempt, "behaved exactly as I expected he would. All he cares for is his position at the Home Department which he has retained; and of course, all his worst traits are encouraged by that odious wife of his."

"I haven't met her. Is she a dreadful woman?"

"Well, Elspeth and I have always thought so. She is one of those women who are forever prating about their charitable works, but when called on to act with charity herself, she is always found wanting."

Augustus chuckled: "Not quite in my line I think! But another thing, these anti-Byng placards and circulars that are everywhere — do you think we should have anti-*Government* pamphlets printed, and get the newspapers to publish articles defending the Admiral's actions?"

"Now that you are here to publicise them — bring them to people's notice I mean, I think it would be an excellent idea. If you can make the arrangements, I will be responsible for the costs."

Augustus eyed him quizzically: "Plump in the pocket are you John? Lucky fellow."

17

"Well I have more than enough for my own needs — and those of my friends."

Augustus took his leave and strolled towards his mother's house, musing over the strange contrast presented by the Dainton brothers. Henry insufferably pompous and self-centred; John so generous and loyal, with that quiet charm that concealed the inner strength of the man, whose qualities of leadership had been so brilliantly proven in his recent command. Yet it was Henry who had retained his political post, while John's career seemed likely to be ruined unless the Admiral could be honourably acquitted. A look of grim determination crossed Augustus's somewhat cynical features — tomorrow he must go down to Greenwich, and then set about doing everything in his power to bring about that acquittal.

The trial of Admiral Byng began at Portsmouth on 28 December on board the *Royal George,* but by that date Augustus had come to share John's view that justice would be the last thing the Admiral could expect to receive at it. The Duke of Newcastle had resigned and Lord Anson had left the Admiralty Board, but their influence was still immense, and their determination to protect their reputations relentless. To make sure that the Court Martial would condemn Admiral Byng, four admirals known to be Government supporters suddenly brought their ships into Portsmouth, and since they were the most senior officers there it was certain that they would be chosen to sit on the court.

As if the sudden appearance of the four admirals were not proof enough of the Government's intentions, another story was circulating the drawing-rooms, that Admiral Boscawen dining one night at Sir Edward Montagu's house, had bluntly said: "Say what you will, we will have a majority, and he will be condemned." So it was in a mood of deep pessimism that John and Augustus travelled to Portsmouth; they had done all they could for their erstwhile commander, but could it prevail against such opposition?

The trial was a protracted one, for in spite of the partiality of the members of the court, nothing could be found on which to condemn the prisoner. In fact the Admiral became so convinced that he must be honourably acquitted that he cut short his defence, and Augustus having given his evidence, found Portsmouth so intolerable, that he returned to London.

It was not until the 27 January 1757 that the court finally announced their verdict — that Admiral Byng was guilty of "an error of judgement" and that under the 12th Article of War he should be executed.

The Admiral had gone on board the *Royal George* in a jubilant mood sure of an acquittal, so when the infamous verdict was communicated to him privately before entering the court room it momentarily stunned him, and the members of his party. To John's intense admiration the Admiral retained his stoical calm, saying after a short pause: "Well, I understand; if nothing but my blood will satisfy, let them take it."

The Government majority on the court had done their work well John thought contemptuously, bringing in the sentence their masters had ordered and then adding a plea that the prisoner should be pardoned to salve their own consciences. He found the knowledge that men could sink so low infinitely depressing, but the enormity of the sentence soon outweighed all other considerations in his mind, for the 12th Article of War ordered death for cowardice, negligence or disaffection, but on all these counts the Admiral had been acquitted. Could it be an illegal verdict? The Admiral, he knew, would want nothing to do with a pardon, he had declared so before entering the courtroom, but an illegal verdict was a different matter. Saying that he would shortly return, John took leave of the Admiral and set out for London to carry the news to Augustus.

It was not until dawn was breaking, that John at last reached his lodgings; Corder had left a letter for him on a silver salver, it bore the Admiralty seal. He opened it mechanically, certain of its contents. It was an order for him to attend at the Board of Admiralty on the 10 February 1757.

The question of the illegality of the verdict raged throughout the month of February, the matter was discussed everywhere and questions were asked in Parliament, but Government influence was too strong and won the day.

On the 10th of the month John attended at the Board of Admiralty where he was told there was no new command available for him at present, so he would be placed on half-pay. In reply, John relieved the pent-up emotions of the past months in a comprehensive commentary on their Lordships' conduct, and tendered his resignation.

The Admiral's execution was fixed for the 14 March, so John made a miserable journey to Portsmouth to bid his chief farewell. His spirits were momentarily lightened by finding that the ingenious Augustus was planning an escape, but the Admiral would have none of it. He was cheerful and composed, and was filling his last days by making long inventories of all his possessions and naming those to whom they were to be given; he was also preparing a memorandum to be published after his execution. John's admiration for his coolness knew no bounds, and his last visit to the man who had befriended him since his boyhood left him heartbroken. He returned to London in the faint hope that a last minute reprieve would be granted, and called at the Admiralty early on the morning of the 14th, only to learn that the execution was to take place at noon. He could not bear to remain idly in the city, so he set out for Wanworth immediately, and was riding through the pleasant Sussex countryside when the fatal hour approached. The warm spring sunshine did nothing to alleviate his misery, neither did the thought of the coming meeting with his brother.

John reached Wanworth in the early afternoon, and found Henry in the library and was obliged to listen to a patronising homily on the folly of his actions. He endured this in stony silence, staring out of the window and reliving the tragic events of the past months. He was so deeply engrossed in this reverie that Henry had to repeat his question "What are you going to do now?" twice, before he could collect himself sufficiently to answer. Finally, he turned, and squaring his shoulders, said quietly: "I have made my plans, so you need not think that I shall embarrass you by staying here for long. I have leased a house on the Island of Portland, and shall go there as soon as I have sorted through my possessions here."

Henry received the news with evident relief, although he would have preferred his brother to have left the country altogether, — he was about to enumerate the advantages of a prolonged continental tour, when a shout from the knot garden, "Papa, Papa," interrupted him. George and Maria were coming up the terrace steps from the knot garden carrying baskets of primroses. Catching sight of their father standing in the library window, they called to him excitedly, and then ran along the terrace to enter the house by a side door.

Henry hardly had time to say urgently to John: "It would be wicked to take the children to such a place — they must remain here," before the door opened and the children ran in to greet their father. John lifted them up in his arms and held them close, his mood lightening as he answered their excited questions. He sat down with one on either knee, delighting in their idle chatter. "Papa, you must see my new pony," from George, and "Papa, you must see my beautiful doll's house, it is in our new nursery," from Maria.

"A new pony, a new doll's house, new nurseries, how your uncle spoils you," said John.

"Uncle Henry said the old nursery wing was cold and damp, so we are in the new wing now," said George proudly.

"I had forgotten you were intending to build another wing, Henry," said John: "So nobody uses the old east wing now."

"Oh, yes," said George, "Aunt Elspeth lives there."

A sudden silence fell upon the room, it was broken by Henry saying testily: "You chatter too much children. Run along to Nurse now — your father will visit you later." Realising that something had made their father furiously angry, the children slipped away. Henry turned deprecatingly to John: "It might seem a trifle unusual I suppose, but we have so many visitors here now, that we felt Elspeth would prefer her own apartments."

"Abominable, Henry, abominable!" and seething with fury, John strode out of the room.

21

Chapter 3

Wanworth Priory, a rambling building standing at the head of a sheltered valley, had come into the possession of the Dainton family after the Dissolution. Humphrey Dainton, the originator of the family fortunes, had been a successful Bristol merchant and shipowner, dealing in furs from Newfoundland. In the Tudor period the transition from merchant to landed gentleman was by way of the law and ownership of property. Edward Dainton, Humphrey's son, practised at Lincoln's Inn, and extended his father's business by trading in furs from Russia. With their accumulated wealth, the father and son purchased the Priory of Wanworth and its productive acres from the Crown, and set about turning it into a sumptuous family house as a visible sign of their entry into the gentry class.

The family were prodigious builders, and as each successive owner prospered he left his architectural mark upon the building, until it had become a vast conglomeration of wings and courtyards, many differing in design and materials — along the way it had lost its beauty but retained its grandeur.

The South front had been rebuilt by the 4th Baron, and consisted of a suite of lofty reception rooms overlooking the terrace, with spacious bedchambers above them reached by a superb carved stairway. This block formed the principal living quarters for the family, and was connected to the east wing, Humphrey Dainton's Tudor building, by the cloisters, the only part of the Priory in its original state.

The afternoon sun did not penetrate the cloisters, and John drew his naval cloak closer round him as he hurried across the covered walk to reach the refectory, the Great Hall of the Tudor house. Even when the life of the house had centred around it, the Hall had been cold and draughty, but now that it had long been relegated to an armoury it held an air of melancholy, accentuated by plaster flaking from the walls, and rust coating many of the ancient weapons. This dreary scene did nothing to alleviate John's wrath — he strode over to the arras, jerked the heavy curtain aside, and stepped into a flagged passage. From a room on the right, the sound of a harpsichord greeted him and he hurried forward and lifted the latch, sure that here at last he would be warmly welcomed.

Elspeth Dainton was seated at the harpsichord, but she turned as the door opened, and rose awkwardly to greet her brother: "John, my dear — oh, but how glad I am to see you — you have been in my thoughts so much!"

"Elspeth, Elspeth, it's so good to see you again!" said John, clasping her to him warmly. "But what are you doing shut away in this wing? I was never so angry in my life, as when Henry had the effrontery to tell me that he thought you *preferred* being here!"

Elspeth smiled: "Poor Henry, his conscience troubles him over what is really the best arrangement for us all."

"How can you be so forgiving, Elspeth? *For the best* indeed! It is the most disgraceful arrangement that I ever heard of!"

"No, John, don't take it to heart so, — the thing is that now Amelia has become a political hostess the house is unbearable; always full of the sort of people you and I heartily dislike, and try as she will, Amelia cannot turn a blind eye to my infirmity, and makes me feel like something from a raree show."

"Does she indeed!" said John wrathfully: "And why does Henry permit such behaviour? — besides, I thought she was supposed to be so saintly, she is forever prating on about her charitable works!"

"I know, she is the most tiresome creature, but do not let us waste more time considering her foibles. Tell me your news — have they really carried out the death sentence on the poor Admiral?"

"Yes, it was to take place at noon today." At the mention of the Admiral, all John's troubles crowded in upon him again, the more so as he watched his sister drag her body across the room to sit near the fire.

Elspeth Dainton had been born a cripple, her left leg was three inches shorter than her right, and the ankle was deformed. As a small child she had been forced to endure a heavy iron weight attached to her foot in the hope that it might stretch the leg. This harsh treatment had only aggravated the trouble by causing her knee-cap to swell and stiffen, until her left leg was stiff from knee to foot, and she could only drag her body awkwardly along with the help of a stick. If her body was infirm, her brain certainly was not, she was blessed with a sense of humour, sparkling wit and a great love of music.

As a small boy John had adored the golden-haired little sister who endured such terrible pain, inflicted, to no purpose that he could see, by unfeeling adults. He would comfort her by taking her with him on fishing expeditions, wheeling her to the lake in a barrow he had constructed himself. She returned his love, and suffered the jolting of his barrow uncomplainingly, for the highlights of her miserable childhood were the times she spent with him.

Although John had been able to spend very little time with Elspeth since going to sea, they had remained very close to each other, his marriage had not loosened this tie, and his bereavement had strengthened it. The thought that he must now tell her that he might never see her again, was too difficult for John to voice, but Elspeth sensed that he was troubled, and said in her gentle way: "My dear, have you thought what you are going to do now, for if so, do tell me about it."

John sat down beside her on the faded couch, and told her of his plan for going to Portland, and of the leasing of the Girt House. He described the Island to her as best he could remember it, and ended by saying: "My going there should satisfy Henry, for there is no society on the Island, in fact there are very few people at all besides the Portlanders themselves."

"No society on the Island", she echoed, her face alight with excitement: "Oh, John, could you not take me there with you?"

For a minute John stared at his sister, and then shook his head: "I cannot think it would be right," he said slowly.

"Oh, do not say so," she replied. "I would try not to be a trouble to you — and I could see you were made comfortable."

He smiled down at her: "You would never be a trouble to me. It is not that, Elspeth. It is just that it would be wrong to condemn you to live in such a solitary place."

"If you will not take me with you, you will condemn me to a solitary life here, and that would be a great unkindness."

"But Henry would never agree to it," he said, wavering.

"You are mistaken. Henry will no doubt raise many objections, but he will certainly come round to such a scheme. Amelia will see to that!"

"Does she dislike you so much? Then perhaps it would be better for you to be away from here, — but are you sure this is what you would truly like? You are not just saying it for my sake?"

"Stupid!" she said, the inflection in her voice turning the term into an endearment: "Truly, I would like it above all things."

John went to bed deeply troubled and depressed. The injustice of his commander's death, and his own failure to help him weighed heavily on his mind; and he had been horrified to find Elspeth living alone in the east wing. But was it right to take a gently bred and cultured woman to live on an isolated island. She was only twenty-three, and would have been known as a beautiful, desirable woman if it had not been for her tragic disability. His children must remain at Wanworth, of that he was certain, however sad he might feel at parting from them. But Elspeth? — at last, several hours later, he came to the conclusion, that if she really wished to go with him, he would take her, and do everything within his power to make her happy.

In the event, Elspeth was proved right, Henry raised many objections, but allowed them to be overruled too easily for John and Elspeth to believe him to be sincere, while Amelia could scarcely conceal her relief. All four felt the awkwardness of the situation should not be prolonged, so John and Elspeth accepted Amelia's offer of her own carriage for the journey and the use of a second coach for the baggage, and within a week were ready to set out for Weymouth.

They travelled by easy stages, putting up for the first night at Winchester. It would have been possible for them to reach Weymouth late on the second day, but John sensing that the incessant jolting of the coach had tired Elspeth more than she would admit, insisted that they put up for the night at The Antelope at Dorchester. When she protested that she would be well able to manage the remaining eight miles after a rest and refreshment, he overruled her saying that it would be a pity to travel on in the gathering dark, as he rather thought a fine view of Weymouth Bay and the Island would be obtained from the next ridge. The landlord, not wishing to lose the custom of a lady and gentleman travelling in style with their own servants and quantities of baggage, added his voice to John's: "Indeed sir, the view from the Ridgeway is famous — if it's clear that is, but as you can see, sir, there's a mist creeping up now, and the descent is treacherous after the winter rains."

This news clinched the matter for John, they would put up for the night. He ordered the best bedchambers and a private parlour, and there they presently partook of an excellent dinner of capons with a rich sauce, a loin of veal, cheesecakes and a floating island.

The next morning dawned bright and clear, although a sharp east wind was blowing. Elspeth, who had an enquiring turn of mind, had questioned the landlord closely as to the local antiquities. He had pressed a pamphlet upon her by the Rev. Edward Stukeley and from this she was able to point out to John, as they left the town, the Roman amphitheatre of Maumbury Rings, and further on they saw the great earthworks of Maiden Castle. The beauty of the Dorset scenery filled Elspeth with delight, and as the horses laboured up the long ascent of the Ridgeway, she looked forward with eager anticipation to her first glimpse of the Island that was to be her home. Nor was she disappointed, at the crest of the ridge John directed the coachman to draw the horses to the side of the road, and she descended awkwardly from the chaise to stand with him and admire the colourful panorama spread out below them.

26

The land descended to the sea in a series of grass-covered ridges, their outlines broken by hedges and small clumps of trees. The town of Weymouth and Melcombe Regis was far smaller than she had imagined, just a line of houses on a narrow strip of land behind which was a great lake surrounded by marsh. At the seaward end of the lake tall masts silhouetted against a further ridge indicated the harbour, and beyond this Elspeth caught a glimpse of the famous Chesil Bank running out in a narrow peninsula to the Island itself.

The sharp east wind caused the blue sea of the bay to be broken by white crests against which the bright sails of fishing boats stood out as tiny flecks of colour. To the west of the Island the sea reached out to the horizon, but the dominating feature of this sparkling panorama was the Island itself, its north face rising in a steep green slope to a lookout tower, in startling contrast to its western face where the high white cliffs rose in dramatic grandeur from the sea, and stretched away southwards.

Elspeth's attention was riveted; the beauty of the countryside conveyed an air of healing and welcome, but the Island was none of these things, it was austere, impregnable and remote. Instinctively she shivered. What sort of welcome would she and John find on that windswept, inhospitable rock fastness she wondered? John had mentioned the Islanders' well-known hostility towards strangers — supposing it was extended to them? Often when Henry and Amelia had been entertaining in the lofty, new reception rooms at the Priory, the sound of music and laughter had drifted across the draughty cloisters to her lonely apartments in the east wing. Then the damp stone walls had seemed like a prison to her, isolating her from those who were physically able to dance and make merry; but at least at Wanworth she had been warmly welcomed in the humble homes of the estate tenants. The thought that even the friendship of the poor might be denied to her now momentarily appalled her. She found herself shaking, and put up her hand to draw her cloak closer round her shoulders to disguise the fact from her brother, and the thought of h'm immediately steadied her for she was not facing the world alone any more, she was with John, and he had chosen the Island for the very reason that disquieted her, it *was* a place apart, even if only a few yards of shingle separated it from the mainland. She turned to her brother to offer him what comfort she could, but it was not needed; the sight of the sea had exerted its life-long hold on him once again, and his face was glowing with pleasure: "It's a splendid prospect, isn't it?" he said, smiling down at her.

"Indeed it is, dearest," she replied bravely, "let us go down and explore the town."

The landlord of The Golden Lion ushered Elspeth into a private parlour, assured her of his every attention, and left to supervise the bestowal of her trunks in the best bedchamber. She sank down on the settle and stretched out her feet to warm them at the blazing fire. A youthful serving maid entered, bearing a tray loaded with coffee, a dish of pastries, a strong-smelling cheese and freshly baked bread. She offered to carry a can of hot water to the bedchamber if madam so wished, but Elspeth felt unable to make the effort to climb the stairs until the arrival of Skinner her own maid; she sank back exhausted against the cushions of the settle, but soon the warmth of the fire and the smell of the coffee revived her spirits, and when John entered she said cheerfully: "This is a most comfortable inn, and such excellent service."

"Yes, Spicer is a capital fellow. I always came here when at anchor in the Roads. Ah, he has remembered my partiality for Blue Vinny cheese, I see. You must try some Elspeth, it's a Dorset speciality, and then we will go out and explore the town a little, if you are not too tired. Spicer is sure to have a gig I can borrow."

Elspeth came to the table and although she felt the cheese to be rather strong, she pronounced the pastries to be delicious, and the arrival of the slower moving baggage coach bringing the faithful Skinner to her, was all that was needed to complete her comfort. Presently Elspeth summoned Skinner to assist her to her bedchamber, while John sought out the helpful Spicer to borrow a gig.

"Of course, sir! At once, sir, I'll tell the boy to harness Bess, who is not only very quiet, but well used to tooling around the streets here. I am that sorry to see your lady sister is so crippled, sir. Have you thought perhaps she might benefit from the sea water bathing? Mr Allen, a gentleman from Bath, was recommended to try it by his physician some seven years ago, and has been coming here ever since, in fact he has had a special bathing machine built for his own use. His house is just across the harbour, sir, the double-fronted one — No. 2, High Street."

John had told Spicer that he would require accommodation for an indefinite period, as he had no intention of subjecting Elspeth to exile on the Island until he had made the Girt House tolerably comfortable for her. Spicer had evidently made up his mind that his new clients would become leading figures in Weymouth society, and John felt unequal to the task of disabusing him of this conception; instead he asked the landlord what places he should take his sister to see, but this only set the loquacious Spicer off again on his own theme.

"Well, sir, if you drive over the bridge and turn left, you will pass Mr Allen's house on the right, then go up High Street and on the left you will see the Old Rooms Inn, it's an old Tudor house that belonged to a Mr Giear who was Mayor and M.P. for the borough in the last century. It is used for the Assemblies now organised by Mr Delamotte — whom no doubt you will wish to meet. There are other old Tudor houses on the other side of the road — it's the best time of year to see that part of the town, sir, for in summer, the Creek (we call it the Cove) is noxious for a lady, and then there's the Town Hall, a quaint old building with a bell tower in High West Street, half way up the hill to Wyke."

"Back in Melcombe, sir — well, if you drive up St Nicholas Street you will come to the White Hart Inn on the corner of the new thoroughfare, what we used to call the Coneygar ditch — it used to be an old fortification running from the sands to the backwater, but it had become a regular sewer and so was filled up last year. Sir James Thornhill, the artist, spent much time at the White Hart, and of course you will be anxious to see his famous painting of the Last Supper in St Mary's Church — " but at this point John, who had no particular bent for historical studies, interrupted, saying firmly:

"Spicer, I shall never remember the half of what you have told me, so I will just take my sister for a drive, and then perhaps tomorrow, when I have to visit Portland on business, you would drive her yourself, and point out all these notable features."

"Of course, sir, I would deem it an honour, sir. Here is your lady sister, sir, at the door now."

John was thankful to see Elspeth, and when Spicer had helped her to mount into the gig, he drove off at a brisk trot. When safely across the bridge, he turned a laughing face to her and said: "Phew! I am glad you appeared when you did. I am not historically-minded you know, and Spicer was about to relate to me the history of every building in the town. I only managed to stop him by saying that perhaps he would drive you round himself tomorrow. I only hope it will not be too much of a penance for you, for of course he will be very upset if you do not wish to go now."

"Poor man! Of course I will go with him, I do not at all wish to hurt his feelings when he has been so helpful. Besides it is a capital scheme, for *I* really am interested in old buildings, and I know you are not."

So they spent a happy hour together exploring both Weymouth and Melcombe, and John pointed out what features he could recall from Spicer's monologue. In fact the town had many quaint old buildings, including the ruins of a Dominican Friary, though sadly some of the buildings on its southern side had degenerated into tenements. Elspeth fell in love with the old shops in St Mary's Street, particularly Mr Hibb's fish shop at No. 45, for this was a delightful Tudor building with a projecting upper storey resting on protruding wooden beams, and latticed bay windows with carved wooden supports. Over the doorway the date was carved, 1550, but she was disappointed with St Mary's Church which stood next to it — indeed the church was a humble three-gabled building, distinguished only by a wooden bell turret, and a bracketed street clock.

To Elspeth the whole expedition was delightful — to be with John whom she loved, was pleasure in itself, for he never made her feel her infirmity was anything to be hidden away and ashamed of, and she was touched by Spicer's solicitous but deferential attention to her welfare. For the first time for years, she was being made to feel a person not an object of pity, and the treatment brought a glow of happiness to her face, and a lightness to her spirits. John noting this, thought that perhaps his enforced resignation from the navy had not been entirely without reward, and went to bed more cheerful than he had been since his return from the Mediterranean the previous summer.

Chapter 4

The next morning John set out to visit the Island, the weather was fine and clear, but with the easterly wind still blowing. John rode slowly up the steep hill from the town, and rested on the crest to study the extensive view before him. The rolling country between Weymouth and Portland was uninhabited except for the village of Wyke Regis, whose ancient church situated on high ground, served as a landmark for miles around. Cantering on John soon reached the church, and turned south to descend the slope to Smallmouth and the ferry.

The ferry was commanded by the Passage House built on the northern side on a sandy bank of land. Before it a thick tree trunk had been sunk into the ground, and from this a stout rope was suspended over the sea passage, and was used to haul the boat across the water. The tide was low and the passage appeared to be about forty yards wide, but John could see that at high water it would be considerably wider.

The ferry boat bearing two passengers, had just set out from the northern side, and as John could see several people awaiting it on the Portland shore he realised he would have to wait some considerable time. The Passage House itself did not look very inviting, so he decided to pass the time by riding a short way along the sandy shore of the Fleet, that peculiar tidal lake which stretched westwards to Abbotsbury where there was a swannery. When he returned, the boat was just landing its passengers from the Island, all of whom carried heavy baskets of fish. A small boy was struggling with a barrel, from which he offered to sell John a freshly-caught live lobster. John refused the offer, and asked the ferryman to take him across at once, as he could see the tide had turned and the sea looked rough and choppy. The passage was safely negotiated, and he rode along the narrow strip of sand and shingle leading to the Island itself.

Nearing the Island, John passed a wide area of marsh, which he remembered was known locally as the "Mare", and beyond this on the lower slope of the hill, was the village of Fortuneswell. John could see that above the village the track divided to the east and west, so he stopped to enquire the best route to the plateau and the hamlet of Wakeham. His enquiries were answered civilly enough, but with a certain wariness that reminded him forcibly of the fact that strangers were not welcome here.

Above the village he turned westwards as directed; here the condition of the track was appalling, with deep ruts which must have been formed by the constant passage of heavy carts, though John found this strange, as on his previous visit the quarrying had been confined to the north-eastern corner of the Island close to the loading piers. The recent heavy rains had filled many of these ruts with water, and turned the rest of the surface into a slippery sea of mud. He climbed slowly, picking his way carefully along the side of the track, beside which were loose boulders of varying size. As he climbed higher, the wind became stronger, roaring along the side of the hill and bringing scuds of rain to add to his discomfort. He glanced up to see a dark bank of cloud approaching from the east, and before he reached the western limit of the track, the storm was upon him. Regretting that cloaks were no longer in fashion, he pulled his hat firmly down on his head, buttoned the collar of his greatcoat closely about his throat, and rode on with his eyes on the treacherous ground.

In an effort to minimise the steepness of the incline, the track wound back on itself in a zig-zag. John had just negotiated the bend, when a warning shout caused him to look up. Advancing down the hill towards him was a low wooden carriage on which was strapped a huge block of stone, pulled by four horses with two others harnessed behind; with horror, John realised the reasons for the carter's warning — the carriage was out of control. A second carter behind it, was shouting and cursing at the rear horses who obediently sank to their haunches, and strove with all their might to pull back the carriage — evidently they had been trained to this terrible task. Momentarily they

33

succeeded, but even as John watched in frozen fascination, they began to be dragged relentlessly forward.

The straining, sweating creatures, their nostrils dilated with fear, evoked for John a vivid mental picture of another scene when men, not horses, had strained their every sinew to save themselves and their fellows. A sudden tornado in the Caribbean Sea had torn the anchor chain apart, and the wind and current were driving the man-of-war on which John was the junior lieutenant of the watch, towards a dangerous reef. He heard his captain's order: "Mr Dainton, throw out emergency anchors, port and starboard." He saw again, the deck awash from the onslaught of the storm-driven waves — the gang of men, lashed together for fear that one of their number might be swept overboard, straining to unloose and pay out the heavy coils of rope. One gigantic wave had sent him sprawling against the rails, to be brought up, with a savage jerk that tore the breath from his body, by the rope that he had lashed to a stanchion. Above the roar of the wind, he could hear the thunder of the waves breaking on the ever-nearing reef — nothing it seemed could save them, but suddenly the onward rush of the ship was checked, and he heard the bosun's voice: "Port anchor holding, sir." In a flash his mind swept forward to the present, and he could see what was missing in the scene before him — there was no drag.

Leaping from his horse, he tossed the reins over its neck, not bothering to tether it, and seized the nearest loose boulder he could lift. This he placed at an angle in what he judged to be the path of the carriage wheels and then forced it into the ground. He turned and found another and jammed this against its fellow, so that the two together formed an arrow-head.

His action was not a moment too soon, for the cart was gathering speed and the rear horses, for all their striving, were being inexorably dragged forward. The carter was desperately trying to control the front horses, for the trace horse, feeling the load bearing down on him, was trying to bolt. For a few seconds more the fate of the animals hung in the balance, and then the near wheel of the cart entered the trap formed by the boulders,

34

rammed up against the arrowhead with a tremendous jolt, stuck fast and held.

The elderly carter busied himself quieting the trace horse, but the boy in charge of the rear horses just gazed spellbound at the motionless cart — then he lifted a chalk-white face to John: "Yer stopped it!" he gasped wonderingly, and John realised with sickening clarity that such an occurrence was only too frequent.

The older man looked up from holding the horse's head: "Ay, sir, you was quick, very quick."

John smiled disarmingly: "Well, I've spent my life at sea, so I've had a lot of experience of drag. Rest your team awhile, and we will think out how best to lay out a series of these stops to get you down the hill safely. You've a spare coil of rope I see, that we can fix to suitable boulders which will help." He held out his hand as he spoke, and after hesitating a moment, the carter gripped it: "Matthew Wiggatt, sir, and that's Sparrow Pierce. Don't stand there gawping, Sparrow! Look to them horses!"

Thus abjured, the boy went to soothe the rear horses, while John studied the incline, and presently he and Wiggatt laid out a series of stops. Before removing the first stop, John instructed the carter to attach one end of the coil of rope to the axle tree and the other to one of the huge boulders embedded in the side of the track. The man looked faintly surprised at receiving what was so clearly an order, but he did what he was told without demur. He studied John covertly with growing respect; at first sight he had supposed him to be a stone merchant, but no kimberlin (as the Islanders called all strangers from the mainland) that he had ever seen had bothered his head over the welfare of carters and their teams; he felt a growing curiosity about this astonishing stranger.

An hour later, after a series of jolting halts, the team reached the gentler part of the slope, and Matthew Wiggatt drew them to a halt: "I can manage now, sir, thanking you. The descent is not so steep from here on. Sparrow, run back up, and fetch the gentleman's horse."

35

While the boy went back up the hill to fetch the horse that they had tethered to a boulder above the bend, John leant against the cart, and ruefully surveyed the ruin of his clothes. He looked up and found Wiggatt studying him with interest: "I look a regular vagabond, don't I? I only hope I won't be turned away from my own door."

Wiggatt stared at him in blank astonishment: "Was you coming to stay on the Island then, sir?" he enquired.

"I wasn't thinking of staying today, but within a short time I hope to do so. I have taken the lease of a house in Wakeham — the Girt House."

Wiggatt's jaw dropped. "Is you the gentleman that has taken the house? My nephew Crabber, and his wife, have been there this past month putting the place to rights. A real finicky gentleman we expected, from the way the London attorney gave his orders that this and that must be of the best. But you'll be wanting to get along, sir, and get dry, and if I were you, I wouldn't try to cross to the mainland today, for by the time you get back to the ferry old Joe Gorman will likely as not refuse to fetch you, for there is a strong wind blowing up, and the passage can be nasty."

"Perhaps it would be best if I stayed," agreed John, gloomily surveying the heavy banks of dark clouds gathering in the east: "But I've no change of clothes with me, and there may not be much food in the house."

"Never you fear, sir, there'll be plenty for dinner! Well, here's Sparrow with your horse now, sir, so I'll bid you good-day. Your best way will be down Wide Street, past the new church, and into Weston." With this enigmatic statement the carter set his team in motion, and Sparrow, having seen John re-mounted, set off after him.

John made his way slowly up the hill again, his mind busy with the implications of the incident he had just witnessed. Sparrow's wonder and relief at the stopping of the cart, had made it clear that horrible accidents were frequent, but surely it would be possible to design some sort of iron "shoe" that would prevent the wheels from turning? Various ideas chased themselves through John's inventive brain, and he was still considering and rejecting them when he reached the plateau.

The weather had steadily deteriorated; dark clouds hung low over the plateau and the driving rain decreased the visibility still further, accentuating the grimness of the treeless prospect. The high ground to the north-east was pasture land, heavily stocked with small, hardy-looking sheep, but southwards, John could make out a cluster of cottages, (which he supposed must be the hamlet he was seeking) and beyond them were two windmills, whose sails seemed to vanish in the low clouds. Slightly apart from the cottages, was a large house with a gabled roof, which John presumed must be the Girt House, but he was puzzled by its position, for Wiggatt had told him to take the road past the church, and this building stood away over to the west of the plateau. Certainly a road led past it, and a wider one than the track to the hamlet — though there was little to choose between the appalling condition of either of them.

Straining his eyes through the driving rain, John could just make out the outlines of another straggle of houses beyond the church to the south. Perhaps that was the hamlet he wanted? But there was no sign of a large house amongst the distant dwellings. John looked eastwards again, and wondered if Wiggatt had given him those directions because of some hazard lying between his present position and the gabled house, making a circuit necessary. There was no-one about that he could see to ask, so finally with a shrug of his shoulders, John set off down the wider road leading to the church, at least it would be interesting to see that at closer range, he thought to himself.

If anything had been needed to emphasise to John the difference between the Portlanders and their fellows on the mainland, the siting of their new church provided it. He presumed the Islanders must have valid (for them) reasons for their choice of site, but to an outsider they were inexplicable, for apart from a single group of cottages, the church stood quite half a mile from the next hamlet, exposed to the full force of the wind from whichever direction it blew. Certainly the position was a commanding one with splendid panoramic views over the Channel, but the underlying reason for the site could not have been the need for a landmark, for two lighthouses had been built at the Bill for that purpose in 1716. Casting his mind back to the village of Fortuneswell, John could not recall seeing a church there, so if this building was to be the parish church for the whole Island, the largest part of the congregation would have to toil up the hill to the plateau to reach it. They were indeed an extraordinary race, John thought, but if Wiggatt was typical of them, then they were admirable too. For John liked what he had seen of the carter with his splendid physique and natural intelligence, but whether any stranger would ever understand them was another matter, and certainly he did not understand why Wiggatt had given him directions, which he felt sure, were leading him away from his goal; for as he neared the next group of cottages, he could see no large building amongst or near them. Wiggatt must have deliberately misled him, but why? Finding no answer to this question, but sure that the house he had first thought to be the Girt House, must be the one he sought, John turned his horse's head into the driving rain, and sought for a track that would lead him back to the eastern side of the Island.

Ten minutes later he drew rein before the tall solid-looking building he felt sure must be the Girt House. Its central porch which extended to roof level and ended in a steep gable, gave directly on to the roadway, and before he could dismount, the door opened and a tall young man with the unmistakable stamp of a seaman came out to greet him: "Good-day, sir. You'll be Captain Dainton, I expect. But you are wet, sir! If you would step inside, there's a fire in the hall. I'll just take the horse round to the stable."

John was faintly surprised by the man's ready acceptance of his unheralded appearance, but he was only too glad to comply with the suggestion that he should enter the house and warm himself by a fire. He found himself in a square panelled hall with a stone fireplace at one end, and a wide oak staircase with square newels and panels of carved strapwork. Although the fire was burning brightly, the hall felt cold and damp, and John shivered as he stood before it in his dripping clothes;

he bent to put another log onto it, and was surprised to see that these were sawn planks.

Very shortly the young man came back into the hall, carrying a can of steaming water, and said respectfully: "Name of Wiggatt, sir, Crabber Wiggatt. You ought to get out of those clothes, sir. If you will come with me, a fire has been lit in the bedroom." He led the way up the wide oak staircase to a large bedchamber, panelled like the hall below, but here the stone hearth surround had been fitted with an iron shield, and a coal fire was burning in a basket grate. Wiggatt opened a door in the panelling revealing a spacious clothes closet, which to John's surprise, contained several coats, and piles of neatly folded shirts, breeches, stockings and other articles.

"Great Heaven," exclaimed John. "Did these things belong to the last owner. Why did he leave them here?"

"He left the Island very hurriedly, sir," said Wiggatt, in a repressive tone of voice.

"But why did he not send for his baggage?" asked John, his curiosity aroused: "Did he meet with an accident or something?"

"Not that I heard of, sir," replied Wiggatt. "But he left secretly and never returned. You see, sir, he was a young man, the grandson of the merchant who built this house — but he would not honour our Island custom."

The matter now being abundantly clear to John, he busied himself with the selection of various items from the closet, and instructed Wiggatt to hang them before the fire to warm, while he threw off his soaking, mud-stained garments. Wiggatt collected these, and said: "If you will excuse me, sir, I'll see to the table. My wife will have dinner ready in about half an hour."

"I am afraid I have put you to a deal of trouble," said John. "I did not intend to stay on the Island today, or I should have sent word ahead of me. Some soup, and cold meat if you have any, is all I need."

"That's all right, sir. There's fresh fish for dinner, and the snalters are back."

"Snalters are back!" echoed John, mystified.

"Yes, sir, we always say that they come back on the first

39

foggy day in March," and with this extraordinary remark Wiggatt left the room.

John sighed, and returned to his toilet — he was beginning to feel out of his depth, and whether "snalters" were fish, fowl or beast was likely to remain a mystery until dinner was served.

He glanced idly out of the window, and several matters immediately became clear to him, for Sparrow Pierce was coming through the wicket gate leading to the stable, sucking a straw. So it was Sparrow who had been attending to his horse! Suddenly John laughed to himself, that was why Matthew Wiggatt had sent him a mile or so out of his way — so as to give Sparrow time to reach the house by some shorter route, and give Crabber and his wife warning of the impending arrival of their new master. That was why the rooms felt so cold although the fires were burning brightly — they had only just been lit. Above all, that was why Crabber had accepted his arrival so placidly.

John fell to wondering just what sort of reception he would have had, if the incident on the hill had not taken place. If the Wiggatts had thought that he had any connection with the owner of the clothes he was now wearing, it might have well been a very chilling one John thought, for the one thing that he did know and understand about the Portlanders, was the importance and sanctity of their Island Custom.

For generations the Islanders had inter-married amongst themselves, but the ceremony of marriage only took place after the woman was found to be pregnant. Courtship was a time of probation to see if the union would produce children, if after a reasonable period there was no sign of a child, the couple would part without any stigma being attached to the woman, who was then free to be courted by another man. If a woman did become pregnant, then very formal proceedings took place between the two families, and marriage always followed. If an Island girl was courted by a stranger, then the Portlanders expected the stranger to honour the custom, and the few that did not were hounded out of the Island.

John well remembered the occasion, when one of his seamen, happy at finding a Portland girl very willing to receive his advances, was horrified to find, on his return to the Roads six months later, that her family had assembled in force to protect her honour, and were threatening to throw him over the cliff unless the marriage took place immediately. After this incident, his men preferred (not unnaturally, considering the discomforts and privations of the lower deck) to go ashore in Weymouth.

John wondered if the Portlanders had threatened to throw the former owner of the house over the cliff — well, he had no sympathy with the young man, and was not sure that he approved of his choice in coats either — they were too narrow across the shoulders for comfort. He delved into the closet again, and emerged with a richly embroidered silk dressing gown. "The very thing," he murmured to himself, holding it up to warm before the fire.

A discreet knock heralded Wiggatt's welcome announcement that dinner was served, and John descended, warm and refreshed, to find that "snalters" were delicately flavoured wheatears roasted on a spit. "We just take what we need for ourselves in the spring," Wiggatt told him. "But in the autumn the boys catch them in their hundreds in stone traps, to sell in Weymouth." The simple but delicious meal was accompanied by some excellent claret, but when Wiggatt had set a decanter of port on the table he asked if John would require anything further that evening: "For if not, sir, the weather's fairing up and with your permission, I'll be off to my pots."

John had intended to make a thorough inspection of the house that evening, but he felt that his unexpected arrival had already given the Wiggatts a good deal of extra work, so he agreed to this request readily enough, saying that he would retire early and make a leisurely inspection of the house on the morrow. He was slightly surprised by the look of evident relief on the young man's face, but supposed that Wiggatt must supplement his wages by selling fish — perhaps he had indigenous relatives to support? He pondered over the question of how much local labour he would be able to employ, but several glasses of excellent port, after the exertions and surprises of the day, soon caused him to feel soporific, so he decided to seek his bed before he fell asleep in front of the fire.

41

The bedchamber fire threw a welcoming glow upon the panelling, the carved four-poster bed looked comfortable, and a warming pan had been passed between the sheets. John drew back the heavy curtains and opened the casement; he was glad to find that the wind had dropped and the moon was just rising, so Wiggatt should have no difficulty in launching his boat. The comfort of his bed made him think of Elspeth, and whether this house would make a suitable home for her; turning the matter over in his mind, he fell into a deep and dreamless sleep, only to be awakened several hours later by a curious rasping sound intermingled with the low murmuring of men's voices.

Chapter 5

John was wide awake in an instant, and curiosity compelled him to get up and creep to the window to identify the source of the rasping sound he had heard. The moon was at the full and shed a pale light upon a most extraordinary scene. The fields in front of the house were bounded, like all the fields on the Island, by stone walls. At intervals along these walls four men were working pulling the stones apart, the curious rasping sound occurring as each stone was lifted from its fellows. The nearest man was only some twenty yards from the window, and when the bottom of the wall was reached a heavy oblong stone was wrenched from its place revealing a hole in the ground.

The four men did not leave their places when the work was completed, but all stood gazing southwards, silent and alert, as though straining their ears for some expected signal. Presently from the group of ancient elms beyond the ruins of Rufus's Castle, the only wooded area on the Island, came the hoot of an owl repeated twice. The man nearest to John cupped his hands to his mouth and gave three soft hoots in reply. Leaning forward to obtain a better view, John heard the sounds of muffled hooves and saw a string of donkeys approaching from the trees. Along the road beneath the window they came, each animal heavily loaded with kegs slung either side of its back. On entering the field the procession divided, and the animals were led to the workers at the wall.

Swiftly and silently the kegs were unloaded and lowered into the holes. The two men nearest to John had just replaced the heavy base stone when a volley of shots rang out from the direction of the Bill. The sound startled the grazing donkey into emitting an ear-splitting bray; cursing his beast, the man hastened from the field and disappeared towards Easton. The other donkey owner followed, and the wall builders bent to their tasks with frenzied energy.

As each man completed his task he left the field without speaking to his fellows, and within a short space of time John was looking down upon an empty scene. He was about to retire to bed when the click of the wicket gate sounded below him; peering down he saw a young woman come through it and glance anxiously up and down the road. Seeing nothing the woman, whom he supposed must be Crabber's wife, pursed her lips and gave a fair imitation of a sea-gull's cry. She stood still listening intently, but no answering call came to break the eerie silence that had descended upon the scene. The woman heaved a deep sigh and turned back into the house.

John continued to stand at the window, his mind busy with the implications of all that he had just witnessed. So Crabber was a smuggler, his anxiety concerning the weather had not been for his lobster pots, but for the illicit cargo he was to bring ashore from some free-trading vessel. And the holes beneath the walls, were they always used, or would the cargo have been secreted in the Girt House but for his untimely arrival? Anger surged through him at the thought, for if it had been discovered, he as the owner of the house, would have been implicated in another scandal.

Where was the boy anyway — what could have delayed his return? His wife had evidently expected him back before now — those shots — could he have been killed or captured? Instinctively John glanced out of the window again, and his attention was immediately caught by something moving across the further field. He leaned forward, his gaze intent upon the distant figure which advanced slowly with a peculiar swaying gait. His brows drew together in frowning concentration as he followed the progress of the figure to the wall, on reaching it the man leaned against it for a while apparently exhausted. After a short rest, the man struggled to climb over the wall, but seemed to be only using one arm. With difficulty he negotiated it, and stood upright for a moment, the moonlight falling directly upon his face — it was Crabber. Then he collapsed and fell into an inert heap on the bank of the near field.

John's first reaction on recognising his newly acquired man-servant was one of fury. That the Wiggatts should engage in

44

smuggling, when he was paying them generous wages for caretaking, was inexcusable he thought, and if they continued in their trade, it might lead to his own unwitting involvement. The whole business was repugnant to him — he could not condone smuggling, although he could appreciate that many of those who engaged in it often did so to prevent themselves from starving — but the Wiggatts could not plead that excuse. Should he dismiss them? If he did so, how could he be sure that any of the Islanders whom he might engage, would not secretly follow the same trade — smuggling was in their blood. It might be, that if he dismissed the Wiggatts, no-one else on the Island would be willing to serve him, and how could Elspeth manage the house with only their own personal servants to wait on them.

Elspeth, his crippled sister, what a fool he had been to bring her to such a place, to a house that was probably used for storing contraband, with servants who left it at night to go smuggling: how would she go on amongst such people, whose actions might, at the least, expose her to the indignity of endless questioning by law officers, and at the worst to involvement in a public trial. After her sheltered existence at Wanworth, it was unthinkable, and as to what Henry would say if he discovered that his brother and sister were sheltering a gang of smugglers — he shuddered to think of it. At all costs he must make sure that Crabber Wiggatt was not found wounded in the house — law breaking was better than that.

He leaned out of the window again to see if the man had moved, but the body was still there — John's gaze swept on, scanning the fields bordering the cliffs, and what he saw there drove him to frenzied activity.

The sky was now clear, and the moon at its highest, the brightness of a thousand stars adding brilliance to its light, illuminating the fields that stretched to the cliff edge, and there silhouetted against the sparkling sea, was a line of tiny figures moving purposefully inland — the Preventives were searching for their quarry.

John scrambled into breeches and a shirt, his mind cool and alert, he snatched up an elegant pair of ivory-handled scissors from the dressing-stand, seized one of the fine linen sheets from the bed, and was off down the stairs.

His footsteps brought a white-faced woman into the hall: "Get water on to boil, have a thick blanket ready in the hall, and then extinguish the lights," he ordered, as he drew back the heavy bolts from the oak door, and sped across the road into the field to where he had seen the prone figure lying.

Wiggatt had come round from the attack of faintness that had overwhelmed him, and was lying propped against the stone wall, staring at his left arm which was bleeding profusely from the shoulder. He looked up at John with mingled fear and suspicion.

"Don't try to speak — just do what I say! They are searching the cliff edge for you, and we have very little time." A few judicious snips with the scissors, and then the linen sheet was torn into serviceable strips, John placed a thick pad over the wound, bound it up tightly and strapped the useless arm to the man's chest: "That should keep it from bleeding until I get you within doors — it's essential we don't leave a trail of blood behind us."

Placing Wiggatt's good arm round his neck, and his own round the man's waist, John propelled him back to the house. Mrs Wiggatt had obeyed his orders, and was standing holding the door open. She bolted it, and then burst into tears at the sight of her husband's bloodstained clothes and bandaged arm.

"Calm yourself woman!" John commanded. "If we are to save your husband from the Preventives there is work to do. He is too heavy for me to carry up the stairs by myself, we must make a stretcher for him from the blanket."

"Where can we hide him?" wailed the woman. "They will search the house."

"Not if I can prevent it," said John grimly, "but if they do, there's one place they won't look for him and that's in my bed."

"Put him in your bed with all that blood, sir, that wouldn't be right!" exclaimed the woman with amazement.

"There is no time for right and wrong now," replied John curtly. "Your husband will have to explain his part in this disgraceful expedition later. Do what you are told!"

Silenced, the woman assisted John to convey the wounded man upstairs and onto the bed: "Strip off his clothes, and hide them in the closet," John ordered, going swiftly to the window. He had just been in time, the line of men was only two fields away now. He drew the heavy curtains close, and went back to the woman kneeling by the bed. She turned an anguished face to him, and whispered: "What can we do for him, sir?"

John spoke reassuringly: "He will be all right, but we must fob them off, before we can set about making him more comfortable. Get back to your own quarters now, and into your night-clothes. I hope they will not question you, but if they do, say that he has gone fishing with a friend off Chesil, and that you don't expect him back till morning. On no account say that he went out from Church Ope Cove, for if they know which boat is his, they may have set a guard on it."

"I can do that sir, and thank you, sir." Unable to say more, the woman cast a loving glance at her husband, curtsied and withdrew.

John threw off his shirt and breeches, and consigned them to the closet. He got into his night-shirt again and pulled on a tassled night-cap, grinning to himself. Then he drew the bed curtains around the young man's still form, settled himself comfortably in an upholstered chair, and blew out the candle.

He did not have long to wait; within a few minutes he heard orders barked out, and booted feet tramping on the road. Then a heavy knock sounded on the door, accompanied by the stentorian demand: "Open up, in the King's Name."

John let a full half minute pass, then he rattled the bed-curtains, lit the candle and pattered over to the window. Throwing open the casement, he leaned out and said in tones of furious indignation: "Who are you? And what are you doing knocking up God-fearing citizens at this time of night?"

The men below him looked up in blank amazement — there were about a dozen of them with a sergeant and one young officer, who gaped at John and said apologetically: "Sorry to trouble you, sir, but we are looking for a wounded smuggler. A cargo of contraband was landed earlier tonight, we tried to intercept the gang and one man was wounded."

47

"Well, what of it?" barked John, "That's your business, not mine, and no reason for you to come demanding respectable householders to open their doors. Why do you think I should know anything about your contraband, or are you suggesting that it is hidden under my bed! And just what" (catching sight of two men emerging from the garden) "are your men doing on my property? How dare you order them on to it, without leave. Where is your warrant?"

"I have no warrant, sir. I did not realise the house was occupied by others than Islanders," said the young officer, taken aback.

"Outrageous!" fumed John, warming to his part. "Outrageous! Preventives walking in and out of private property at will without so much as a search warrant, on the flimsy excuse that the owner is not present! The authorities cannot be aware that such liberties are being taken with the rights of private ownership. Furnish me with your name and rank immediately, for my brother Lord Wanworth at the Home Department shall hear of this."

"It's Manvers, sir, Lieutenant Manvers — I am very sorry, sir, I can explain — "

"Not at this time of night," interrupted John, "I shall very likely catch an inflammation of the lungs, if I have to stand here any longer in my night-shirt! You may wait on me in the morning, at ten o'clock, and it's an apology I want, not an explanation!"

With this he closed the casement with a snap, and drew the curtains across it again so sharply that the rings rattled together. He went back to the bedside and stood still, straining his ears, to catch the murmur of voices below; presently he heard orders being issued and then the tramping of feet. He trod softly to the door, and stole along the passage to where another window overlooked the road. Keeping well into the shadows, John counted the men as they marched off towards Easton — fourteen, and the officer and sergeant. He gave a deep sigh of relief, evidently his bluff had succeeded in setting the young officer's suspicions of the house to rest.

He watched the departing figures until they were lost in the shadows of the night, then he stole along the passage to a window that overlooked the garden and stable yard, but there were no soldiers lurking there. For a further hour, he kept his vigil to make sure that none returned to spy on the house, and then he sought out Mrs Wiggatt, whom he was thankful to find had recovered from her shock, and was very ready to obey his orders: "Bring hot water, and some clean linen, and we will do what we can for your husband now," John told her.

He went back to the bedchamber to find that Crabber was awake and looking far stronger. With Mrs Wiggatt's aid, John washed the wound, dressed it with some basilicum powder discovered in the dressing-stand, and bound it up tightly again. Luckily the ball was not lodged, but had gone right through the fleshy part of the arm, and it was the loss of blood that had caused Crabber to swoon: "There, that should do for the present. Now you had best get some sleep before we present you to the Excise men, but first, where does your uncle Matthew Wiggatt live?"

"In Weston, sir."

"That is fortunate, for at first light your wife must go and fetch him, and she should be able to do so without being seen by anyone if she goes by the windmills. The thing is that we must make it seem as if you have cleaned out the stable and groomed my horse. If your uncle could do it before he goes to the quarries, then when the Preventive officer comes, he will find you in the stable, with a curry comb in your hand, apparently having done all the work. Do you think you will feel strong enough to stand by the horse while he questions you?"

"Of course, sir," replied Crabber, grinning. "I won't let you down, sir, after what you've done for me."

"All I shall say on that head for the present," said John sternly, "is that I do not intend to be compromised like this in the future — if you wish to remain in my service you will have to give up smuggling. But now you had best get some sleep where you are — if your arm should break out bleeding again, it had better do so in this bed."

"I will light the fire in the parlour, and heat some coffee, if you would care for it, sir?" offered Mrs Wiggatt, eager to make amends for their folly. She hurried off to do this, and presently, having seen John comfortably settled before a blazing fire, she set out to find the carter.

Matthew Wiggatt was in no way pleased at being roused from his bed, but when he had heard the tale he exclaimed: "I knew him for a right 'un when he stopped the carriage yesterday, but to rescue young Crabber — well, I never looked to be grateful to a kimberlin, but it seems it's the hand of Providence he's come here. I'll come right back with you Mary, and do what I can."

Meanwhile, though warm and comfortable, John was finding sleep elusive. One of the problems that beset him was how to cover up the tracks made when he had brought Crabber back to the house, and it was also probable that there would be blood on the wall, and on the bank beneath it, where the young seaman had swooned. No satisfactory solution presented itself to him beyond praying for a heavy downpour of rain. He decided that he must go out early and inspect the field, and if, as he feared, there was a lot of blood about, he must somehow stop the Preventive officer from seeing it — but how this was to be achieved he could not imagine. He mentally rehearsed his interview with the officer, and in so doing fell asleep.

He woke to a delightful medley of sound made up of men's voices, children's laughter, the jingle of harness and the stamp of hooves. A glance at his watch told him that it was past seven o'clock, and he rose guiltily and went to draw back the curtains. He stared out of the window, and then began to shake with silent laughter, for all his problems had been solved.

The cultivated fields of the Island were farmed in strips according to the ancient feudal practice, and it seemed that in the field opposite the house each strip must be owned by a different man, for there were some twenty or thirty of them assembled, accompanied by swarms of children who were racing about, and jumping on and off the walls. There were six horse-drawn ploughs which were apparently going to be used by all the men in turn, for while six were already at work, the

50

others were lounging about in groups on the banks. Evidently the greater part of the day was to be spent in work and jollity, for at strategic places, the walls were covered with children's shawls, rush baskets, stone jars of liquid refreshment and gaily coloured handkerchiefs containing food.

The door opened, and Mrs Wiggatt entered bearing a loaded tray: "Good morning, sir. I thought you might like an early breakfast by the fire. Uncle brought some fresh-caught mackerel, and he's made all ship-shape in the stables, and given me a hand in the house, so we're all aforehand."

After a substantial breakfast John felt much better, he instructed a pale but indomitable Crabber in his part, and then made a thorough inspection of the house. This proved to be a disappointment, for although it was commodious, he did not think that it would be suitable as a permanent home for Elspeth, as all the rooms seemed to be on different levels, and he knew that she found climbing stairs particularly trying. However, he ordered Mrs Wiggatt to make ready what he thought were the most attractive rooms, and then settled down by the fire to compile an extensive list of necessary repairs and alterations. He was still at work on this when Lieutenant Manvers was announced.

The boy was clearly ill at ease, he began by making a formal apology for disturbing John, but it was apparent that he was much aggrieved at being censured for endeavouring to carry out his duty. It was clear that he loathed the Islanders who constantly outwitted him, and as his forces were totally inadequate for the task he had been set, John began to feel quite sorry for him. He unbent a little, and tried to draw the boy out, for he particularly wanted to know if there was any hard evidence to connect Crabber with the smuggling gang.

Lieutenant Manvers thawed visibly; he had put John down as a pugnacious old meddler, who would no doubt wreck his career by reporting his failure to produce a warrant to the authorities, and as he had very little faith in the real, as opposed to the academic, desire of the landowning class to stop smuggling, he felt his position was hopeless.

The night had been a great disappointment to Lieutenant Manvers, for once he had actually witnessed the landing of illicit cargo, instead of finding that false information had lured him to the wrong side of the Island as was usually the case; but how the gang had mysteriously melted away on the side of the cliff he could not imagine, except through witchcraft, which he felt, was quite probable, as the Islanders were notorious for their belief in the Black Arts.

A question from John concerning the amount of co-operation he received from the naval cutters, set any lingering suspicions to rest, and he poured forth a diatribe against the Islanders and their nefarious dealings, from which John was able to extract the information he wanted, namely that the whole population was under suspicion rather than any individual. Whereupon he rose and said: "Well, we had best ask my man Wiggatt whether he has any information that may help you."

Lieutenant Manvers knew from past experience that any information offered by an Islander would be deliberately misleading, but he felt too much in awe of John to say this, and so followed him meekly to the stables.

Here they found Crabber vigorously grooming the horse, or so it seemed from the fact that the smock he was wearing was generously covered with dust and hairs, (his uncle Matthew having thoughtfully left it for him to put on.) When questioned, Crabber assumed an expression of bovine stupidity, and said that he could not have heard anything as he had been fishing off Chesilton all night. He gave it as his opinion that the patrol might well have frightened the Frenchies into dumping their cargo, and he recommended the Preventive officer to put his patrol on to searching the shore.

"While the donkey train is led openly through Fortuneswell, I suppose," replied the Lieutenant sardonically, which remark quite endeared him to John, but caused Crabber to reiterate his innocence, and add, in aggrieved tones, that he was only trying to be helpful.

"Helpful!" repeated the Lieutenant, thoroughly incensed. "No-one on this God-forsaken Island knows the meaning of that word," and forgetful of his manners, he stalked out of the stables followed by John.

He took his leave, apologising for his show of temper by saying that a prolonged tour of duty on the Island would certainly end in him being sent to a mad-house. He then mounted his horse, glared at the jollification taking place in the field, and cantered off towards Easton.

John went back to the stable to find Crabber weak but triumphant. "That numskull couldn't snare a rabbit," he prophesied. Whereupon John sternly reminded him that he, Crabber, had almost been snared the previous night, and that furthermore he felt a certain amount of sympathy for the wretched boy, who was only trying to do his duty and, like everyone else, had his living to earn. But such broad-minded sentiments were totally alien to Crabber, and John left him gasping in outraged astonishment.

"Cor!" muttered Crabber to himself, suddenly feeling faint. "Feel sympathy for a Preventive officer — the man must be queer in his attic."

Chapter 6

Elspeth thought that John looked tired and depressed when he returned to The Golden Lion for dinner, but she refrained from commenting on this, merely saying that she was glad that he had come back to dine with her as she had ordered dressed crabs to be served, which she knew to be one of his favourite dishes. She kept up a flow of amusing small talk about her sight-seeing expeditions, and was delighted to see that by the time he had consumed the crabs, a pigeon pie and a delicious white wine syllabub he was beginning to look more cheerful.

"And what do you think I have discovered, dearest," she said, when the covers had been cleared and Spicer had set fruit and nuts on the table, together with a bottle of his best port, "the most excellent music shop, where the proprietor, a Mr Wainwright, was most helpful. He had several clavichords there that he had built, and also one of the new pianofortes made by a Mr Silbermann in Hamburg. Apparently he had procured it, after a great deal of trouble for, as he put it, 'a great lady of the district,' and then she had not liked it, so the poor man had been unable to recoup his expenses. Apparently the only person who had shown any interest in it was a Colonial gentleman — a most knowledgeable musician Mr Wainwright thought, but I was especially taken with it and, oh John, I do hope you will not think me recklessly extravagant, but I have bought it."

"Elspeth, I'm delighted, really delighted that you have done so, for it will help pass the time for you here. The thing is that there are several repairs that need to be done in the house, and if you would be happy to stay here for a while, you need not be subjected to the noise and inconvenience of workmen in the house. Perhaps we should call on this Mr Delamotte, Spicer mentioned, and write our names in his subscription book? Assemblies are held in the Old Rooms Inn, I gather, and you might make the acquaintance of this musical gentleman."

"I am afraid there is no question of that, because Mr Wainwright discovered that he was only staying in the town and he returned to America shortly after his visit to the shop. But you need not fear that I shall find the time long here, for there are so many interesting things to see, besides Wainwright has promised to deliver the pianoforte tomorrow." She rose and went to the settle beside the fire: "But tell me all about the house, dearest. Was it a disappointment to you, or are there other difficulties about us going to live on the Island?"

Touched by her kindness and selfless devotion, he began to relate the happenings of the previous day. He passed over the incident of the horses and the stone waggon lightly, as he knew it would distress her, and embarked on a detailed description of the house and the flight of its previous owner. He then recounted the smugglers' nefarious dealings, but ended his tale of the night's adventures morosely, saying that he could not imagine what Henry would say to him for bringing her to such a place.

She went off into a peal of delicious laughter. "Neither can I, but it would be almost worth telling him about it — just to see his face."

He grinned, but said solemnly, "But Elspeth, it's most reprehensible!"

"Should I be shocked? Well I am not. I daresay it comes from having suffered a surfeit of sanctity at Wanworth. I never could stand those worthy bores Henry and Amelia surrounded themselves with . . . . But, dearest, if this house is not suitable, why should we bother to do more than the most necessary repairs? — Why don't we build ourselves a new house at once."

"But you might find you did not like living on the Island," he protested.

"Of course I shall like it, if I am with you, — though I own I should prefer a southern or western aspect, and also I do not care for the entrance leading directly onto the roadway. Spicer has been telling me that the southern end of the Island is almost deserted, — could we not find a suitable site there, well away from the quarrying?"

He took a turn about the room considering the matter, and then said: "It would cost a great deal of money, because all the timber would have to be brought over from the mainland."

"Does it matter how much it costs? Between us we have a great deal of money, and for once in our lives, no one to consider but ourselves."

"Would it really please you?" he said, smiling down at her. "Because if so, I will agree to it willingly. For you richly deserve a comfortable home, after all you have suffered."

Her face lit up with sudden happiness. "You are too kind to me, John. You always have been — and I am not the only one to have suffered. But I do think we shall be happy together, in fact I *know* we shall be! Now, where shall we build our house?"

Fired with her enthusiasm, John fetched a map of the Island, and they pored over it together. Then Elspeth got out her sketch book, and time passed unnoticed, as they discussed the shape and size of the house, and the layout of the rooms.

Spicer, entering unobtrusively, to replace the guttering candles, was called upon for the names of architects and masons. Never at a loss, he replied that the Bastard brothers had earned a fine reputation in the county for their work at Blandford, after the disastrous fire there in 1731, and that a Mr Thomas Gilbert, a local man, was in charge of the building of the new church on the Island itself.

Having taken the decision to build a new house, there was much to be done. As the Island was a Royal Manor, a grant of land would have to be obtained from the Crown Steward, who together with the members of the Court Leet, was responsible for administering the Island. Before making any formal application, John was anxious to find out if there were any particular places which the Islanders would resent being leased for the purpose of building a house, and to this end, he returned to the Island four days later and sought out Matthew Wiggatt to tell him of his plans. Wiggatt, appreciating this courtesy, told him that there were a large number of freehold tenants with special rights regarding the disposal of their property within the Manor; but if John really wished to live on the southern half of the Island, which was mostly Common Pasture, he was sure that some satisfactory arrangement could be made with the Court Leet. Anyway, he would speak to the Bailiff about it, and if John found a site that he fancied, he could meet the Bailiff to discuss the matter, before applying to the Crown Steward, who did not live on the Island.

John was much relieved to hear this, for to bring his sister to live in an isolated position, surrounded by a hostile population bitterly resentful of any encroachment of their ancient rights, would not have been a pleasant situation; and although he hoped that by stopping the waggon and saving Crabber from the Preventives, he had made a happy start in his relationship with the Islanders, he was well aware that it would be only too easy to become the focus of their traditional hatred of foreigners.

Woken early the next morning by the sun streaming through a gap in the curtains, John rose and flung open the casement to find that the mist that hung over the cliffs on the previous evening, had cleared, and the day promised to be fine with that softness in the air which ushers in the returning spring. Filled with restless energy, he dressed hurriedly, and having fortified himself with a mug of steaming coffee and a round of Mrs Wiggatt's freshly baked bread, he set out to search the southern half of the Island for a site.

John was determined to build the house beside the sea, so he turned off the road leading into Southwell and made his way along the cliff edge above Freshwater Bay. The small, hardy sheep were grazing the spring herbage, and the air was filled with the song of the wheatears (the Islanders' "snalters") which had returned in large numbers from their winter migration. Many of these delightful birds with their distinctive black eyebands and their white rumps, were perched on the stone walls from where they darted forth in swift sallies to catch their prey, and then returned to their watching places. John was fascinated by their activities, but they were very shy, and if he approached too close, they flew off, or ran to seek shelter beneath the nearest bush, and he understood why they were so easily trapped.

His progress towards the Bill was slow for he stopped frequently to study the extensive view of the Channel, and of the Dorset cliffs stretching eastwards to St Aldhelm's Head. The sea was calm except for the turbulence of the Race, and a bevy of fishing boats were busy on the deep blue water. The land sloped gently away towards the Bill until it was only about thirty feet above the sea, whose treacherous shore was guarded by the lower of the two lighthouses, and on reaching this John realised, with disappointment, that no suitable site for a house had presented itself to him. He certainly did not wish to live near the Bill, but he could not resist cantering across the Sturt to look again at the dramatic change of scene immediately west of the promontory, for here the cliffs were much higher and rose in perpendicular splendour from the swirling mass of white water at their base.

For a long time he sat there, held in the thrall of his old enchantress the sea, glorying in the power of the waves, as they hurled themselves against the rock face with such force that clouds of spray rose thirty feet in the air to fall on the broken ledges in frothing rivulets, and be sucked back by a receding wave to rise again in perpetual motion.

At last he dragged himself away, and cantered along the path which ran directly north from the upper lighthouse, and turned to the sea again at Wallsend Bay. He continued along the cliff edge, deep in thought, and had rounded a further headland before he was suddenly halted by the beauty that lay ahead of him. At this point the sea had won its elemental battle with the rock, and had carved out a cove, sheltered from the north by the stark headland of Black Nor, which shut out the view of the Roads and Weymouth Bay; but westwards John could see the whole magnificent sweep of Lyme Bay, and beyond, in the far distance, the misty outline of the Devon hills stretching away to Starte Point.

He drew in a deep breath of pleasure, for this was an enchanted bay, secret and secure, its shingle beach, although littered with loose boulders and huge square blocks of stone from the fallen cliff, as yet unsullied by the waste from the quarrying operations. As he watched, a pair of ravens ejected themselves from their nesting ledge on the cliff face, and encircled the bay before moving inland to settle on the pasture. His glance followed them, and he noted that the cove was parallel to the hamlet of Weston and about half a mile from it. A footpath led from the hamlet to the centre of the cliff top, and when he reached there he saw that it twisted down the cliff face to the beach below. He sat still, gazing at the clear blue water as it lapped around the boulders beneath the headland, his ears filled with the song of the larks which rose from the pasture and intermingled with the harsh cries of the gulls wheeling about the cliff face. He knew that he had now found the site for his house; some might think the cove too stark, too remote, but to John, born with a love of the sea and its wild shores, its solitude spoke of the infinite.

For a while longer he remained there motionless, drinking in all that he saw, and then he wheeled his horse round and galloped inland, spurred into action by his desire to share his discovery with Elspeth, and to open negotiations for the securing of the land without delay.

On entering the stable-yard at Girt House, he was surprised to find a low curricle standing there, and to see Dingle, Elspeth's groom from Wanworth, emerge from the stables to take his horse.

"What are you doing here?" John demanded anxiously. "Have you brought a message from my sister?"

"Miss Elspeth sent me over early this morning with her baggage, sir," replied the man politely. "She is following by boat."

"Following by boat!" John echoed mystified.

"Yes, sir, Miss Elspeth and Mr Spicer have fixed up something between them. Miss Elspeth's light carrying chair will come on the boat, and two of the men are to bring her to the house. You don't need to worry about Miss Elspeth, sir, Miss Skinner will be with her."

"I see," said John, quite at a loss. "Well, the sea is calm enough I suppose, but where did you get that curricle from?"

"It is Miss Elspeth's own, sir, and it arrived from Sussex yesterday. Miss Elspeth don't care to feel that she is being a trouble to anyone, sir, so she likes to make all her own arrangements. She always did so at Wanworth, and me and Miss Skinner see that everything's all right."

Nonplussed by this new insight into his sister's character, John retired into the house to find himself very much in the way, as Mrs Wiggatt was bustling about, feather duster in hand, and when she caught sight of John she expressed the hope that he would not be requiring any refreshment for a while yet, as she wished to make all ship-shape for the mistress. John sought refuge in the bookroom, but finding that he was unable to settle to anything, he decided to walk down to the cove to meet his sister, but as he crossed the hall he heard Wiggatt shouting to his wife that the mistress was now coming up the hill.

His sister's stately arrival filled John with amusement and gathering admiration, for it reminded him strongly of a picture at Wanworth depicting Queen Elizabeth being carried on a royal progress. Two burly, but profusely sweating boatmen carried her chair, beside which stalked the gaunt Skinner, clutching a jewel box, while two stout lads brought up the rear, one carrying a couple of portmanteaus, the other a heavy wicker basket. Wiggatt, holding open the door goggle-eyed, could do no more than bow, but Dingle, emerging through the wicket gate to greet his mistress, took charge of the proceedings and having directed the boatmen to put down the chair in the hall, shepherded them off to his own quarters, leaving John to welcome his sister and introduce the Wiggatts to her.

"I do hope you don't mind my coming here like this," said Elspeth anxiously, when the Wiggatts had been dispatched to serve up a light luncheon. "But Spicer said the sea was very calm so I had better not miss the opportunity."

"Of course not, I'm delighted," John replied. "Besides I have never been privileged to see such a regal progress before — do you often travel like that?"

"Now you are quizzing me," said Elspeth, smiling. "But I do find the chair most useful. The knot garden at Wanworth was one of my favourite retreats, but I found the flight of steps to it very trying, so Dingle suggested that the carpenter should make a carrying chair for me. Of course I shall not use it unless necessary, for my curricle has arrived — have you seen it?"

"Yes, and it's the very thing for here, it should travel very smoothly over the short turf of the pastures — and, Elspeth, I'm so glad you have come because I have found a splendid site for the house."

"Oh, that's famous! Tell me about it!"

He plunged into such an enthusiastic description of the cove that Elspeth said she could not wait to see it for herself, and why did they not drive over there that very afternoon; but John would not hear of this saying that she must rest after her journey, and then he wished to go over the house with her to decide what alterations must be undertaken.

The next morning they set out together in Elspeth's curricle which John declared to be very well sprung. John was anxious in case Elspeth might not care for the cove, but her delighted reaction to that starkly beautiful place was all that he could wish for, and they spent a happy hour watching the ravens, who were very active flying to and fro between their nesting ledge and the adjacent bay, and discussing the exact siting of their house.

Elspeth was in the gayest of moods, and persuaded John to take her to inspect the Bill itself, so they drove along the cliff path to Wallsend Bay. Here John's attention was caught by the sight of a squadron making its way westwards; the gate marking the end of the Great West Field made a convenient hitching post for the horse, so they left the curricle and descended the cliff path to where a wide grassy ledge afforded a delightful stopping place. John stared out to sea while Elspeth studied the shore below.

"John, the ravens and gulls are eating something down there."

"Only an unfortunate sheep that has fallen over the cliff, I expect," he replied, absorbed in his study of the warships.

"I'm afraid it isn't a sheep, dearest," she said in a queer constrained voice. John glanced down to see that her face was ashen:

"Elspeth, what the devil is the matter?" She swallowed, unable to speak, and pointed to the northern shore of the bay.

One hundred and fifty feet below them the gulls were mobbing the ravens over the body of a young man, the upper half of which was spreadeagled on the corner of a huge square boulder, around which the incoming waves were gently lapping. The legs appeared to have been broken in the fall, for one was hideously twisted beneath the other, wedging the lower half of the body between the boulder and the jagged ledge from which it had fallen. The man's skull was broken, but the remains of the face with its empty eye sockets was turned upwards to the ravaging birds. The tide was running in fast,— a stronger wave broke over the boulder and mercifully obliterated the body, but not before John had recognised it — Lieutenant Manvers, the young Preventive officer had done his duty to the bitter end.

Chapter 7

For a short time John remained where he was, staring down at the swirling water, a particularly grim expression on his face. Then he turned to his sister who had moved a few paces away, to where a grassy bank made a convenient sitting place. He sat down putting his arm round her for comfort, and was greatly relieved to find that she was composed, although still very white.

"Elspeth! Are you all right? My dear, what can I say to you?"

She looked up and said quietly: "Yes, I shall be quite all right if I just sit here for a moment or two. I think it was the birds I found so shocking — though why I do not know, for I am well aware of what they do to the lambs — and I do think the young man must have died at once — don't you?"

"Yes, of that I am quite sure," said John reassuringly, filled with admiration for her courage, for the only outward sign of agitation she showed was the wreck of the fine cambric handkerchief she was twisting to pieces between her fingers.

"John . . . you recognised him, didn't you?"

"Yes, it was the young Preventive officer I was telling you about."

"John . . . you don't think . . . I mean to say . . . this couldn't have been done by Crabber Wiggatt for revenge, could it?"

"I wouldn't have thought so," he replied frowning. He got up, and paced restlessly up and down the greensward. "The trouble is that we don't know these people well enough to make judgements. Amongst themselves there are very few crimes, but whether they would consider the killing of an Excise man to be a criminal offence, or a justifiable action in defence of their ancient trade, I don't know."

"It couldn't have been an accident, I suppose?"

"An accident! Are you suggesting that the man came here *alone*, and just fell over the cliff!? If it had been an accident, there would have been someone with him to report the matter. What could have made him come here alone anyway? It was a crazy thing to do! Did he come here to meet someone, or had he discovered some secret connection with this place?"

Involuntarily Elspeth shivered. "Well, I do hope that Wiggatt didn't have anything to do with it, for we should be most horribly involved in it all."

"I'm afraid we *shall* be horribly involved in it all whatever happens, but at least I can find out whether Wiggatt is responsible, and the sooner the better."

"What do you intend to do?"

"Well if you feel up to it, we will go back to Girt House now, and say nothing. Then after luncheon, you will retire to rest, and I shall tell Wiggatt I want his advice about the possibility of bringing a boat into our cove — as a local fisherman he would be the person I should consult in the normal way. I'll bring him over to the cove late this afternoon and then I can easily think of some excuse to come on here. If I watch him carefully when he discovers the body, I shall know whether he is innocent or not — but I must wait until the tide has turned."

"John, you'll be careful." For the first time there was real perturbation in her voice: "You'll go armed!"

"Of course I shall have a pistol with me, but there will be no danger. Wiggatt seems to me to be a very level-headed young man — it would be madness for him to get rid of me, having set out with me in front of our own servants." He reached down his hands to help her to her feet, saying ruefully: "Now I've got you into another scrape."

"Yes, but I daresay we shall come about. That poor young man, it is too dreadful: I am glad it didn't happen in our bay though."

"You are a woman in a thousand, Elspeth, and although I know I should not have brought you to the Island in the first place, I can't think of anyone I'd rather have with me now."

They drove slowly home having decided on their plan of action. Before reporting the finding of the body to the magistrate,

John was determined to take Crabber Wiggatt to the bay to discover how much he knew, if anything. To this end, Elspeth was to give out that she was suffering from a migraine, and intended to retire to bed for the rest of the day, so no formal dinner would be required, as John's purpose could not be accomplished until the tide had turned and exposed the body again.

All went as planned; Crabber readily agreed to visit Mutton Cove, which did much to strengthen John's belief in his innocence. He was evidently a competent seaman for his advice was sound, and he entered into all John's plans with enthusiasm. He showed no sign of fear at the mention of Wallsend Bay, and was most willing to visit it. He merely said it was not suitable for landings, as there was only a short strip of rocky beach at its northern end.

They walked over to the bay together and descended the path as John and Elspeth had done earlier in the day. Crabber went ahead saying: "In a moment or two you'll see what I mean, sir — we should get a clear view of all the beach there is from the next ledge . . . " The words died on his lips as he caught sight of the body. He stood staring down at the sodden corpse, his body frozen into immobility, an expression of implacable hatred on his face: "Oh Gawd!" he muttered. "They done him — the devils!"

"Who are they?" The note of authority in that quiet voice jerked Crabber out of his stupefaction. He swung round to stare into John's face, reading the knowledge there. "You *knew* it was here," he said slowly. "You brought me to see it, didn't you? Gawd, you don't think I done it, do you?" clenching his fists in a menacing fashion.

"No. From the first I was convinced that you did not. and for the past half hour I have *known* that you did not, but that is why I brought you here, to prove to myself that my conviction was right. If you consider my position, for a moment, bringing my sister, who is a helpless cripple, to live amongst strangers and be waited on by a man who is an acknowledged smuggler, you will understand why I had to have proof."

"I suppose I do see," agreed the young man reluctantly, the anger and resentment dying out of his face: "But smuggling's one thing — murder's another."

"Exactly." agreed John. "That is just how I thought you would feel." He sat down on the grassy bank and signed to Crabber to join him: "Now that we are agreed that you are entirely innocent, you had better tell me everything you know, because I shall have to report the matter to the proper authorities immediately."

A blank mask of reserve descended on Crabber's face and he sat silent for a minute or two, staring out to sea. "I don't rightly *know* anything," he said carefully. "It's just what I thinks. Leastways, there is one thing I do know. I wasn't the only one to get shot that night you carried me in."

John looked up, frowning. "Who else was, then?"

"One of the Frenchies — brother of the captain Boisson, — he was in charge of the landing party, and got hit in the stomach. They got him off back to the ship — but he died the next day."

"How do you know this? Has there been another landing?"

"No, but it's what I heard. Boisson is an evil bastard — he'd stick at nothing. Well, two days ago a Jerseyman, owned by a man called Latour, put in to the Roads and tied up at Castletown pier — for urgent repairs to the rigging, it was said. Now, Boisson is a crony of Latour, and it's rumoured he was aboard. Naturally the Preventive officer inspected the ship, but I'm dazed if I know why he had to eat his dinner on board, or go off to Weymouth with Latour and Boisson afterwards — at least I suppose they didn't go there — but that's what was horned all over."

Interpreting this lapse into the vernacular as best he could, John asked how Crabber had obtained this information.

"From me Uncle Matthew — they was loading stone from Castletown pier the next morning, and the Frenchmen said they'd finished mending their rigging and were moving over to Weymouth to pick up Boisson, who, they said, had gone carousing with the Preventive — a fine joke they made of it, how Boisson had duped the Preventive proper, but all the time they'd lured him up here and murdered him, the devils!" He spat expertly onto a stray pebble to show his contempt for all foreigners, and then added: "But he must have been loose in the haft to go with them without his patrol."

"I quite agree with you," said John. "I can't imagine what sort of cock and bull story they could have told him to make him do it. Perhaps it was connected with the lighthouses in some way, but speculation is useless."

"Ay," agreed Crabber, "I daresay we could fret our gizzards green but not find the answer."

This remarkable statement effectively silenced John and he stared out to sea deep in thought; this inaction fretted Crabber and he set off down the cliff path for a closer inspection of the corpse. On his return he gave it as his opinion that it only needed a change of wind, and the swell would shift the body.

"Then the sooner it is reported to the authorities the better," said John, startled out of his reverie: "But first we will call on your Uncle Matthew to see if he has gleaned any further information."

Matthew Wiggatt made John welcome, but listened with growing concern to what he had to say and then questioned his nephew as to the exact position of the body. "Was it near Girt Jar, Crabber?" he asked.

"No," replied his nephew, "on the northern side, and I can tell you the sight of it made me feel as clammy as a cockle snail."

Matthew paid no heed to this eloquent description of his nephew's feelings, but said quietly to John: "There is a hidden path behind the Girt Jar stack, Boisson and Latour would know of it, and I was wondering if they had lured the Preventive up there on the pretence of showing it to him. You get an excellent view of it from the opposite cliff — it's a sheer drop there, and it would be only too easy to push him over while he was studying it. Anyway now I see why the patrol was searching the quarries today, and asking endless questions of all the men."

"Were they doing so?" said John. "Well, I'd best report it to the Bailiff and the Sergeant immediately, and they can arrange for a message to be sent over to the nearest magistrate.

67

Perhaps you would direct me for I don't want Crabber involved in this."

"Ay, I'll do that," said the carter, adding grimly, "but there's no denying that it'll mean a load of trouble for the lot of us!"

Matthew was right: the ensuing enquiry was both protracted and fruitless, and only served to exacerbate the Islanders and widen the gap between them and the authorities on the mainland. The Portlanders' indignation at being suspected of a crime which they knew had been perpetrated by a foreigner knew no bounds, but although they asserted to a man that the Frenchman Boisson was the culprit, the authorities refused to believe them. The workers on the pier were very ready to expound on how Latour's crew had boasted about duping the Preventive officer, but were unwilling to reveal the existence of the secret path behind Girt Jar, and maintained an obstinate silence when asked if there was any particular significance in the body being found at Wallsend Bay.

John's dealings with the authorities had not been entirely happy either, for he had unwittingly set up the back of the magistrate, Mr Willerby, a pompous little man full of self-importance, who was convinced that one of the Islanders was responsible for the murder, and was determined to gain credit for himself by bringing the criminal to justice.

In an interview with John, Mr Willerby expounded his theory that the smuggling trade was the root cause of the trouble. John could not but agree with this, but added, in his fair-minded way, that the authorities themselves were partly to blame for the tragedy.

"The authorities are partly to blame for this crime!" repeated the outraged Mr Willerby, bristling with indignation, "I never heard of anything so preposterous in my life!"

"Nevertheless it is true," replied John with unimpaired calm. "The authorities must bear some responsibility, because Manvers's task was impossible with the tiny forces at his disposal. It was desperation that drove the boy to his last foolhardy action."

But Mr Willerby would accept no such viewpoint, and began to suspect that John was in league with the smugglers. This might have led to serious trouble if it had not been for the intervention of the Crown Steward, on whom John had made the most favourable impression, and who, unlike Mr Willerby, had no desire to see any of the Islanders accused of the murder.

The Crown Steward's sole concern was the peaceful administration of the Island. He had been present when John had given evidence at the inquest, and had been struck by his quiet yet commanding manner. He recognised in John a useful ally, someone whom he could trust and whom the Islanders respected, so when Mr Willerby confided his suspicions to him, the Crown Steward ridiculed them, and said that he for one was thankful that John had come to live on Portland, and he intended to do everything in his power to encourage him to take an active part in the life of the Island.

The long-drawn-out enquiry was to prove very unsatisfactory for Mr Willerby. He harassed and harangued every official on the Island, but only succeeded in making himself extremely unpopular, until even the members of the Preventive patrol, which had been hastily reinforced, were heartily sick of the whole business, and the new officer was heard to say that it was a pity that no-one had thought of throwing that pernickety old fool of a magistrate over the cliff.

Nothing came to light, and finally Mr Willerby was forced to put the case aside with the verdict — "Murder by Persons Unknown." But the Islanders did not put the matter aside — indeed they could not afford to do so, for smuggling was a means of supplementing their slender incomes, and the re-inforcement of the Preventive patrol had virtually brought the trade to a halt. The trouble was that the Islanders had no more idea than Mr Willerby why Boisson should have murdered Lieutenant Manvers, but it was of vital importance for them to discover the reason.

With only a small number of soldiers on Portland, the Islanders had had very little trouble in carrying on their trade, for their intimate knowledge of the winds and tides had made it possible for them to change the landing places frequently, and to make landings in places which the patrol thought impossible for boats to come ashore. However, now that treble the number of soldiers were available, all this was at an end. Every evening at dusk four parties of troops left Portland Castle. Two parties climbed the hill to the plateau and then divided, one to patrol the east coast from Nicodemus's Nob to the Bill, the other the west cliffs. The other two parties watched the lower part of the Island, one patrolling below the Verne, the other the West Weares and Chesilton.

The Islanders working their strips or digging their gardens (for every cottage had a garden to produce vegetables and accommodate chickens and pigs), watched the patrols with growing concern through the lengthening evenings of spring. But apart from harassing the soldiers with lurid tales of flickering lights on the southern end of the Island, (usually an effective means of raising an alarm) for indeed, the marsh gas did give the appearance of lanterns flashing, there was very little they could do, except to organise their own watch-keeping force. They gathered nightly at The Lugger Inn at Weston to collect their information, but the spring and summer passed and no solution to the mystery presented itself.

Very early one morning in late September, Crabber left the Girt House to inspect his lobster pots, for Elspeth was very fond of lobsters particularly if they were served in a cream sauce. The dawn was just breaking as Crabber pushed his boat out from Church Ope and raised the single sail. The wind was very light, but the tide was on the ebb and carried him swiftly southwards through Freshwater Bay to where he had sunk his pots off the Cave Hole. The corks, marked with a W cut in their face to identify them as his own, were bobbing on the surface of the calm water. He reefed his sail and dropped anchor, in this case a mooring stone, for the Islanders never used ordinary anchors on that rocky coast.

The first pot contained a fine lobster; he paid out the anchor cable and rowed to the next pot, glad to be active for a damp chill was penetrating his thick knitted jersey. He glanced towards the shore, and then bent to his oars, frowning — a mist was forming over the low cliffs — he must be quick or he might be caught in thick fog.

Twenty minutes later his worst fears were realised; the fog rolled off the land forming an impenetrable wall of chill greyness around him. Crabber shivered, but he knew there was only one thing to do — to anchor until the tide turned slewing round the head of his boat; then he could drift homewards on the flood tide. Since he had spent the years of his boyhood fishing off the Island in a small boat, he could roughly estimate the time lag between Cave Hole and Church Ope; but once he had covered the estimated distance he must drop anchor again, and wait until the fog lifted before attempting to guide his boat into the cove, because he knew from bitter experience how easily all his sense of direction would become disorientated in the fog.

It was about half-an-hour before the head of his boat turned. With a sigh of relief, he drew up the mooring stone and the boat moved swiftly forward on the flood tide. He took a sand-glass from its wrappings in a locker beneath the stern seat, and watched it carefully. When he had seen it fill twice, he put it away and dropped the stone again — if the tide had not carried him too far out into the bay, he should be off Church Ope now.

The eerie silence was broken only by the gentle slapping of the waves against the stern of his boat, all around him the fog hung in a thick pall isolating him in an opaque world of his own. He sat still, straining his eyes to catch any transient lifting of the fog that might reveal a glimpse of the familiar coastline, and tell him where he was.

Suddenly the menacing silence was broken by a loud splash, a man coughed hoarsely, footsteps sounded and then died away. The silence returned. Momentarily startled by the nearness of the sounds, Crabber mentally cursed the hostile pall which enveloped him, cutting him off from the sight of his fellows, for he was a sensible young man not easily given to conjuring up bogeys, and the sounds he had just heard were familiar ones. A boat must be anchored near him — someone on that boat had come up on deck, thrown the slops overboard and gone below again.

"Gone below again." The words conjured up a picture of warmth and hot food — instinctively Crabber sniffed — was it his imagination, or did a faint aroma of boiling onions hang on the air? He leaned forward straining his eyes to catch a glimpse of the outline of the hidden boat, if he could find her he could go aboard, and await the lifting of the fog in comfort. He had more than enough lobsters for Girt House, he could offer some of them in exchange for a meal. He shouted, but there was no reply; could all the crew be below, he thought curiously?

Very gently he released a little of his anchor cable, the *Mary* moved forward with a rush, to be checked again as the cable tightened. The third time he allowed the *Mary* to move forward he was rewarded by the sight of a rope seemingly swinging in mid-air ahead of him — it was the anchor cable of the boat he was seeking. With the skilled judgement acquired through years of boat-handling, he manoeuvred the *Mary* alongside the cable and grasped it. He was about to hail those on board, when a slight breeze swirled away the wall of fog for an instant, showing him the stern of a brig and her name painted in bold black letters, *Marie-Louise*. The words died on his lips — for *Marie-Louise* was the name of Boisson's brig.

Boisson! A spasm of anger shook the young fisherman. What was the dirty swine doing here? There had been no intimation that he was about to bring over a cargo — and certainly the Islanders could not deal with one while the Preventive patrol was so alert, they would be certain to be caught red-handed. The French bastard had caused them enough trouble already — what was he trying to do now — get them all strung up?

Suddenly his ears caught the rhythmical sound made by oars rising and dipping into the water. It grew louder — someone on board the *Marie-Louise* heard it too, there were footsteps, muffled voices, a splash as a coil of rope was thrown over the side.

A voice from the approaching boat hailed the brig, and was answered by one that Crabber knew to be Boisson's. He made out the words "Mon Capitaine."

72

A brisk, cultured voice answered Boisson. Crabber did not understand more than a few words of French but he recognised the note of authority in that stream of language. Boisson's voice again, ingratiating, servile and then changing as he shouted orders to his crew. Running footsteps, the rattle of the halyards through the blocks, the creak of sails lifting, familiar sounds from a ship about to weigh anchor — but surely, Crabber thought, Boisson was not such a fool as to risk sailing in dense fog, or had he been ordered to do so regardless of the danger? The thought spurred Crabber to action, for if Boisson's mission was so secret, no witness of it would be tolerated. Hauling on his anchor cable, he began to ease the *Mary* away, it was hard work against the flow of the tide, but fear lent him strength and now the fog was his ally, shielding him from those on board the *Marie-Louise;* he prayed it would not suddenly lift and betray his presence. He redoubled his efforts, the sweat pouring from him; the stern of the *Marie-Louise* faded into the fog, and the silence returned.

Crabber slumped over the tiller utterly exhausted, only to be jerked up again by a horrible spasm of sickness. He stared at the miserable outpouring of his body in disgust, wanting to disbelieve the evidence of his eyes and nose because for him the smell of his wretchedness was the smell of naked fear.

Presently, when he judged that the *Marie-Louise* had made her get-away, he took his baler and began a meticulous cleansing of the bottom of his boat; but his actions were wholly automatic for his conscious mind had moved back in time to a night two years before, when he was lying hidden in the rocks under Rufus's castle, but then the cove at Church Ope had been lit by the merciless light of the moon and the groans and curses of dying men had been carried to him on the gentle breeze.

Chapter 8

Crabber had first joined the smugglers when Mary conceived their child. Their serious courtship had begun some months before when Mary was sixteen and following the Portland custom, the arrangements for the marriage began as soon as she became pregnant.

Crabber counted himself fortunate in inheriting a tiny cottage in Wakeham from his great-aunt, for whose timely demise he fervently thanked his Maker every night. The handsome bed, (retrieved almost undamaged from the wreck of an East India Merchantman) in which the kindly old woman had slipped quietly from this world, was the only luxury he could offer Mary for her lying-in, for besides his annual quit rent of a farthing, he owed the largest part of his meagre income to the Weymouth boatbuilder from whom he had purchased the *Mary*, and would continue to do so for several years to come.

Faced with the necessity of supplementing his income, he turned to smuggling. At first he worked with the donkey train, but his skill in boat handling soon came to the notice of the gang leader, Abel Norster, and within six months he was one of the most trusted members of the group.

The extra money was a great boon to the little family, and the boat work was far more to Crabber's taste than urging on the recalcitrant donkey which had been assigned to him; soon he began to enjoy his nefarious adventures. Pitting his wits against the Preventives added a zest to his life for he had an active brain, an eye for detail and a good deal of solid common sense, qualities which combined to make him a formidable conspirator.

Possum, as he was always called, was just two when to Mary's delight, a dark, curly-headed daughter was born. But from the first Alice was a sickly child, and at nine months became seriously

74

ill with a putrid sore throat. The Island herb woman could do nothing for her, so Mary wrapped her in a warm shawl and holding her close, walked to Weymouth to consult a physician. Mr Richard Portbury, M.D. examined the child and shook his head gravely. He wrote out a prescription for the apothecary to make up and refused to take any fee, but to Mary's consternation the money she had with her would only buy a very small quantity of the medicines ordered for Alice. She returned to Wakeham worn out and greatly distressed, to find Crabber consuming the last portion of cheese in the house in preparation for a long and arduous night's work with the smugglers.

The sight of the empty platter was more than the exhausted Mary could bear: "Oh Crabber! You've finished the cheese, and I'm that weary and leary I don't know how to stand!"

Crabber jumped up guiltily, and drew her gently towards the tiny fire: "I'm sorry, Mary, love. I wern't thinking like, and I shall be working all night. I'll heat some milk for you and Alice. Is she very bad?"

She nodded, unable to speak and sank into the high-backed chair. He put some milk to warm on the hob, and then came and put his arm round her shoulders loosening her cloak. She lifted her free hand to clasp his, and leant back against him gratefully: "I didn't mean to bite your head off — it's just that she's so very ill."

The child in her arms stirred, and wailed plaintively, Mary cuddled her close, crooning and soothing. She drew the small bottle of medicine from her pocket: "The milk should be warm now. Add some of this to it and don't spill any, for it cost all the money we had in the house."

"No need to be muopen about money — I'll get Abel to pay me to-night." Crabber measured the cordial carefully into the milk and brought the mug to Mary.

Alice swallowed the liquid convulsively and then gave a cry of pain. Crabber bent and stroked her damp curls: "She do look sickly, poor twoad," he said pityingly, . . . "I must be off," his hand gripped Mary's shoulder reassuringly, "take heart, love, by daybreak I'll have all the gold we need for her."

The light was failing as Crabber made his way to Church Ope, but every inch of the steep cliff path was familiar to him and he welcomed the onset of the concealing darkness. He had spent the afternoon preparing his lines and his boat was ready just above the high tide mark. He pushed it out through the bubbling fob and rowed out into the bay. Five minutes vigorous work against the flow of the tide brought him to the rendezvous — a small buoy he had carefully positioned some months previously. He dropped his mooring stone gently overboard and set out his lines.

A passing shoal of mackerel absorbed his full attention, and it was not until his basket was half full that he noticed the enfolding darkness, the *Marie-Louise* was late. The conditions were perfect for the run now — darkness and a gentle breeze; but soon the tide would turn and two hours later the moon would rise and expose them in its merciless light.

He listened intently but there was no sound of the *Marie-Louise's* approach — only the gentle lapping of the waves against the side of his boat broke the silence of the night. Suppose the Frenchmen didn't come? How would they be able to buy the medicines for Alice? Desperately he threw out his lines again, a full basket of fish to sell in Weymouth would be better than nothing!

Suddenly a voice hailed him and a rope was thrown, but at that moment the head of his boat slewed round with the turning tide. The rope fell into the water with a resounding splash, and immediately an owl hooted twice from the shore.

Crabber caught the trailing rope and made it fast to the buoy. The bulk of the *Marie-Louise* loomed up alongside, and a Frenchman swung himself over the side and climbed down into the *Mary*. A heavy hand gripped Crabber's shoulder: "Were you asleep, mon ami, to miss the rope?"

"Asleep! On this job! Didn't you see the head of my boat slew round? The tide is on the ebb. You're late!"

"No need to be so touchy about it! Better late than never, as you English say." The good humour in the voice failed to soothe Crabber's irritation, although Marcel Lamont was the only member of Boisson's crew he genuinely liked. Marcel was short and fat, but his barrel shaped girth belied his great strength and when he laughed the sound seemed to come bubbling up from the depth of his belly shaking his whole body. These paroxysms of mirth fascinated Crabber who was privately convinced that "Jelly", as he had wickedly nicknamed him, would one day die from laughing.

Curt orders issued from the darkness above them and the *Marie-Louise's* longboat was lowered into the water. A carelessly handled net of kegs bumped against the side of the brig calling forth a stream of abuse. Jelly caught the net deftly: "He's in a dangerous mood that one. There was trouble over the money — that's why we're late."

"Trouble over the money!" Crabber echoed, pausing in the act of stowing the first keg: "In what way?"

"Had to pay more than he liked — and so will Abel! Mark my words, there'll be some wrangling on your beach to-night!"

"God Almighty! Not to-night!"

The desperation in Crabber's voice caught the warm-hearted Frenchman's attention: "You are in trouble? Can I help?"

Crabber shook his head. "It's Alice — she's that sickly, poor twoad, and the medicine Mary bought for her took all our money. It's foolhardy to be hanging about after a run, and with the moon up it'll be downright dangerous, but I must see Abel and get paid at once."

Marcel nodded sympathetically, and glanced up at the sky. The clouds had dispersed and the heavens were ablaze with the constellations of late autumn, when the moon rose it would be as bright as daylight. "Best get the job done quickly," he muttered grimly, stowing away the last barrel. He seized an oar, and together they sent the *Mary* skimming towards the beach and the waiting donkey train.

An hour and a half later when they had completed three more journeys to and from the *Marie-Louise*, Crabber's worst fears were realised. The full moon rose majestically above the horizon revealing the illicit activities at the cove in its cold, merciless light.

77

The last of the donkeys had reached the dispersal point above the elm grove and Marcel had helped Crabber pull his boat up the beach to its usual resting place, so the basket of mackerel, their glossy scales phosphorescent in the moonlight, could have seemed the proof of an innocent night's fishing were it not for the presence of the French longboat at the water's edge, and the *Marie-Louise* riding serenely at anchor in the bay.

Marcel seated himself on a block of stone and relaxed with an evil-smelling pipe: "Well, the kegs are safely away; but now," pointing his pipe towards the longboat, where Manton, Boisson's lieutenant, was arguing hotly with Abel Norster, "Jules is demanding a new price for them, as I told you he would, and will stay here till daylight if need be to get it."

Crabber groaned. "It's madness! They're exposed to the full view of any patrol by this blasted moonlight. The Hunter's moon we call it — but I don't care to be hunted!" He shook his fist at the two protagonists in exasperation. "Will they never cease this argle-bargle?"

"It seems they have done so." Marcel rose and knocked out his pipe as he saw a bag of money change hands. "But, Mon Dieu, it is too late! Look up there!" He gripped Crabber's arm and pointed to the top of the cliffs.

A solitary figure was silhouetted against the skyline, it moved stealthily forward and vanished into the obscurity of the elm grove, but not before Crabber's sharp eyes had caught a tiny spark of light. Without hesitation he put his fingers to his lips, for he knew that what he had seen was the glint of moonlight on polished steel. The harsh croaking of a raven echoed across the cove.

Despite his great girth, Marcel was halfway to the boat before the sound had died away, but Crabber remained where he was in the shadow of the quarried stones coolly assessing his chances of escape. He knew he must wait until the patrol emerged from the grove to see whether they split up or all came down the main path, before deciding which part of the cliff to climb himself.

He gazed upwards watching tiny glimmers of light moving through the trees, but suddenly a brighter flash caught his attention. Another figure was visible at the cliff top, but there was nothing stealthy about his movements — he was signalling with a lantern.

"Sending for reinforcements, damn them!" a voice muttered in Crabber's ear, and Abel leant back against the stone, panting.

"It seems like it. Did Jelly make the boat?"

"Ay, but they'll have a long row by the looks of things — that Devil's going!"

"What?!" Crabber spun round incredulously; the longboat was already some hundred yards from the shore, the crew straining at the oars, but the *Marie-Louise* had weighed anchor and was gliding serenely out of the bay on the ebbing tide.

Crabber stood as though transfixed, gazing at the increasing distance between the brig and her longboat: "Bastard!" he muttered under his breath. "Stinking bastard!"

"Ay, that he is, but I didn't mean they'd have to row to France. He'll probably anchor out of sight in Freshwater Bay and wait for them because Jules has got the money."

"Money! That's what I'm after. Abel, I *must* be paid now!"

"All right, all right! But we'd better save our own skins first, and fast too. Look at what *this* set of bastards is doing, they're ringing the whole cliff! We'll have to get out round the headland. Leave those dratted fish!"

"That I won't! I've been night fishing regular like lately, to make an alibi for myself. That cursed sergeant knows my boat and knows I do it, and he ain't such a fool as he can't tell when fish be freshly caught. I might as well stand here and give myself up as leave the basket behind!"

Abel saw the force of this argument and wasted no more words. He grabbed one of the basket handles and together, keeping in the shelter of the quarried stones, they ran towards the water's edge at the northern end of the cove. Here ancient landfalls from the cliff sprawled out into the sea in a rugged, irregular rock mass. While they paused to get their breath in the safety of its dark shadows, Crabber studied the shining wet shingle calculating the state of the tide: "We'll have to swim," he muttered, stripping off his clothes and tossing them into the basket.

79

Abel reluctantly followed suit, cursing the moonlight under his breath, for he was a quarryman and hated the water.

Crabber cut him short. "You shouldn't have stood there argling-bargling for all the world to see if you didn't want to get wet. Downright foolhardy, I thought it!"

Before Abel could think of a suitably crushing reply to this well-justified criticism Crabber was already waist-deep in the water. Abel followed him gingerly, hoping that his great height would save him from having to swim, like all quarrymen he was immensely powerful and taller than most, standing six foot seven inches in his stockinged feet. He worked his way carefully past the last steep shelf of cliff towards the mass of fallen rock which ran out into the sea forming a natural breakwater.

The water lapped around his shoulders, and ahead of him Crabber was swimming with long, easy strokes, doggedly manoeuvring his basket through a thick field of seaweed. Abel disliked seaweed almost as much as he disliked swimming out of his depth, he looked about for a convenient ledge to climb on to, and lost his footing on the treacherous rock floor. He came up spluttering with shock and thrashing wildly. Crabber seized his arm and drew him in amongst thick fronds of seaweed beneath an overhanging rock: "Stubble it!" he hissed, as a lantern beam flashed across the cove.

Chapter 9

The beam of light was crossed by others weaving eerily to and fro along the deserted beach. They flashed together and fell apart in an intricate pattern of dancing light as the ring of Preventives closed in at the base of the cliff. To the watchers below the rock the crunch of shingle beneath heavy boots sounded as loud as the rattle of rifle fire; and then the light and sound resolved into the grim reality of a group of armed men conferring at the water's edge.

Anger and frustration were manifest in every action of the group, but to the Portlanders' surprise no shots were fired at the retreating longboat; instead the men kept looking back towards the cliffs, and then began a thorough search amongst the blocks of quarried stone.

Abel drew in his breath sharply: "It's us they're after!" he whispered.

A lantern was raised, and slowly the beam of light travelled along the side of the cliff they had passed penetrating the dark shadows. Suddenly it flickered and died. Abel relaxed his numbed body with a sigh of relief, only to freeze into immobility again as a second brighter beam replaced the first.

Nearer and nearer it came, moving in an irregular pattern as the holder of the lantern studied each patch of blackness between the jagged rocks. Crabber, reacting instinctively to the ebbing of the tide, ceased to tread water and planted his feet firmly on a rough shell-encrusted rock. He shifted the basket slightly so that it floated before them, the rushes intermingling with the fronds of seaweed to form a solid shield of fibrous material, screening their faces from the piercing light.

The beam was very near them now, momentarily it rested on the over-hanging rock and then fell to search the clinging seaweed. Invisible behind the barrier of the basket, the two men stood rigid, hardly daring to breathe. The water rippled gently around them carrying the shock waves of tension from one to the other. The light hovered over the dark, shining, brown mass and for an interminable fraction of time, shone directly onto the basket.

At last it moved — passed swiftly over the outlying rocks to the point and swerved sharply back to the beach. For a moment it wavered wildly in the direction of the cliff path as the officer gestured to the patrol, and then vanished.

"Quick! Now's our chance!" Crabber shook himself to relieve his cramped muscles, and waded out from under the rock. "They've gone to search the huts!"

Abel followed carefully, his teeth chattering: "Ugh-h-h! M-much longer in that hellish hole and I'd have floated out like a corpse! We must get up to the Castle quarry, we'll be safe there!"

Keeping low, they scrambled over the wet, slippery rocks, oblivious of the sharp, merciless edges tearing at their numbed fingers and toes. They were stark naked, but the fresh, drying breeze was almost welcome after the shocking cold of the water, and by the time they had rounded the bluff of the cliff they were sweating with exertion.

There was no beach to the north of Church Ope cove, long ago a massive portion of the cliff had fallen away forming a series of ridges which were now covered with gorse and rough vegetation. Abel pulled himself up onto a convenient ledge grasping the coarse grass with a deep sigh of relief — at last he was on dry land again. He scanned the moonlit cliff anxiously for any sign of the Preventives, but the castle and the quarry to the north of it were silent and deserted.

Abel got to his knees. "All clear! For Gawd's sake let's get our clothes on . . . " But the rest of the sentence was drowned in a croaking gasp, as Crabber who was close behind him, knocked him to the ground.

"Down! Down!" he hissed, as a well-aimed bullet whistled over Abel's head and buried itself in a tangle of gorse behind them.

Abel recovered his breath. "Struth!" he muttered. "Where the hell did that come from?"

"Look out to sea, and you'll discover where from!" replied Crabber grimly.

Abel peered cautiously over the hummock, from the direction of the Roads, lights ablaze, and all her sails set, a naval cutter was racing towards them. He ducked again swiftly as a second bullet struck an outcrop of rock on the seaward side of the hummock and exploded in a shower of broken scree: "Hell and damnation! That pesky marksman knows what he's about!"

"Ay, and you made a splendid target in this blasted moonlight, but they've altered course now to clear the headland." Crabber wriggled back into the safety of a hollow and opened the basket: "We'd best get our clothes on right quick, and make for the quarry."

"The quarry itself won't be safe enough — not now they've heard those shots! Under the castle is our only chance!"

"Never! We'd be caught like rats in a trap!"

"No we won't! I'll show you something we discovered quarrying a while back." Abel squeezed his bleeding feet gingerly into his shoes and scanned the cliff purposefully. Fully clothed again, albeit in garments that were wringing wet, and mercifully released from the alien element of the sea, the landsman's self-confidence returned and he immediately resumed command: "Keep low, and follow me!"

From time immemorial the Portlanders had sited their quarries along the cliffs because the marketable stone was covered to a depth of ten to thirty feet by useless rubble which was easily disposed of by tipping it into the sea. The Castle quarry was being worked in this time-honoured manner making the ascent of the cliff extremely hazardous.

The basket was a terrible impediment for Crabber, striving to find a foothold amongst the sliding rubble. He cursed the ancient practice under his breath, and heartily wished he had made his escape by swimming along the coast. Struggling against the ebbing current would have been far less strenuous than attempting this horrible climb, he thought, although it would probably have meant separating from Abel, a poor swimmer as ever he'd seen, without obtaining his money. Remembering Alice and his desperate need of the money, spurred him to greater efforts; but when he finally pulled himself up onto the level floor of the quarry in the last stages of exhaustion, Abel had disappeared.

Instantaneously anger replaced exhaustion. Swearing viciously to himself, Crabber stood upright searching the deep shadows cast by the huge stone blocks for any sign of his companion, but the quarry was empty.

The vein of marketable stone had been of very high quality here, so the thrifty Islanders had quarried right up to the castle walls, leaving the ancient building perched precariously on a man-made knoll. The wall of the knoll was in shadow, the deep, natural fissures in the rock making strange, menacing patterns of dense blackness leading the eye upwards to the ghostly, broken battlements of the keep; the eerie darkness accentuated by the moonlight shining on the stark, white limestone of the far side of the quarry.

Involuntarily Crabber shivered; the silent quarry was a hostile, repellent place — if he remained here he would be snared as simply as a snalter. He glanced along the shadowed wall again and stiffened, the colour draining out of his face — one of the stone blocks stacked against the knoll wall was moving slowly outwards.

For a few seconds he stood still, paralysed into inaction like a rabbit before a stoat. A dark fissure yawned behind the stone and a beckoning figure appeared. "Witchcraft!" Crabber muttered, hastily crossing himself.

"Hurry, you fool! Hurry!" Abel hissed.

Relief and fury sent Crabber across the quarry at breakneck speed: "Why in hell's name didn't you wait for me?" he demanded seizing Abel by the shoulder. "Scaring the wits out of me with this wizard's act! I wish I'd let that pesky marksman get you!"

"This stone is damned difficult to move, that's why!" Abel retorted. "Stop blathering, and help me to pull it back!"

The huge stone blocks had been cleverly stacked to hide the base of the fissure, in which a man could stand upright in comfort, and a layer of smaller blocks placed neatly on top of them. A heavy iron staple had been driven into the back of the movable one, from which hung a length of stout rope. Standing sideways, one behind the other, Crabber and Abel heaved it back into position entombing themselves in the intense darkness.

"Cor!" muttered Crabber, "I ain't been in one of these gullies before. How far does it go?"

"A fair way, but it's too narrow to walk ahead — lean against the wall and move sideways. We'll keep the basket between us for contact, but mind your step, it's devilish rough underfoot!"

Keeping their backs against the cold stone wall for guidance, the two men began to edge their way along the gully, (the quarrymen's name for the widest of the natural joints in the limestone.) Through fishing at night, Crabber had developed the ability to see adequately in the dark, but here the suffocating blackness seemed to bear down on him, temporarily blinding him, making every crab-like step a hazard over the debris-littered floor: "Thought I'd got eyes like a cat," he gulped cheerfully, determined to get even with Abel for fooling him in the quarry, "but I can't see no more than a mole in here! The air's bad too."

"Ay, you'd best save your breath. It gets worse before it . . . " The sentence ended abruptly in a stream of swear words as Abel's foot slithered in a patch of soft, evil-smelling dung, and he stumbled to his knees. The sounds vibrated strangely in the confined space, disturbing a colony of bats who swept past Crabber's face with an indignant whirring of wings.

The fetid atmosphere had seemed stifling before, but now the stench released from the dung left both men choking and gasping for breath. Bats, however, held no terrors for Crabber, and Abel's discomfiture had somehow restored the balance of honour between them. Moreover his eyes were becoming accustomed to the dark, and he could make out a faint greyness ahead of them.

"Hi!" He tugged at Abel's jacket: "Does this lead through to the cove?"

"Ay. This joint meets an East-Wester just ahead. It's a tight squeeze along that, but only for a yard or two, and then we're in that deep gully you can see from the path — a regular cave that is!"

"How will that help us? There's no way up or down from that."

"No way up, but one can get down. I'll show you."

A few paces further on Abel stopped abruptly, confronted by a solid wall of stone. He twisted his body into the right angle and began to grope his way along the transverse joint, which was indeed so narrow that Crabber half expected to see the quarryman's powerful frame become sandwiched between the confining walls of limestone for ever. But somehow Abel managed to struggle through the impasse, which presented no difficulty to the slimly built Crabber, following impatiently, for the greyness was growing stronger and the air less fetid. Almost immediately the rock wall to their right fell away sharply and they were standing in a wide, moonlit gully, with a fresh, southerly breeze bringing the tang of the sea to their eager nostrils.

Abel, exhausted by his contortions in the "East-Wester", leant back against the wall gulping in the clean, life-giving air, while Crabber gazed at the cavernous proportions of the gully in amazement: "Who'd have thought . . . ", he began and then stopped abruptly, stiffening like a hare poised before flight, as the sound of boots rasping against rock reached their ears.

Both men stood still, listening intently. Suddenly the rasping noise stopped. There was a startled exclamation, and then the sound of someone running which gradually grew fainter. Crabber and Abel dropped to their knees and crawled towards the gully entrance, which was broad enough at its base for them to lie side by side. Cautiously, Abel raised himself on his elbows and looked out over the cove.

He stared down at the moonlit scene below him in consternation: "Gawd help the poor devils!" he muttered. "They've got them!"

"Not Jelly!" Forgetting caution, Crabber slithered forward and leaned out of the gully. The naval cutter was anchored in the bay, and astern of her, the empty French longboat told its own tale.

Crabber passed his tongue over lips that were suddenly dry. "What could have happened? I didn't hear no shots when we were coming up the cliff. And where's the *Marie-Louise*?"

The gully was set like an eagle's eyrie high in the wall of the knoll, and from it the view extended southwards over Freshwater Bay to the English Channel. To Crabber's experienced eyes the turbulent waters of the Race were clearly visible in the bright moonlight, but the sea was empty except for one ship coming in from a night's fishing.

She was rounding the headland from Freshwater Bay, a brig with black sails close hauled to catch the wind. Evidently she had had trouble with her trawl nets for these were draped in disorder over her side, and the men on her deck were busy disentangling them.

Crabber studied the brig in growing amazement. "The *Marie-Louise*!" he breathed. "But it can't be her. *She* has white sails."

"Ay, but I've seen Boisson change them before — and he'd have had plenty of time to do it as she drifted out on the ebb."

"But what can he do? How can he hope to rescue Jelly and the others?"

"He can't rescue them — that would be impossible." Abel's face was very grim. "Silence them perhaps?"

Crabber stared at him in horror. "You mean he's going to blow them out of the water — his own crew!"

"I can't guess what he'll do, any more than you can. I only know he's utterly ruthless."

"Spawn of the Devil, that's what he is!" Crabber spat the words out contemptuously, and watched the spittle fall away slightly in the breeze with alert, professional interest: "Talk of the Devil, where did he conjure this breeze from, to bring him back against the tide?"

At the suggestion of witchcraft both men crossed themselves, for like all Islanders, they believed implicitly in the power of evil spirits. Crabber leant forward to test the strength of the wind with his hand, and as quickly drew back: "That sentry we heard — he's near the bottom of the cliff path and shouting to the others. Do you think *he* recognised the *Marie-Louise*?"

"More likely saw her draw out from Sand Holes. Boisson could have anchored there out of sight."

Whatever warning the man might have intended to give, it was too late. The *Marie-Louise* was already nearing the cutter on a parallel course. The watchers in the gully heard the cutter hail her, ordering her to heave to, but the *Marie-Louise* came steadily on and as she drew abreast of her unsuspecting prey, the mass of netting was deftly drawn aside revealing the open gun-ports below her built-up deck.

She was armed with only three light cannons, but at such close range they were able to inflict appalling damage. The first shot, aimed high, tore away the shrouds bringing down the mainsail in a jumbled heap. The second exploded amongst the group of men gathered on the deck amidships, creating a charnel house of death and mutilation. The third cut through the hull planking and buried itself in the sail locker. The gaping hole was just above the waterline but it did not remain so for long, for as soon as he had fired his third cannon Boisson altered course to starboard, bringing the stern of the *Marie-Louise* within a stone's throw of the cutter's bows, and the waves of her wake slapped against the victim's side and flooded through the shattered planking.

The element of surprise and the speed of the manoeuvre had so far brought complete success for Boisson, but now two of his crew, busy on the after deck, were cut down by musket fire. As they fell a burly figure, who the Portlanders recognised as Boisson himself, raced towards the stern, bent over a smoking cauldron and lobbed the burning rope-ends from it, onto the crumpled heap of sail on the cutter's deck.

The smouldering pitch ignited the canvas, and fanned by the breeze, the tongues of flames leapt up and spread across the forward deck.

Crabber sprang to his feet, his face ashen: "Jelly!" he cried.

"He and the others will burn to death, for they'll be bound hand and foot!"

Abel seized his arm roughly. "Keep down! Do you want to hang yourself, boy! There is nothing we can do to help them."

Crabber subsided unwillingly against the cold stone wall and was violently sick. But a deafening explosion drew him to the gully mouth again. The heat from the burning deck timbers had set alight the sail locker below, and sparks from the smouldering canvas had fallen into the powder store, detonating the powder and blasting the shattered hull out of the water in a lurid pyre of foam and flame.

The echoes of the explosion reverberated round the cove, intermingled with the groans of the dying, the despairing cries of the survivors and the shouted commands of the Preventive officer supervising the launching of a dinghy to rescue them.

Abel tapped Crabber on the shoulder and pointed to the confused activity on the beach: "Now's the time for us to go. Watch me, and then hand down the basket."

Below the mouth of the gully there was a sheer drop of some eight feet to a narrow ledge, but a firm handhold had been chiselled out of the rock floor making it comparatively easy for an active man to lower himself down the vertical wall and drop to the ledge. Five minutes later they parted company near the castle causeway.

At the top of the cliff path Crabber paused and glanced seawards again. The *Marie-Louise* was far out in Weymouth Bay now, her course set for France. Beating to windward would be hard work for her depleted crew, Crabber thought, and suddenly the gold in his pocket felt as heavy as lead.

It was almost two o'clock when Crabber reached his cottage, but a light was still burning in the kitchen. He lifted the latch quietly in case Alice was sleeping in Mary's arms, but it was his aunt, Martha Wiggatt, who rose to greet him, and one look at her face told him that Alice no longer needed the gold he had brought.

He put down the basket of fish but made no attempt to come further into the room, for his body seemed incapable of movement and he was cold and desperately tired, but part of him knew that he must drive it to still further effort. He straightened his shoulders under the wet, salt-ridden clothing and smiled numbly: "It was good of you to come, Aunt Martha. When did it happen?"

"About ten. I came over soon after eight with some soup I'd made for you all. The poor little twoad was very weak and could take nothing, but I got a good fire going and Mary nursed her by it. She slipped away from us very peaceful like."

Crabber nodded dumbly: "And Mary?"

"She was right plucky. She said she'd really known from Mr Portbury's face that there was no hope, but she wouldn't let herself believe it. She helped me lay Alice out, but then she could do no more. She wanted to sit up for you, but I got her to take some hot soup, put a couple of bricks in the bed and persuaded her to try and rest. She said she'd never be able to sleep, but she was that exhausted from walking to Weymouth and back, she went off as soon as she was in bed and warm."

Martha bent and stirred the steaming liquid in the cooking pot and then looked up at her nephew: "You seem right weary and leary yourself, Crabber. Come to the fire and have some soup." She moved towards him and took his jacket: "Why, your clothes are soaking and hard with salt! Get them off at once and give yourself a rub down!" She bustled about like a motherly hen, finding him a nightshirt and a blanket to put round his shoulders, and very soon had him seated in the rocker before the fire with a bowl of steaming soup between his hands.

"Something went wrong on the run, then?" she enquired, her comfortable features wrinkled with anxiety.

"It did — but we got the brandy away safely."

"Is your boat all right?"

He nodded, and she forbore to ask him any more questions. She picked up his clothes, remarking sagely: "Well troubles never come singly, that's for sure," and left him to his soup.

After two bowls of the delicious soup Crabber felt quite different, he was warm and dry and no longer hungry, but rest eluded him. Confused images of Alice, Jelly and the dramatic sinking of the naval cutter revolved endlessly round in his brain, all interwoven in cause and effect by his desperate need for money. Perhaps if Mary had taken Alice to Weymouth sooner she might still be alive. If Boisson had not been late, if Jules had not argued so long, Jelly might now be indulging in one of his paroxysms of mirth. But Jelly had not died of laughing as he, Crabber, had predicted, either he had been burnt to death or killed by an exploding cannon ball in order to guard his captain's secrets. Gradually the spinning images crystallized into a deep and bitter hatred of the ruthless Frenchman. One day, he vowed to himself, he'd get even with that Devil's Spawn.

The resolution, once taken, brought him peace and relaxation, or was it merely the heat of the fire that was making him soporific, for suddenly all that mattered was that he was warm again.

Chapter 10

It was the warmth of the sun that jerked Crabber's mind back into the present. The fog was lifting, revealing the familiar outlines of the cove, with a sigh of relief he fitted his Kops oars into the pins and made for the sandy beach.

The sun was high in the sky now and he was guiltily aware that Mary would be waiting impatiently for the lobsters and worrying about his failure to return. But when he had hauled his boat up above the high water mark he did not set off for the Girt House immediately. Instead he walked a little way along the beach studying the sand. He soon found what he was looking for — two sets of footprints led back towards the cliff path and were crossed by returning prints. Two men had visited the cove during the night, but for what purpose he could not imagine.

Boisson he knew to be an evil lawbreaker, but the mysterious stranger whom Boisson had addressed as "Mon Capitaine" had spoken in a cultivated voice. What could such a man be doing on a smuggler's ship? Deeply troubled, Crabber walked slowly back to his boat and picked up the tub of lobsters intended for the Daintons' dinner. The thought of John Dainton's commanding but sympathetic personality sent him striding up the cliff path to pour out his problem to the one person in authority who could be trusted not to betray his own unlawful dealings with Boisson.

Mary Wiggatt had spent the morning in growing anxiety for she loved her husband dearly, but did not share his love of the sea. Her father had been drowned off Chesilton when she was eight years old, and the memories of the resulting poverty suffered by a large family of young children would always haunt her. Her mother had toiled bravely to bring them up and had succeeded, but it had been a bitter struggle and Mary could remember many days when they had been cold and hungry.

She could never go out on the cliffs in wild weather without recalling the night of her father's death, or understand Crabber's fascination for gazing down the narrow shaft of the Cave Hole to watch the waves crashing over the rocks forty feet below. The turmoil created by the retreating water meeting the onslaught of each fresh wave was awesome in its elemental power, and filled her with dread. The much deeper shaft at the Blow Hole she avoided altogether.

Fog was another of the hazards that Mary feared, so when Crabber at last appeared at the Girt House, she relieved her pent-up anxiety in a flow of abuse: "Well, w'er have you been dawdlen to? And me all joppety-joppety thinking you wer drowned! And wi' never a thing to serve up to the mistress for dinner! You'd best get to boiling those lobsters at once!"

"Cease thy blather, woman, and boil them yourself. I must see the Captain." — and without further explanation of his belated arrival, Crabber dumped the tub of very active lobsters on the kitchen floor and strode off to the front of the house.

Affronted by his offhand behaviour, Mary muttered darkly to herself over the unfeeling habits of men. She had never been adept in the handling of live lobsters, but fearing that her dinner would be late, she extended her hand gingerly into the tub, whereupon one of the creatures seized her fingers in a vicious grip. Her yells of pain brought Dingle in from the stableyard, and she gratefully handed over the responsibility for their dispatch to him.

Meanwhile Crabber had sought out John and poured out the tale of his discovery of the *Marie-Louise* and the clandestine visit to the cove of two Frenchmen. "But where they went, I'm dazed if I know," the young man ended, "for they're been loading stone from the cove, and 'tis a very lippy time."

Correctly interpreting this to mean that the footprints ended in the morass of mud created by the recent rain, John sighed and rose. He had listened to the story with growing concern, for although he knew nothing about the incident at the cove two years before, he had never forgotten the expression of contempt and hatred on Crabber's face at the sight of Manvers's corpse at Wallsend Bay. He was well aware that none of the Islanders had been involved in smuggling since Manvers's death, so he could not imagine what the Frenchmen could have been doing at the cove, and ruefully envisaged himself being subjected to further questioning and annoyance by the authorities.

"I will come down to the cove with you. We had better search those quarrymen's huts on the beach, and the old church, though I do not suppose we shall find anything. It's possible that the Frenchmen may have come to meet someone — a spy perhaps? We must find out if any strangers have been seen on the Island, but whatever we do or do not discover, I am afraid we shall have to report the whole matter to the Preventive officer, because we are at war with France. I shall not, of course, mention that you recognised the ship."

Crabber agreed to the first part of this plan, but as his dislike of the Preventives far outweighed his patriotic fervour, he was reluctant to commit himself to the second. He assumed an air of martyrdom and mumbled in an aggrieved undertone that he supposed his master knew best, but for his part it seemed likely that if the perishing Preventives were brought into it, all that would happen would be more poking and prying into things which every Islander wished to conceal.

John laughed. "I sympathise with your views. Do you think I want that officious little magistrate, Willerby, yapping at my heels again? But I'm afraid our duty is clear."

Crabber sighed, and retired to the kitchen to ponder over the eccentricities of the gentry, while partaking of a substantial, if belated breakfast.

The steep cliffs of Church Ope were constantly being eroded by landslides and where fresh falls had occurred huge piles of jagged rock stood out in naked contrast to the accumulated debris of older falls now covered with rough grass and tangled thorn bushes. Halfway up the cliff in the centre of the cove stood the old church of St Andrew, for hundreds of years the only place of worship on the Island. A century before the Portlanders had done their best to prevent it falling into the sea by building a substantial stone wall around the perimeter of its graveyard, but the immense labour had been in vain for the cliff face had continued to fall away until finally, in 1753, the church had had to be abandoned.

The mid-day sun beating down on the path to the cove was rapidly turning the mud into a series of hard-baked ridges and ruts, but John revelled in its warmth after the weeks of mist and grey skies. He glanced towards Weymouth Bay and his attention was immediately caught by the sight of four ships of the line, their topgallant sails set to catch the light breeze from the land, as they made their way towards the Roads on the last of the flood tide: "Your friend Boisson was wise to make his getaway in the fog. He'd have had to run the gauntlet of that lot if he had waited for the fog to lift."

"Ay," agreed Crabber sourly. "I saw them turn in from mid-Channel when I was beaching my boat. But there, the Devil always minds his own, my Gramf'er says." He spat to signify his disapproval of the Devil's vigilance, and then turned to the business in hand. "There are the footprints I told you of — and here they seem to end."

John stared at the footprints which ended abruptly near the recent landslide, and then studied the mass of fallen rock and rubble below and to the right of the broken wall of the church-yard. Behind the church a grove of elm trees flourished in an ancient valley, whose stream had long since disappeared below ground to bubble up in a spring of fresh water at the base of the cliff. Was it the landslide that had deterred the Frenchmen from venturing up the cliff path John wondered? But what they could have been seeking in the church or the grove beyond he could not imagine.

Crabber, growing restless, turned away to search the huts on the beach. John called to him to look in the boats drawn up near them, and then started to climb the steep path on the southern side of the churchyard. Although weekly services were now held in the Tabernacle, a small stone building erected for the purpose in Easton, marriages were still celebrated in St Andrew's, in spite of its dilapidated state. The graveyard at least showed

95

signs of loving care, its grass had been recently scythed, and the path leading to the massive oak door was clear of weeds.

Certainly the church had little architectural merit, John thought, as he pushed open the door. It was a long, low building with a tiled roof, roughly rebuilt after French raiders had burnt it to the ground in 1475. The interior, which was bare of ornaments, was in a ruinous condition — the cracked walls were running with water, the pews were covered with a damp mould and in places their supports were rotting. A perfunctory search of the vestry revealed nothing that could have been of interest to the Frenchmen, so John left the main building and entered the square tower, which was a separate structure standing some thirty feet away from the west door of the church.

Here no effort had been made to check the decaying effect of the weather; the rain had poured in through the leaking roof, rotting the floor of the loft and forming a slimy pool on the sunken slab floor. A rickety ladder with several broken rungs stood against one wall, but it was covered with cobwebs and the debris of birds. Trails of ivy had entwined themselves round the window mullions, but enough light penetrated to show John that the floor was thick in dust which bore no footprints other than his own — evidently the Islanders considered it unsafe to enter the tower, and indeed had no reason to do so, since it had no clock or bell.

John returned to the sunlight to find Crabber sitting on the stone wall conversing with a ragged child who was kneeling by one of the graves, plucking at the weeds with a sharp knife. A scythe, propped up against the wall, proclaimed its puny owner to be the caretaker of the churchyard. Crabber rose and came to stand beside the boy: "This is Will Wollage. He keeps the graveyard tidy. He hasn't seen any strangers about here lately."

Will gave a quaint little bow and nodded, his grimy hands twitching nervously.

"So you are the gardener! I didn't see anyone about when I came up here, and wondered who did the work." The words were spoken kindly, but their effect on the child was shocking. Beneath the dirt his face turned ashen, and he stared up at

John with fear-stricken eyes. Momentarily nonplussed by the boy's reaction, John could think of nothing to say. It was Crabber who broke the tension by placing a protective arm about the waif-like figure.

"You've no need to look like that, Will. The Captain won't tell on you."

"You're sure, really sure?" Emboldened by Crabber's expression the child's face regained some of its colour, and he gave a deep sigh of relief. "He'd give me a terrible drapping if he knew I'd been to Betsy's for dinner. People are supposed to pay him if they want their graves done special."

John's curiosity was now thoroughly aroused; he sat down on the wall and said reassuringly: "Of course I won't tell anybody anything. Who'd give you a drapping — your father? Who is he?"

"Aint' got no father — or mother either. I bides with my Uncle, Uriah Heap. He's sexton."

"It's sad you've no mother or father, and you look in need of several good dinners. Don't you get enough to eat?"

"Somedays I do. You see Fridays is Betsy Stone's baking day — she lives in the cottage above the grove, and she gives me dinner. A real big pasty I had today — hot too!" The memory of that wholesome meal brought a glow to the grubby cheeks: "So I keep her grave nice — it's that one over there — her father and mother." He pointed to a plain headstone surrounded by neatly clipped grass, on which a bunch of freshly picked flowers had been laid.

"Do you work here every day?" John asked.

"No. Tuesdays and Fridays mostly, but I've got to be here tomorrow 'cos Uncle says Parson's coming down here Sunday. Other times I do Uncle's garden — a big garden he has, and mind the pigs and fowls. Winter time I muck out Mr Lowman's horses."

"You do work hard. How old are you?"

"Rising eleven."

"Well, when you come here tomorrow you come up to the Girt House at noon, and Crabber will see you get a good dinner, and on Tuesdays too. You needn't mention it to your Uncle, it's just between the three of us."

"Something hot Tuesdays *and* Fridays! That would be primer that would."

The child's eagerness smote John's heart. Was the sexton really so poor that they lived on bread and cheese all the week? He must look into the matter. He turned to Crabber: "You didn't find anything on the beach I suppose? There was nothing in the church."

"No, nothing, and I daresay we shall fret our gizzards green before we do. I've been thinking — "

"It is time we got back to the house," interrupted John, not wishing to discuss the matter in front of Will Wollage: "We can talk as we go. I shall expect you at noon tomorrow, Will." He strode off up the path, and when out of earshot of the boy, said: "What have you been thinking, Crabber?"

"Well, sir, it's like this. I can't see no need to tell the Preventives about what I heard this morning — not till we discover something anyway, or I'll look a regular gawkhammer. Maybe if I went off to The Lugger tonight, I could hear if any strangers have been about. I could see my Uncle Matthew too, and find out if anyone has been visiting the quarries."

John's determination to report the matter to the Preventive officer had been steadily diminishing throughout his fruitless search of the cove, and a glance at the obstinate lines around the young man's mouth confirmed his suspicion that Crabber would be as unco-operative as possible. He decided to temporize: "Very well, we will keep the matter to ourselves for a day or two, while you and your uncle make some enquiries. Tell me about this man, Heap. Is he so very poor?"

"Poor! That old skinflint! Why I don't know how many golden guineas you might not find if you searched his house. No, he's just a miser he is, and that hard on the boy it makes your heart bleed. But there, I suppose he's no worse off than if he were on the Parish in Weymouth — she died in Weymouth, his mother did, and his father was drowned some years before. Uriah prides himself on his goodness in taking in the boy — but I've no time for his sort — Holy is as Holy does, I say!"

Elspeth pronounced the dressed lobsters to be delicious, but John signally failed to enjoy them. He was haunted by the memory of Will's fear-stricken eyes, but how he could help the child, if his mentor considered himself to be a model of virtue, he could not imagine. It seemed unlikely that Heap would allow Will to be employed at the Girt House, for the child was too useful to him.

There appeared to be no immediate solution to the matter, or to the more pressing problem of how best to deal with the mysterious visit of the *Marie-Louise*. Elspeth was full of the adventure. Having been regaled with a highly embellished version of the tale by Mary Wiggatt, she wholeheartedly supported Crabber's determination to keep the event secret for a while. John smiled at her enthusiasm, and teasingly accused her of becoming a regular vagabond.

She laughed delightedly: "Well, I suppose some people might think so, dearest; but then they are not living here. I think it would be a pity to antagonise the Islanders until you find out more. Besides, now that the Frenchmen have found out that the landslide has occurred, I do not suppose that they will come back."

John was fully aware how easy it would be to antagonise the Islanders, and although he could not agree that the Frenchmen were unlikely to return, he kept this thought to himself. He was still mulling over the problem when he retired for the night. He could not believe that the Frenchmen would have risked visiting the cove, or have made their get-away in thick fog, unless they had had something secret and important to do there. No satisfactory answer came to him, for Will's frightened eyes kept intruding upon his thoughts, and stirred the bitter memory of another child's sad face, a beloved son who had hugged him tightly, saying : "*Must* you go away again so soon, Papa?" His own children had been abandoned to an uncle, but not, John strove to re-assure himself, to hunger and ill-treatment.

It was some hours before he fell into a fitful sleep, to be awakened, almost immediately it seemed, by the sound of marching feet. The Preventive patrol returning from their nightly vigil he supposed; but surely they were leaving the cliffs earlier than usual? Unable to subdue his curiosity, John rose and pulled back the heavy curtains to find that the dawn was just breaking. He went back to bed, but sleep eluded him. Restless and out of temper, he dressed and let himself out of the sleeping house, and made his way to the cove.

The light was stronger now, and when he reached Bow and Arrow Castle he understood why the Preventives had left the cliffs before dawn. The four ships of the line were making their way out to the Channel on the ebb tide. He sat down on a convenient outcrop of rock and taking his telescope from his pocket, watched their progress with professional interest.

The weather had changed overnight, and now a strong breeze was blowing from the east turning the calm sea of yesterday into a myriad of rippling waveheads. He glanced down to the cove, here the waves were bigger for the conflict of the wind and the ebb current was causing a heavy swell; but something was floating amongst those foaming crests — a log or spar, twisting and turning as it was driven shorewards by the wind, only to be pulled out again by the ebb stream as it sunk into the trough of each wave. John watched it idly, and then stiffened — something was clinging to that spar — a man's body thrown across it, trying desperately to guide it in towards the beach.

Pocketing his telescope, John raced down the steep cliff path. The spar was closer in now, and he could see the man fighting valiantly to gain a foothold in the shallow water. Twice the ebbing current pulled him under, then a stronger wave threw him up onto the beach to lie face downwards on the wet sand, with the spar some feet away from him.

John reached the spar first and stopped in surprise, for it was no ordinary piece of timber, but a carved panel some five feet in length, depicting the creatures of the sea. Oblivious of his errand, John gazed down at it, for it was not the crude scratching of an idle seaman, but the exquisite workmanship of a master craftsman. The graceful dolphins of the centrepiece seemed to leap towards him in life-like mastery, stirring a chord in his memory — but before recollection came, the prone figure stirred, and gave a moan of anguish.

John hurried over and knelt beside the man, understanding his agony, for his back from shoulders to waist, was covered with dark, raw weals, with deep, suppurating wounds where the knotted cords of the "cat" had torn into the flesh. Gently, John turned the figure to lift it, and gasped in shocked recognition — "Hudson!"

The man who was hardly conscious, opened his eyes and stared up at John through mists of pain. He let out his breath in a sharp sigh of relief and croaked: "It's true then, what they told me, you are here, sir.... I... I... " But no more words came. The salt water he had swallowed formed a foam on his mouth, he lifted his arm to wipe it away, and writhed in agony. Then, mercifully, he fainted.

Chapter 11

Staring at the unconscious man in his arms, John was shaken with fury. Barney Hudson had been his master carpenter in the *Barchester*, a fine craftsman with an excellent record for good conduct. What could have occurred to put him in conflict with authority? Who could have ordered a man with his record such a flogging, and how could he have swum ashore in such a state?

Then he remembered the carving. Hudson would have known that the ebbing tide would carry him past the Island, and must have prayed that the east wind would help him gain the shore. The salt water would have cleaned those terrible wounds while he was in the sea, but now he must be suffering the torments of hell.

John slipped off his coat and removed his shirt. Gently he covered the man's back with the fine linen, and tied it securely round him with his cravat. He glanced out to sea, the ships of the line were moving steadily out to the Channel; they would not return for their deserter, but no-one must witness Hudson's arrival at Girt House, though how to convey him there, unless Hudson could walk with his support, he did not know.

He felt in the deep pockets of his coat, and thankfully drew out a small flask of brandy. He poured the liquid down the man's throat. Hudson choked and some colour returned to his face. He lifted bloodshot eyes to John: "I can explain it all, Captain."

"But not now. I must get you away from here. My house is quite near, but first we've got to climb that cliff path."

The man turned his head to study the terrain and drew in his breath. "I'll make it somehow, Captain," he muttered.

Slowly they progressed across the beach, but before they had reached the shelter of the cliff, a small figure came racing down the path from the churchyard, clutching a fork.

"I see your friend can't walk properly, Captain, so I've brought my fork for him, and I can help too. Cor, he does look poorly — perhaps he needs a drink from the spring."

Will seemed to see nothing unusual in finding his new benefactor supporting a half-drowned man across the beach. He cheerfully placed his small form beneath Hudson's other arm, and somehow they reached the spring. Hudson fell on his knees, drank deeply and was then terribly sick.

"Perhaps he'll feel better now he's shot the cat," said Will hopefully, but it was clear to John that Hudson could never climb the cliff path in his present condition.

"Will, go up to the Girt House and find Crabber. Tell him I want him and Dingle here immediately. They must bring a blanket to use as a stretcher. Hurry, and don't say anything to anyone else."

The boy set off eagerly. Hudson propped himself sideways against a rock, and closed his eyes. John was about to sit beside him, when he remembered the carving and went to retrieve it. He came back to find Hudson looking stronger. "I can go on again now, sir," he offered.

"Splendid! I've sent Will off to bring help, but if you can go a little further, I think we should do so."

The man nodded; grasping Will's fork, he rose painfully to his feet, and with John's support began to climb the steep path. They had reached the tangle of thorn bushes to the right of the churchyard when Will appeared on the wall. He took a flying leap, and landed beside John, his face alight with excitement.

"Captain, the Preventives are coming down through the grove. I saw them marching down Wakeham. I always keep well out of their way, so I ran back and hid in the grove. When they turned in, I thought I'd better come straight back to you — thinking your friend mightn't care for them either."

"You did quite right, Will. We must hide Hudson here till they pass, but where? And I must get that carving out of sight too."

"I'll hide him, Captain. I know all the cliff. Can you crawl?" He turned to Hudson, who nodded. "Then follow me," and without further ado he plunged into the undergrowth and was lost from sight. Hudson crawled slowly after him.

John raced down the path, picked up the carving and stowed it in the bottom of a nearby boat beneath a pile of netting. Then he ran swiftly up the path, and was seated nonchalantly on the churchyard wall, with his telescope to his eye, when the patrol rode out of the grove.

The Preventive officer, a Major Collins, was clearly discomfited at the sight of John. He dismounted and came over to him, saying stiffly: "You are abroad early this morning, Captain Dainton."

"The reason is clear to see," replied John equably, "or was," and pointed to the distant ships. The officer gazed seawards, and then raised his own telescope.

"I watched them come in yesterday," continued John, "and guessed that they would leave on the ebb tide this morning. I have watered in Portland many times myself, when serving with the Western Squadron."

"I see, sir," replied Collins more genially: "And do you miss the life at sea?"

"Damnably!" It was some time since anyone had asked John that question, and he was surprised at the depth of feeling it evoked within him.

Collins, somewhat embarrassed by the effect of his innocuous inquiry, was unable to think of any suitable rejoinder. To cover his confusion he shouted an order to his sergeant, and to John's consternation the men spread out in line and began to search the undergrowth.

Collins turned back to John and read the concern in his face, but thinking that his previous blunder must have been its cause, said in his most conciliating manner: "Well, sir, I must bid you good-day and take a look in the tower. Sergeant Howe reported that he found fresh footprints in there, which seemed highly suspicious to me because the Islanders told me it was unsafe to go in there, but maybe that was just a blind and they are using it as a store for contraband."

John, inwardly cursing the sharp-eyed sergeant, was in two minds whether to tell the Preventive officer that the footprints in the tower were his own or say nothing, but a shout from one of the search party decided him to take the first course — somehow the hounds must be drawn off the scent before they discovered Hudson.

He rose and joined Collins: "I expect your man saw my footprints. I went into the tower yesterday. I was curious to find out why it stands a yard away from the main building. It's such an unusual feature, don't you think?"

Collins looked at him suspiciously. "You went in the tower? Didn't you know it is unsafe, sir?"

"I took a chance on that. I wanted to see if there were any signs of fire there. It occurred to me that it might be part of the original medieval building which was burnt to the ground by the French in 1475." He saw that Collins was beginning to look less suspicious and warmed to his theme: "My sister is very historically-minded, and has been looking into some of the old records. If you are interested in that sort of thing, I am sure she would be delighted to tell you about her finds."

"I should indeed be interested to hear about Miss Dainton's studies." Collins was visibly gratified at the hint of an invitation to the Girt House. They reached the tower and he pushed open the door saying: "Did you discover any signs of fire here? I cannot say that I have ever noticed any."

"No — but I can prove that these footprints were my own," said John, placing his feet carefully in the prints.

Collins laughed. "Yes, I see they are." He glanced round the decaying structure: "Well, we need not risk our lives by remaining here. I must recall my patrol."

Immensely relieved, John followed him across the churchyard where Will was hard at work clipping the grass. Collins hailed his men, but their backs were towards him and the wind carried his voice away from them — they continued their search unheeding.

"There's no chance of making them hear me with the wind this way. I shall have to go to them," said Collins, vaulting off the wall into the undergrowth.

John watched the retreating figure apprehensively, would he reach his men before they discovered Hudson? He sat down on the wall unable to think of anything further he could do, his eyes riveted on the distant figures of the searchers. Will continued to clip the grass, but his kneeling figure drew closer until he was beside his benefactor. He touched John's knee with one grubby hand to attract his attention, and smiled mischievously up into his anxious face: "They won't find your friend, Captain. He's snug underground. I put him in the cave where the guns are."

"The cave where the guns are!" John repeated in astonishment: "What guns?"

"French guns, Mr Manvers said they were — hundreds of them."

"Mr Manvers! Do you mean the other Preventive officer?"

"Yes — the one they murdered."

"With good reason I suppose, if he'd discovered their secret hoard," said John grimly. "Will, how many other people know about this cave?"

"I don't rightly know — a lot of older Portland people I suppose. My mother told me about it. When she was a maid everyone used the water from there if the summer was dry. She said it had been built as a water supply for the castle hundreds of years ago — but the path to it fell in a landslide."

"How did you find it, Will?"

"I fell in it blackberrying a year back. The shaft was full of loose scree then, and I hurt my ankle bad. Cor, it did swell up, I couldn't work for ten days. Uncle was that angry with me I didn't dare tell him what I'd been doing — said I'd fallen coming down the grove. When I went back I took a fork, but there was no need to, for someone else had been there — the shaft was clear, so I went down it —" he paused dramatically, his eyes gleaming with excitement at the memory of that momentous discovery: "It's a wonderful place! Fan-shaped it is, with the floor sloping down to the water at one end, and stone pillars to hold up the roof. There was a lot of water there then, but it had been even higher — you could see that from the slime on the walls and pillars."

"How high up the walls did this water reach?"

"About two feet, I should say."

106

"Two feet!" John laughed derisively. "Will, you can't store guns in two feet of water."

"Oh, the guns are dry enough. They are in the higher cave beyond the wall." He saw the look of patent disbelief on John's face, and touched his arm entreatingly: "They are there, honest, Captain — I'll show you when that lot have gone," nodding towards the searchers on the cliff face.

John saw that Major Collins had joined his men and rose hurriedly. "Will, I mustn't be here when they come back. The ships I was supposedly watching are almost out of sight. Get on with your work now, but as soon as they have gone, come up to the Girt House and find me, but don't say a word to anyone about Hudson or the guns. I'll come straight back here with you, and when we've got Hudson safely within doors, I'll take a look at these guns of yours."

John made his way up the grove, his mind in a turmoil. The child's astounding revelation of the French arms store could well be the reason for the secret visit of the *Marie-Louise*, but how had Will been connected with Manvers? Why had Manvers not reported his discovery, or had he wanted to arrest Boisson before doing so? Did any of the Islanders know about the guns? An ugly thought this, and one he rejected outright, but how had the Frenchmen concealed their nefarious doings from their confederates in the smuggling trade?

At the top of the grove Betsy Stone was sweeping her porch. She gave John a cheerful greeting, and brought to his mind the most urgent question of all. How was he to convey Hudson to the Girt House secretly in broad daylight?

This did indeed seem an insuperable problem, and he was still considering it when he opened the side door. The welcoming aroma of freshly baked bread wafted to him from the kitchen quarters, from which Crabber (having seen him enter the garden) emerged. He stared at his master, taking in his frowning countenance and disordered dress: "Is anything the matter, sir?"

"Indeed it is! And I shall need your help. I'm devilish hungry too, some coffee and fresh bread will do. But first bring me some shaving water. Tell Dingle I shall want him too."

107

These brusque orders confirmed Crabber's fear that some dire misfortune must have occurred, and he hurried off to the kitchen to chivvy Mary into activity. Mary, having already baked the day's bread and provided the servants' breakfast, was inclined to be resentful of these summary commands, for she was enjoying one of her most pleasurable moments of the day, supervising Possum's consumption of a large helping of porridge. The memories of childhood hunger still haunted her, so to watch her son eat his fill, was a never-ending source of gratification to her.

"All in good time I'll get the Captain's coffee," she said testily. "There was no sense in my making it before feeding Possum, for he likes the water freshly boiled, and *you* said he'd gone out."

"Ay, but he's in now, and in a rare taking," replied Crabber, filling a brass can from the steaming kettle on the hob. "I disremember when I've seen him look so grim. Leastways, not since that Manvers was murdered I haven't, so bustle about woman; and, Possum, you stop dawdlen over your dewbit and tell Mr Dingle he's wanted in the breakfast parlour."

"Lawks a' mercy!" ejaculated Mary. "You don't think those pesky Preventives are causing trouble again, do you?"

"I don't know what to think," replied her observant spouse. "But something's afoot, for I aint never seen the Captain walking out without his shirt on before, or wearing a handkerchief round his neck — proper fussy he is about his neckcloths!" With this cryptic remark, he vanished round the bend in the back stairs, leaving Mary, now thoroughly agitated, to prepare a hasty meal.

Ever since the night of his arrival on the Island, when the Captain had shielded her husband from the Preventives, Mary had been devoted to him and a kinder or more considerate master she could not imagine. She could not conceive what kind of trouble he might be in now, or see how her humble services might help him, but at least she could make sure that he did not lack for nourishment. So when, some twenty minutes later, freshly shaved and with his disordered attire set severely to rights, John descended to the breakfast parlour, he found her hovering by the side table which bore, besides an imposing silver coffee pot, a dressed ham and a sirloin of cold beef.

"Ah, Mary, a large breakfast is just what I need," said John smiling warmly at her. "But fetch Skinner will you. I want to talk to you all."

He helped himself liberally to both the ham and the beef and began to eat, while Crabber and Dingle waited expectantly. He looked up when Mary returned with Skinner and said without further preamble: "I've sent for you all because I need your help. I intend bringing a seaman who once served under me, to this house to be nursed back to health. He swam ashore from his ship this morning, so if his presence here is discovered, you could all be in trouble for aiding and abetting a deserter."

He glanced from one to the other, sure that however much Skinner and Dingle might disapprove of his action, they would serve him loyally, but it was Crabber who spoke first.

"Well, he ain't likely to be discovered, for you can count on Mary and me to hold our tongues. Besides, he'll be safe enough on the Island for there's none of us as care overmuch for law officers. Where is he, Captain?"

"Will Wollage has hidden him near the churchyard," replied John, choosing his words carefully. "He was nearly spent when he reached the beach, and in acute pain from his back which is raw from a recent flogging." He paused as Mary gasped, and then went on: "Hudson was my master carpenter — a man I liked and trusted. I don't know what led to such punishment, but I can't believe it was deserved. I had hoped to get him back to the house before anyone was about, but unfortunately a Preventive patrol came to search the cove. Will saw them coming and hid Hudson. He'll come up here as soon as they leave, but now we shall have the devil's own task to get Hudson back here without being noticed."

Dingle, who had been standing with his arms folded, engrossed in thought, looked up and said: "I believe I know how it may be achieved, sir. Miss Elspeth mentioned to me the other day that she wanted some large stones to make a rock garden here. I'll harness the cob to the covered baggage cart; then your man can lie under cover and we can have two or three slabs sticking out over the tailboard and no one won't think to question what's inside."

"A splendid idea, Dingle! Put in some sacks for Hudson to lie on, and take Crabber with you. He can be at the back of the cart to make sure the slabs don't slide off coming up the grove."

"Ay, that will be dandy that will," agreed Crabber. "Moreover we can stop and pass the time of day with Betsy Stone as we go down, and then she'll know what we're about."

"I'll harness the cob now, sir," Dingle opened the door to find Will and Possum hovering nervously in the passage.

"Will wants to see the Captain urgent like, but no one heard him knocking," explained Possum.

"Forgive me, sir," Mary stepped out into the passage. "That's a good boy, Possum. Now you run back to the kitchen, and Will, you come in to the Captain."

Will slid nervously into the breakfast parlour. Uneasily aware that the four servants were staring at his mud-bespattered person, he swallowed convulsively. "I come to see the Captain private like," he muttered, wringing his hands in distress.

John smiled reassuringly at the boy: "It's all right, Will. I have told everyone here how helpful you were hiding Hudson. The Preventives have gone, have they?"

"Ay. They've gone over towards Weston."

"Is Hudson all right?"

Will rubbed his nose doubtfully. "He says he is, but he's bibbering terrible."

"Bibbering?"

"He means shaking with cold, sir," interpreted Crabber. "Where did you hide him, Will?"

"In the cave where the . . ." Will glanced at John, who gave an almost imperceptible shake of the head. "The cave where the water for the old castle is." He finished lamely.

"The water supply cave!" ejaculated Crabber, in what was to John's relief, obviously genuine astonishment. "You're gammening me, boy! Why the entrance to that cave was blocked by a cliff fall years ago."

110

"I know the *path* to it was," agreed Will. "But I told the Captain how it was I fell in the shaft blackberrying a year back."

Crabber still looked unbelieving, but John said quietly: "I suppose it is quite possible that only a thin layer of debris covered the actual shaft — but until we see the cave for ourselves, we can only surmise what must have happened. Our first consideration must be to rescue Hudson. Dingle, you must start for the cave immediately."

He swallowed the last of his coffee and rose, but Skinner detained him: "Which room should be prepared, sir?" she asked in reproving tones. "Miss Elspeth cannot manage the stairs to the attics. And knowing her, she will insist on preparing the remedies for the man's back herself; for I take it, you will not be wishing to call a surgeon."

John halted, reading the disapproval in the old servant's face: "Miss Elspeth! I must see her myself." He crossed the hall and mounted the wide oak staircase, reflecting ruefully that he was about to involve his crippled sister in yet another scrape.

Chapter 12

Elspeth was seated at her escritoire studying the projected elevations of their new house at Mutton Cove. By habit she was an early riser, for her hip caused her acute discomfort after lying in one position for any length of time. The effort of dressing, even with the assistance of the faithful Skinner, always exhausted her, so unless some expedition was planned, she spent the first hours of the day in the panelled bedchamber above the porch, which she had furnished as a morning room.

"Ah, John," she smiled up at him, as he bent to kiss her, "I am so glad you have come to visit me early, for I thought we might drive over to the site at Mutton Cove this morning. Gilbert is coming to see us on Monday, and there are one or two improvements I have thought of."

"Elspeth, I can't go this morning, Nor can you, for I need Dingle for a while. The thing is . . . " He paused, frowning, wondering how best to tell her about Hudson.

Intuitively she realised that something was troubling him: "Is it about the *Marie-Louise*? Did Boisson come back?" she asked.

"No, but we may have stumbled on the reason for his visit," he answered, and told her all that had happened at the cove.

She sat listening quietly, with her arms resting on the escritoire, a quill clasped in her hands, her eyes shining in sympathy as he unfolded the story. She could see little danger of Hudson's identity being exposed, for she knew they could trust her own servants, and Mary had told her that not only Crabber, but Matthew Wiggatt too, held John in high esteem. There must be some rare quality in him she thought, that made men serve him with the utmost fidelity.

At the end of his recital she laid a hand on his arm: "Of course you are right to bring the man here. Skinner and Mary shall put a truckle bed in the room over the dairy — for I find the attic stairs very difficult to manage. If you will help me down to the still-room, I'll prepare a salve for his back, while you go to the cove."

"You are a woman in a thousand, Elspeth," exclaimed John fervently, bestowing a light kiss on her forehead, as he stooped to help her to her feet.

As he approached the cottage at the head of the grove, he was amused to see that the baggage cart was still drawn up before it. Dingle had dismounted from the box and was gossiping with the garrulous Betsy Stone, while Crabber was leaning idly against the side of the cart sucking a straw. Both actors appeared to have entered into the spirit of their parts with relish, for on sighting John, they hastily abandoned their positions as though not wishing to be caught loitering, and set off down the grove without more ado.

Will was waiting for them at the entrance to the churchyard with a serviceable hook in his hand. Beside him, a pile of fossilised rocks and several stone slabs, were proof that he had not been idle since leaving the Girt House. He led them to the north eastern corner of the graveyard and began slashing at a thick clump of brambles growing up the wall. He clambered over and hacked away with the hook, revealing a steep flight of stone steps which ended abruptly in a thicket of thorns and brambles, beyond which was an outcrop of rock.

Negotiating the steps, John realised that they must have originally led down to a wide ledge in the cliff, forming a path from the church to the old castle which was now obliterated by fallen rock.

Will plunged headlong into the thicket, and after a moment's hesitation, John followed. But to his relief, the seemingly impenetrable barrier proved to be nothing more than a thick screen fronting the original rock ledge. Once through it, John reached an open space and saw that ahead of him the original cliff face had been quarried out in the distant past — either to build the medieval church, or earlier, to form part of the fortifications of the Norman castle, he supposed. The rock below his feet was covered with trails of ivy and other creeping plants, but to his left it had been pulled away to reveal the yawning shaft of the cave.

Will nudged his arm: "Here it is, Captain," he said triumphantly, and started down the shaft like an over-eager terrier.

Dingle, who had followed close behind John, produced a tinder box and lit the lantern he had had the forethought to put in the cart.

"Competent as ever, Dingle," grinned John, who had descended into the shaft. He took the lantern and shone it ahead. The shaft was short, but dropped away at a steep angle, and in a few moments John found himself in the chamber Will had described. Holding his lantern aloft, he marvelled at its fan-shaped construction and the graceful pillars supporting the roof, as he swept the beam around searching for the entrance to the Frenchmen's cache. Suddenly he held the beam steady. High up in the corner furthest from the water, some of the rough-hewn stones of the wall seemed to have fallen away and a dark cavity loomed.

A cry of distress from Will: "He's here, Captain. Come quick!" caused him to turn. The beam of the lantern showed Hudson's figure slumped in Will's arms beside one of the pillars near the water. He hastened over the uneven floor — Hudson was unconscious and ice cold. Will gulped: "Do you think he's gone, Captain?" he whispered. "He's terrible cold."

"No. He is not dead yet," replied John, feeling the man's slow pulse, "but he will be, if he has to stay here much longer. Where are Dingle and Crabber?"

"Coming now, sir." Dingle's voice sounded from the shaft, and he entered the cave bearing a make-shift stretcher constructed from a blanket tied to two poles, followed by Crabber carrying more blankets. "Seeing how steep the shaft was, sir, I thought as how we would need a stretcher, and it was easier to do it in the daylight," Dingle explained.

For a full minute Crabber paid no heed to the group about the pillar, but gazed around intently, and in gathering anger. Then he strode up to Will and shook him roughly by the shoulder:

114

"You're a rum 'un, not telling anyone you'd found the shaft to this cave. The times we've struggled up that dratted path, sweating lest the Preventives should get wind of the run before we'd disposed of the casks. This would have been a splendid place to store them!"

Will was spared the necessity of replying by John, who interposed firmly: "I can see that it would have been. You can come back later and look over it, but first we must get Hudson to the house. Strip off his soaking breeches and wrap him in those blankets. My shirt will protect his back."

"So that's what you done with it," commented Crabber sagely, his anger fading as he took in Hudson's condition. "His feet are freezing! We'd best look sharp, or we'll be putting him to bed with a shovel."

With some difficulty they hauled the unconscious man up the shaft. No one was about, so John left the others to negotiate the steps with their burden, and hastened down to the beach to retrieve the carved panel from the boat where he had hidden it. He rejoined the others to learn that Hudson had come round once, but had fainted again when he was lifted into the cart. "The best thing for him," commented John, stowing away the panel beneath some sacks. "It will spare him the jolting of the cart. Load on the stone now and be off as quick as you can. I'll stay here for a while — it will look more natural if I return later."

The cart was soon lost to sight amongst the elms of the grove, and John turned to his young conspirator: "Now for your guns, Will. They are beyond that cavity in the wall, I suppose."

"Ay, all that part of the wall comes away like."

A few minutes later they stood in the cave again. John stripped off his coat, and together they began pulling away the stone slabs. It was heavy work, and John was soon sweating profusely in spite of the dank chill of the cave. When they had taken off a sufficient number, Will climbed through the gap and held the lantern high. To his amazement, John saw that the boy was standing in an inner chamber of natural rock, extending deep into the cliff. It was on a higher level than the water supply cave, and although the air was fetid, it was completely dry.

115

Will's eyes were blazing with excitement. "What did I tell you, Captain," he exclaimed. "Look here." He swung the lantern to the right, and the wavering beam revealed a line of wooden chests stacked one above the other against the rock wall.

"Great Heaven!" John vaulted into the inner Chamber and put his hand on the boy's shoulder: "This is a splendid adventure, Will. We must check what is in them." He took the lantern and began to inspect the chests. They were fastened with heavy iron locks and bound with coils of rope. John walked down the row counting them.

Will nudged his arm: "Mr Manvers opened one, the second time we cum'd." He pointed to one of the further chests, the lock of which, John saw, had been prised off.

Thrusting the lantern into the boy's hands, John opened the heavy lid and whistled. Will bent forward eagerly — the chest was full of long narrow casings of oiled cloth. John lifted one out and untied the tapes securing it — the barrel of the musket glinted in the lamp-light, the protective covering having kept it in perfect condition.

"Mr Manvers was right! They are French muskets! Are there powder and balls as well, Will?" Will nodded, and moved further into the dark recesses of the chamber to where the powder kegs were stacked, and beyond them the smaller boxes of balls.

"A complete armoury!" exclaimed John grimly. "Will, exactly when did you tell Manvers about this, and why?" He frowned down at the boy, and saw that he was shivering. "No, don't tell me now, it can wait until we are back in the fresh air again." He replaced the musket in its covering and closed the chest, and a few minutes later they were once again in the sunlight.

John seated himself beside the wall: "Come and sit here, Will, out of the wind. Don't look so scared. I'm not angry with you, I just want to know what made you tell Manvers about the guns?"

"*I* didn't find them — he did. I didn't tell no one about the cave, or go there again, 'cos I work for Mr Lowman winter-time. Then in the spring a deal of stone was loaded from the cove —

116

the path was that muddy and slippery it was hard work bringing up the water from the spring near the beach to use in the graveyard. The butts there are rotten, you see, but Uncle wouldn't get new ones, 'cos the church ain't going to be used no more, so I thought about that water in the cave. I 'spose I'd taken it from there two or three times, when Mr Manvers caught me coming out of the bushes carrying a bucketful. He made me show him where I'd got it from — I didn't see nothing wrong in it." Will hesitated before uttering what was virtually heresy from an Islander. "You see, I liked him."

"I thought you said you always kept clear of the Preventives?"

"I do . . . but Mr Manvers was kind . . . it's lonely working in the graveyard, and he used to sit and talk to me. He spent a lot of time about the cove just then."

"I see." Knowing the miserable life he endured with his uncle, John could well understand the child's response to any sympathetic adult. Besides, he had liked Manvers himself: "Go on with your story."

"I showed him the way to the cave, then the cat was in the cream pot proper like, for he found another track to it — it's gone now under that new fall. He asked a lot of questions — had I seen it when I first fell in the shaft? But I was sure I hadn't — it was all brambles then. He went off and got a lantern, and we went down the cave — and there was that gap in the wall! I hadn't seen it before, 'cos I didn't need no light just to get the water." The scared expression returned to Will's eyes, and his voice dropped to a whisper: "I was afear'd then. Perhaps I'd led him to run casks — I thought I'd be lynched!"

He fell silent, reliving that terrifying moment. John put a protective arm round his thin shoulders, and said gently: "Tell me what happened next."

"He found that the stones were loose, like we done just now. We lifted them off and got through. When I saw them chests I wer all joppety-joppety, but when he said they were French guns I felt better, for I knew no one on the Island would have had anything to do with them. I said so to Mr Manvers, but I don't know as how he believed me. . . . Anyway he told me not to say a word to anyone about the cave or what we'd found there; and then two days later those Frenchies murdered him. After that I didn't dare say anything to no one."

"But you hid Hudson there to help me. I cannot thank you enough, Will."

The child raised trusting eyes to John's face: "Anything I'll do for you, Captain, anytime."

"Capital, Will! And I shall not forget you. You had best go back to work now. You can rely on me to see that no one makes any trouble for you over this, but don't say anything about it for the present."

Will made his quaint little bow, and scrambled over the wall. John was preparing to follow him in a more leisurely fashion, when a bellow of rage from the graveyard sent Will back over the wall like a ricochet from a gun. "It's me uncle," he breathed, his face aghast.

"Is it indeed!" exclaimed John grimly. "I have been wishing to meet him. You will be quite safe with me, Will."

Unconvinced of his new benefactor's ability to protect him from his uncle, Will cowered behind John, clutching the skirt of his coat. The threatening roar grew louder. "You won't escape from me, you lazy varmint! I'll give you a taste of my stick to teach you not to go loping off when you should be working!" Heavy footsteps sounded, and a burly figure leant over the wall, brandishing a stick.

John stared haughtily at the newcomer, searching the unpleasant face for any sign of Christian charity, but there was none. Above a protruding jaw, the mouth was set in hard, cruel lines and the small gimlet eyes reminded John forcibly of an angry boar. A strong odour of onions exuded from the sexton's person, and it was evident that neither kindliness nor cleanliness was part of his creed.

"Were you addressing me, my good man?"

The note of authority in that ice-cold voice took the sexton aback. He whipped off his greasy hat and stammered: "Beg pardon, sir. I must have mistook . . . I thought my nephew . . ." He caught sight of Will, and resumed his belligerent attitude: "That's the young rascal I'm after, and a good thrashing he's going to get. It's no use you hiding behind the gentleman, you lazy good-for-nothing. Come here!" He raised his stick menacingly.

Will crept forward, but John thrust a restraining arm in front of him. "One moment, Heap! For I presume you *are* this child's guardian, although you do not appear to be a proper person to fulfil such a position. From all that I have heard on this Island, you have treated Will abominably, while priding yourself on providing for him, so I will relieve you of what is evidently a most irksome duty. The boy has the makings of an excellent gardener, and it is time that he gained more knowledge of the subject. My sister is a noted herbalist, so I shall place him under her instruction."

"Take him away from me, Guv'nor! You can't do that, I need him!"

"Maybe. But I shall not charge you any premium for this apprenticeship, so you will be able to hire an older youth to do your work."

"Pay good money for a lad to do the work that Will does for nothing! It's not likely that I'll agree to that!"

"If you do not do so, I shall have no alternative but to discuss this matter with the parson, and inform him that I consider his employing as sexton, a man who has ill-treated and half-starved a child in his care, is highly undesirable. Furthermore," continued John, relentlessly pursuing his advantage, "I shall make a point of letting my views be known to the Crown Steward, whom I intend visiting this evening."

Rage and chagrin were plainly visible on the sexton's face, but having no wish to be ignominiously dismissed from his post, he was forced to acquiesce in the arrangement.

John turned to the small figure beside him: "Have you any possessions of your own, Will?"

"Only me mouse and me bird. Oh, please may I bring them? He'll kill them otherwise!"

"Of course. But have you nothing else of your own?"

Will shook his head: "He sold the things me mother gave me."

"To pay for your keep, you ungrateful rascal," blustered Heap, his face red with fury at this disclosure of his despicable action: "I wish that I had put you on the Parish!"

"Be silent, man, and stand aside!" John commanded, mounting the steps. "I have already been delayed too long over this disgraceful matter." He strode away through the graveyard, without a backward glance, his newly acquired garden boy trotting blithely behind him, leaving the fulminating sexton to give vent to his rage by calling down vile recriminations upon the authoritarian kimberlin in a most unchristian manner.

Chapter 13

John found Elspeth recruiting her forces with a dish of tea in front of a bright fire in the breakfast parlour. A small table, placed beside her wing chair, bore a plate of cold sliced chicken and some thin slices of Mary's freshly baked bread, thickly spread with butter.

"Tea at this time of the day!" exclaimed John, teasingly. "My dear, are you feeling quite well?"

She chuckled. "It is a luxury, I agree, but such a delightful one. And I thought I might indulge myself, after a morning spent in attending to your seaman. He will survive, I think, but he was dreadfully chilled when they brought him in. However, a warm bed and a cordial of cinnamon water soon restored his body heat and he is now sleeping soundly. . . . Those terrible wounds on his back! I have dressed them with crushed acanthus, which I hope may be soothing and healing. I have not many of the leaves by me, so we must hope that the suppurations will dry quickly and then cowslip ointment can be used. . . . But tell me about the cave. Are there really guns hidden there? Is that what has delayed you?"

"Indeed, the guns are there. I will tell you about our discovery. But I have also acquired a garden boy . . . and made an enemy."

"Made an enemy! How did that come about? John, I will not be fobbed off with such a Banbury story, but mean to know everything. Will you not carve yourself some of this excellent chicken? Or there are the breakfast cold meats on the side table, and Crabber has drawn you a fresh jug of ale. Come by the fire, and explain the whole matter to me."

John carved himself some chicken and ham, and took a chair opposite her, saying: "This is most cosy, and it seems a devilish long time since breakfast." He stretched out his legs to warm them at the blazing fire, and took a satisfying draught of ale before relating the events of the morning, ending: "Will is a delightful child. I am sure you will like him."

"Of course I shall, and if this man Heap is unpopular I do not suppose he will be able to do us much harm. But I do not quite understand about the guns. For whose use were they intended? If the French were planning an invasion, surely the troops would come armed?"

"I agree, that is what I find queer too. Will was quite certain that no Islander would have been involved in treasonable dealings, though Manvers obviously found it hard to believe him."

He sat staring into the fire for a few minutes, and then rose, saying, with a shrug of his shoulders: "Well, I suppose I must get on with this business, but I wish I could see my way through it. I will return to the cave now, with Crabber and Matthew Wiggatt and hear what they have to say. Then I must ride over to the mainland, and lay the whole matter before the Crown Steward. I am certainly not going to carry this story to that tiresome little man, Willerby, without some support."

On his return to the house at noon, John had despatched Crabber to find his uncle Matthew Wiggatt, and bring him back to the Girt House. Crabber had set off willingly, for he was most anxious to discover whether his uncle knew anything about the cave. That he should have remained in ignorance of the existence of such a splendid hiding place for run goods, let alone a safe retreat in time of need, was a source of growing resentment to Crabber, and he arrived at his uncle's cottage in a thoroughly bad temper.

When tackled by his disgruntled nephew, Matthew Wiggatt said he remembered getting water from the cave as a young boy, but confessed that he had not thought of its existence for years: "And there's no need for you to look hountish at me, nevvy," he said severely, "for that cave was covered over by the great cliff fall of thirty or more years back — before you were born, or even thought of!"

Somewhat appeased, Crabber delivered his message and then regaled his uncle with a dramatic version of the seaman's rescue, and the Captain's subsequent dealings with Heap. Since both

Wiggatts were at one in disliking and despising the sexton, they were delighted at his discomfiture, and their mutual enjoyment of the story went far to restoring the harmony of their relationship. They arrived at the Girt House eager to spend the afternoon exploring the cave, but their mood changed abruptly when John showed them the contents of the inner chamber.

At the sight of the gleaming musket barrel in John's hands, Crabber sprang back as though recoiling from a snake, his face dark with fury: "'Struth!" he muttered. "The dirty bastard's trying to get us hanged!"

Matthew stared at the musket, open-mouthed in astonishment. Then he bent over the chest, counting the oiled casings: "Ten — and there's twelve chests." He sat down on one and mopped his brow: "120," he pronounced, after a pause and much counting on his fingers, "you're right, nevvy, it's a hanging matter and the whole Island under sentence, for there's no one on the mainland likely to believe we knew naught about these things being hidden here. It's a rare pickle we're in, for sure!"

Instinctively they looked to John for guidance. "What'll we do Captain?" Crabber asked despairingly. "It's as Uncle says, no one won't believe us innocent."

"I do for one," replied John, "but I agree that it's a devilish situation, and I do not see my way through it, although our first action must be to report the matter to the authorities. But I cannot understand why the Frenchmen should have hidden the guns here. Whatever use could they be to them?"

"Oh, they could use them all right!" exclaimed Crabber. "They've only got to wait for the right weather!"

"Do you mean for a raid of some sort?"

"Or more than that — an invasion! A strong south-westerly is all they need."

"Tell me what is in your mind, Crabber?"

"Well, sir, it's like this — in a strong south-westerly all shipping must keep out of the West Bay, as you well know. So when a small fishing fleet — four or five boats say — comes up out of the west and rounds the Bill, no one thinks anything of it — it's natural like. They keep close in to the Island — but no one can blame them for that for they must avoid the Race, and anchor off the cove, as bold as brass. What if they are boarded by the Preventive patrol — there's no contraband aboard and their story rings true. They can say that they haven't gone on into the Roads because they mean to leave as soon as the wind backs, so no one ain't suspicious. As soon as it's dark, they land the soldiers (who've been dressed as the crew), pick up the guns and take the old castle. One hundred men in there, and they could cover any landing."

"You mean the Bow and Arrow Castle?"

"Ay, the one here."

Abruptly John left the cave and climbed back on to the cliff path. Away to his left, the ancient castle stood on its isolated knoll of limestone dominating the cove. He saw at once that Crabber's idea was feasible — for a short space of time the castle would be impregnable, it could only be reduced by heavy guns. He stood frowning at the prospect before him, turning over in his mind the problem of such a landing. Crabber, who had followed him out of the cave, shuffled his feet impatiently: "You see what I'm getting at, sir?"

"Yes, I see that it could be possible — but the fishing boats might have to remain off the cove for several days before the wind enabled the transports to cross safely."

"Ay, it would all depend on the weather and skilled seamanship, but there's plenty of French captains knows their way into Weymouth in bad weather."

"No doubt you are right." John saw with sympathy, that the young man's face was grey with anxiety, and that Matthew, who had joined them, seemed to have aged ten years in as many minutes. Anger gripped him, they were simple straight-dealing men caught in the intrigues of an enemy country. "It's a damnable situation!" he exclaimed vehemently: "But you may be sure of one thing, that I trust you implicitly, and will do everything in my power to help you through this trouble. I feel that my best course is to go over to the mainland at once, and lay the whole matter before the Crown Steward. Not only do I like him and respect his judgement, but I am certain, that as chief administrator of the Island, he will be the best person to act on your behalf."

Crabber looked up in surprise: "But surely you'll speak for us yourself, Captain?"

"Of course; but you will need an advocate who is more popular with the authorities than me." He met Crabber's astonished gaze squarely and added drily: "You must remember that the only reason that I am among you is because of the failure of my efforts to defend my late commander."

An awkward silence fell, but was broken by Matthew, who said philosophically: "Ay, that was a bad business, but an ill wind for one is fair for another, and it is a good thing for all of us that you are come amongst us, Captain." He paused, and considered the weather, and then knocked out his pipe on a convenient outcrop of rock: "But we'd best not be dawdlen, for there's a strong east wind and the ferry's none too safe after dark."

Before leaving for the mainland, John visited Hudson's room where he found the acid Skinner in charge; she informed him that the seaman appeared to have shaken off the fever; but was still in a deep sleep. Glad to know that Hudson had survived his ordeal, and thankful that his problems could be set aside for the time being, John took leave of Elspeth, warning her not to expect him until the morrow when he would probably be accompanied by the Crown Steward.

John rode slowly down the hill to the ferry, his mind full of the difficulties that lay ahead of him, not only in dealing with the urgent matter of the hidden arms, but also the problem of concealing a deserter in his household. He knew very well that if Hudson's identity was discovered he would be in serious trouble with the authorities, but that was not going to deter him from helping a man whom he knew to be of exemplary character. He was well aware that his own paternalistic attitude towards his crew was not shared by many other naval officers, and that the hardships endured by the seamen in many ships were viewed with callous indifference from the quarter deck. If Hudson had been driven to some act of insubordination it must have been through desperation and misery, and he was determined to get to the bottom of the matter at the earliest opportunity.

It was close on seven o'clock when John rode across the bridge separating Weymouth and Melcombe. A cold mist hung over the harbour, but on the quay men were busy with the unloading of a tall-masted ship. John entered the yard of the nearby Golden Lion, thankful that he could afford the luxury of a permanent suite of rooms there; his mind was too full of his own and the Portlanders' problems to endure the noise and bustle of the coffee room.

"Captain Dainton! Why, sir, this is a pleasure!" Spicer, the inn-keeper, emerged from the door of the hostelry, his jovial face beaming. "You come right in, sir, out of this damp. Martin will see to your horse." He took John's saddlebags from the middle-aged ostler who had unstrapped them, and led the way into the inn. "Jem, light the fires in the Captain's room immediately, and tell Jenny to carry up a warming pan. Annie will be that pleased to know you're here, sir, and she has an eel pie ready baked and three chickens roasting on the spit, for there are half a dozen passengers from the barque just in from Bristol in the coffee room." As he spoke, he led the way up the twisting oak stairs to the rooms on the first floor that were always in readiness for John. Jem, the pot-boy, was already busy at the hearth fanning the dry wood into flames which threw a mellow light over the comfortable room.

Spicer, having momentarily paused in his monologue to light the branched candles, began again with enquiries after Elspeth's health, but John interrupted him, saying firmly: "My sister is well, but she has not accompanied me, because I have urgent business with the Crown Steward. You don't happen to know if he is at home, I suppose?" The Golden Lion was a posting house, so its landlord was well acquainted with the movements of the local gentry, who used its extensive stabling when visiting the town.

"It's more than likely he is, sir, because a gentleman arrived to visit him from London yesterday. A colonial gentleman, I believe."

"Then I had best go to his house at once. Have a fresh horse saddled for me, and tell Annie to set aside a portion of her eel pie against my return."

On being admitted to the Crown Steward's house, John learnt with relief that the owner and his guest were at home, but had not yet left the dining-room. He was shown into a handsome library, but had not long to wait before the Crown Steward joined him, saying civilly: "Captain Dainton! This is a most pleasant surprise. I beg you will join me in a glass of port."

"That would be very welcome. You must forgive me for intruding upon you at such a late hour, but something of the utmost gravity has occurred on the Island, and I felt it my duty to acquaint you with the matter immediately."

Briefly, John recounted Crabber's encounter with the *Marie-Louise*, and his own subsequent discovery of the cave through Will. He eliminated any mention of Hudson, but laid stress on the Wiggatts' reaction on being shown the guns, and ended by saying that, having studied the terrain, he felt that Crabber's suggestion of a landing was feasible.

The Crown Steward had listened to the tale in growing amazement, his eyes never wavering from John's face: "An extraordinary story, Captain Dainton! And one that could have far-reaching consequences. But you really believe that the Islanders had nothing to do with this store of arms?"

"I do. It is an extremely serious matter for all of them, for there are many who have had dealings with the French through the smuggling trade. That is why I have come to you, for it would be difficult to convince, Mr Willerby, for instance, of their innocence."

"I agree — but at least we are fortunate in that one respect, Mr Willerby is away visiting his relatives in the north."

"I am thankful to hear it. I do not know anything about the other local magistrates, but surely there must be some who are not prejudiced against the Islanders?"

"Yes, indeed. I can think of two who would look on the matter sympathetically. The trouble will not come locally, but from the government in London. Are you aware of the situation there?"

"Only as far as I can learn of it from the newspapers and journals."

"Then you will know that we have suffered crushing defeats abroad, and the morale of the nation is at a very low ebb. Even the redoubtable Mr Pitt has described the situation as 'A gloomy scene for this distressed and disgraced nation.' If the discovery of this arms store was publicised it might engender an invasion scare, and public feeling might be whipped up against the Islanders."

"I know only too well how easily that can be done," exclaimed John savagely.

The Crown Steward nodded sympathetically: "Yes, indeed! I understand your feelings." He stared into the fire in frowning silence and then spoke again: "With your permission, I will ask my guest for his opinion. He is a Virginian lawyer called Charles Mason who has just come from London." He gave a wry smile: "Charles has been trying, with little success I gather, to negotiate tax concessions on Virginian tobacco. He has been in and out of the various government offices for the past month, so he must be well aware of the feelings of the Ministry."

"By all means do so. I am in your hands."

The man who entered the room a few minutes later was dark and very tall. His lean limbs gave him a lackadaisical air at variance with his highly intelligent eyes and broad forehead. His beaked nose was distinctly crooked, his mouth curved upwards in good humour above a firm chin. John judged him to be in his early thirties, and liked him instantly. It flitted across his mind that, in spite of the irregularity of the Virginian's features, he might be extremely attractive to women.

Charles Mason found the story fascinating, and asked a number of shrewd questions. A second bottle of port was called for, and the three men settled down to discuss the situation at length. It was almost midnight when the Crown Steward rose, saying: "Then we have settled that this incident should be hushed up if possible. Tomorrow I will visit Tom Gollop, the Governor of the Island — that is if he can see me, for he has been very ill, and obtain his agreement to our plan. On Monday, I will ride over to the Island, see this Major Collins and arrange for the arms to be taken to the castle." He turned regretfully, to his guest: "I am afraid this will mean my leaving you on your own tomorrow, Charles, for Tom's wife, Mary, died recently and the household is in mourning."

"Do not heed me," replied the Virginian in his slow southern drawl: "Besides, Captain Dainton's story has whetted my curiosity to see this Island. Perhaps I might hire a horse and ride over there, or does one go by boat?"

John laughed: "A shrewd question! But there is a ferry that carries both men and animals. My sister and I would be honoured if you would visit us, and I hope" (turning to his host) "that provided we can arrange this business satisfactorily, you will dine with us on Monday and remain for the night."

Chapter 14

In expectation of receiving the Crown Steward, Elspeth had risen early and had dressed with care. She was fully aware of the difficulties of John's mission and was determined to help him in the only way she could, by making sure that her household arrangements were above criticism, and that she herself was looking her best.

To this end, she ordered Skinner to lay out a new open robe of pomona green silk with a matching petticoat ending in a wide ruffled hem. Her hurried departure from Wanworth had left no time for the acquiring of new clothes, and those that she possessed were sadly outdated. However, during the summer Elspeth had spent a week in Weymouth in order to stock the Girt House with necessities for the coming winter. Accompanied by Skinner, she had put up at The Golden Lion where the overhelpful Spicer, anxious to be of service, had suggested that Mr Allen should call on her to recommend his famous seabathing cure.

The projected visit did not take place because Mr Allen was called away on business, but the suggestion gave Skinner the opportunity she needed: "It is as well the gentleman has been called away, for I have my pride, and to be forced to dress you in any one of these old gowns of yours, Miss Elspeth, would have filled me with shame!"

Elspeth protested that her dresses were comfortable and in good condition, but Skinner was adamant: "They may have done while you were shut away in that mouldering wing at the Priory, Miss Elspeth, but now you are Mr John's hostess; and who knows but the Governor or some such gentleman may call at the Girt House."

Realising that argument was useless in the face of the relentless persistence of an old servant, Elspeth had given way and had ordered three new gowns from Weymouth's leading modiste. Until this morning, she had had no occasion to use them.

She had chosen the pomona green silk because it was worn over a bell hoop which effectively disguised her disability. Its stiff stomacher was decorated with echelles of dark green velvet ribbon, with embroidered robings running from shoulder to hem. Its neckline was fashionably low-cut — too low, Elspeth considered, for morning wear, and had ordered a handkerchief of finest lawn to match the pleated ruffles at the elbow. A tiny cap of Nottingham lace completed the ensemble.

Shortly before noon John arrived at the Girt House with his guest. He found Elspeth seated on the couch in the south parlour, and was delighted to see her so becomingly attired: "You look very charming this morning, my dear" he said gaily, as he bent to kiss her, "and you will be glad to hear my mission went off very well. Let me introduce Mr Mason to you. He was visiting the Crown Steward, who has had to go and see the Governor of Portland over this business, so I have brought him to stay with us."

Elspeth extended her hand in greeting: "You will forgive me not getting up," she said in her low-pitched, musical voice, as she smiled up at the visitor; and Charles Mason, unaware of her crippled condition, thought that he had seldom seen such an attractive woman.

Her red-gold hair was swept off her high forehead, and allowed to fall in loose curls below her ears. Above a firm mouth, her deep blue eyes held a hint of laughter in their depths, but the arresting quality of her face did not lie in the charm of her individual features, but in a subtle expression of great strength of character. "As steel is tempered by the flame" he thought, and wondered what trials of endurance she could have undergone. He sat down beside her, engaging her in light conversation, explaining the purpose of his visit to England.

Presently she suggested that he might care for some refreshment, and rose awkwardly to her feet, reaching for her ebony stick.

As she dragged herself laboriously across the room. Charles stared after her, realising with a wave of sympathy that her battle was against physical infirmity, and the knowledge that it would be a continuing test throughout her life filled him with admiration for her courage.

He became conscious of John's eyes upon him and sought to make amends for his seeming lack of manners. He glanced round the room and his eyes fell on Elspeth's pianoforte. "A Silbermann pianoforte!" he exclaimed: "I have only ever seen one instrument like this, I discovered it in a shop in Weymouth on my last visit to England."

Elspeth turned in surprise: "In Mr Wainwright's shop? Then this is the very instrument you saw, I purchased it from him last spring. He told me that the only other person who had been interested in it was a colonial gentleman."

"An extraordinary coincidence," he agreed, smiling down at her, "I hope you will give me the pleasure of hearing you play it."

During the serving of a light repast of cold meats, cream cheese and crisp rolls of bread, with a syllabub, sweetmeats and fresh fruit to follow, John noticed that Crabber was looking unusually grim. On arrival, he had informed the young man that his mission had gone off far better than he had expected, but this information did not seem to have had the reassuring effect that he had supposed it would. So after the meal, he sent for Crabber and told him that the Crown Steward had promised to do all he could to protect the Islanders, and that if all went according to plan, the arms would be removed to the Castle the following day by Major Collins's men.

"*If* they've not been tampered with before then," replied Crabber sourly, "and anyway Major Collins will not remove them — he left the Island with his whole troop this morning."

"Left the Island? How did you hear of this?"

"From Joe Gorman, the ferryman. They crossed over to the mainland at dawn, bound for Poole."

"Are you sure of this? Gorman never mentioned it to me, when I came over."

Crabber said nothing, but looked at his master with an expression akin to one humouring a simpleton.

John glanced up and caught that expression: "I see. He didn't tell me because I am a kimberlin. Is that it?"

"Ay, that's it."

John digested this in silence for a moment: "Well, what other information did he withhold? Do you know why Collins has gone to Poole?"

"It's rumoured a run will take place there." Crabber's tone implied his disbelief in such a rumour.

"You mean it's a false scent? . . . Is there going to be a run here?"

"Ay — but I'm sure that's a false scent too."

"Why?"

"Because the weather's right."

"Right for what?" Exasperated by Crabber's deliberately unforthcoming attitude, John felt a fleeting sympathy for the Preventive officers — theirs was an impossible task when pitted against the solid hostility of the Portlanders. He studied Crabber's sullen countenance. What was the matter with the boy? He was always so willing and helpful — something was very wrong! John thought over the conversation again, what was the weather right for? And what did Crabber's opening remark about the arms being tampered with mean? Was that the clue to his apparent hostility? "You said something about the arms being tampered with; has anyone else on the Island found the cave? Are they going to take the arms for themselves?"

"No; but . . ." Crabber stopped abruptly.

"But what? Crabber, you must tell me what is on your mind. How can I help, unless I know the facts. Surely you can trust me not to betray your people." He raised his eyes, and looked the young fisherman squarely in the face. Crabber met that forthright gaze for a second, and then looked down, twisting his hands together in a gesture of indecision.

When he looked up again, his expression had changed: "You know I trust you, Captain," his voice was very low, "after what you done for me and mine, I'd give my life for you." He paused, and added fiercely: "And Uncle Matthew and me aint blathered about the arms either! Lethal, they are! For there's some we could name who'd take a few of those for their own use — just in case of need like!" He paused, shaking his head in perplexity; "That's the rub of the matter, and Uncle's in a rare takin', for Pipit Pierce is ill and we can't think of above two or three others whom we could trust to come with us to-night and leave those chests intact at the end of the business."

At last he was coming to the crux of the matter; John chose his words carefully: "Why do you think you'll need trustworthy men to-night? What do you think is going to happen?"

"The Frenchies! They'll come back to-night, as sure as cocks 'll crow!"

"The *Marie-Louise!*" exclaimed John sceptically. "Rather unlikely I should think . . . but I suppose it's possible." He paused, considering all the facts: "You think that was why Collins has been lured away from the Island?"

"I'm sure of it!" Crabber leaned forward eagerly. "It all fits, you see. That night they came and found the landslide, they couldn't do anything because the fog came down, and the patrol might have come on them, sudden like. If they're to find the cave, they need plenty of time, *and* be sure of being undisturbed. So they spread this rumour of a run at Poole — that's easy enough to arrange, and if they've paid out enough gold there'll be a string of ponies for Collins to find — only all they'll be carrying is fish to Wimborne."

John laughed, his sympathy for Collins deepening: "Who would be on Preventive duty ashore! Thank Heaven I was in the Navy! Go on."

Crabber grinned. "So there's no patrol on the Island, and they've made sure none of our people will be at Church Ope — they've arranged a run off West Bay. The message came last night." He look at John defiantly: "You know there's been no run since Manvers was murdered. Well, there's those who haven't felt gold in their pockets since then, so they weren't likely to miss the chance of getting some now, although there's been a deal of grumbling about the short notice *and* the place. The tide is wrong, you see."

"Wrong for the landing, you mean? Where is it to be, off Chesilton?"

"That's where it *should* be, but there's a flood tide to-night, so the small boats will have to come into Mutton Cove or Wallsend. That's why there'll be no-one at Church Ope — every available man will be needed to carry the barrels up the West cliff. We've done it before to avoid the Preventives, but there's no sense in such sweated labour when there are no troops on the Island. That's what suspicioned Uncle Matthew — the *Marie-Louise* will be able to come in, unseen, on the flood, and make her getaway six hours later on the ebb."

John sat drumming his fingers on the writing table — Crabber's argument was certainly convincing; he picked up a lunar almanac seeking further evidence. He found it — the moon would be at the full at two minutes past midnight. Inwardly, he groaned, foreseeing a long, cold, and probably fruitless vigil ahead, but too much was at stake to risk ignoring Crabber's theory.

The issue decided, he turned to the practicalities: "Very well, we will watch. We must be in position by eight o'clock. How many men can you depend on?"

Crabber counted on his fingers: "Uncle Matthew, Willy Flann, Shad and Isaac Stone, my brother-in-law Mark Attwoll, Mr Dingle and me."

"Seven, and myself. Well, it must suffice. Get a message to the others to meet in the harness room at seven, wearing warm, dark clothes, and tell Mary to put together some food for each of us. Now I must return to my guest."

Charles Mason had persuaded Elspeth to play for him, and the rich melody of one of Handel's Suites for the harpischord greeted John as he returned to the parlour: "You must forgive my neglect of you," he said, addressing his guest, "a matter of business has kept me."

"There is nothing to forgive," the colonial responded genially, "your sister plays brilliantly. I have never heard that particular suite performed with so much feeling."

"Have you been to see Hudson, John," interposed Elspeth. "He is much recovered to-day."

"No, but I must do so later on. I have been speaking to Crabber, and have some most interesting news." He sat down to tell them about the young fisherman's dramatic disclosures, and of the plan for keeping watch, ending: "There will only be eight of us, but it may well prove to be a fool's errand anyway."

"Nine," interjected the Virginian laconically, rising to stand before the fire, "I have always been accounted a useful man in a fight."

"But we cannot embroil you in our affairs," said Elspeth sharply.

"Embroil myself! — See if you can keep me out of them!" His lazy manner had been replaced by a sudden intentness, reminding John of a gliding hawk about to strike. "A good dog-fight is just what I should like after kicking my heels in Government offices for months. Besides," he added, with a twinkle, "a few dead Frenchmen are just the evidence we need to clear your Portlanders. Can we go and study the terrain?"

Seeing that his mind was made up, Elspeth turned to her brother: "Ring for Skinner, dearest, and I will change into a driving dress. What could be more natural than we should take our guest on a tour of the Island."

"Have you pistols with you?" John asked, when Elspeth had left the room.

"A pair of Mantons," Charles replied. "Will the other men have arms?"

John chuckled: "Not conventional ones, I should suppose. But I don't doubt they will have the means of defending themselves."

His prediction was right, of the seven men assembled in the harness room only Dingle, who had been taught to use firearms in case of being held up while driving Elspeth, carried a pistol. Matthew sported an ancient musket he had rescued from a wreck, but the other men were armed according to their trade.

John guessed, at a glance, that Willy Flann and the Stone brothers were quarrymen, for they were all over six foot and powerfully built, and carried the heavy kevels used in cutting stone. Formidable weapons, John thought with satisfaction, for he had often watched the quarrymen at work, and marvelled at their strength and agility in handling the double-ended tools which weighed anything from eighteen to twenty pounds.

One end was a hammer, the other an axe, with its razor sharp edge so foreshortened that it could be used like a pick.

Mark Attwoll was a fisherman like his brother-in-law. He was younger than the others, but tall and wiry. Both he and Crabber carried staves with grappling hooks fitted to the end, and wore leather belts from which hung small axes and the long sharp knives they used for gutting fish.

John outlined his plan, and then split the groups into twos, so that each man of the pair was differently armed. Crabber and Willy Flann were to be on the beach. Their task was to eliminate the guards left on the boat, and render it unusable. Matthew and Mark Attwoll, because of their intimate knowledge of the cliff path, were to be near the spring, and to follow the climbers, taking any stragglers by surprise. Charles Mason, Dingle and Isaac Stone were to be hidden near the cave shaft.

John chose Shadrick Stone to be his companion in the cave. He liked the man's air of sturdy imperturbability; and thought that his bull-like strength would be an asset in the hand-to-hand fighting in the cave. "If they do come," he warned the group, "no-one must shoot before their leader has entered the cave. We must have proof that the arms are their objective."

The Islanders began to look more cheerful, for it seemed that this Captain Dainton meant business. Matthew and Crabber had had some difficulty in persuading them to come on the expedition under the leadership of a kimberlin; for from what the men knew of Crabber's master, they realised that he would expect his orders to be obeyed to the letter; and they had feared that the evening would turn out to be the sort of tame entertainment in which they were merely expected to round up their opponents and hand them over to the authorities.

Their opinion of the Captain was further enhanced by the appearance of Mary bearing two large jugs of home-brewed ale, substantial portions of bread and cheese and extra rations for each man tied up in coloured kerchiefs. So when they presently dispersed, to make their separate ways to the cove, it was in the jovial expectation of an opportunity to pay the hated Frenchmen a little of what was owed them.

John and Dingle were the last to set out. Charles Mason having gone ahead with Crabber who had undertaken to guide him through the elm grove, and find him a suitable hiding place near the shaft. The careful Dingle carried an improvised stretcher, a coil of thin rope and a lantern, all of which articles, he informed his master, he intended to conceal in the church in case of trouble.

John also carried a lantern, and his preparations included the wearing of a dark fisherman's jersey, a stout leather waistcoat, thick woollen stockings and a pair of workman's shoes.

The moon had not yet risen when they approached the dark grove of elms, but by now they were sufficiently familiar with its rough pathway to make their way through it, and when they emerged from the trees a faint silver light had begun to illuminate the scene, enabling them to make out the outlines of the abandoned church ahead of them. Dingle deposited the stretcher, rope and lantern in the tower, and they moved across the churchyard. At the bottom of the steps, Dingle slipped aside to take up a position in the shadow of the wall.

As John pulled aside the rough bushes screening the shaft, Shadrick's bulky form moved out of the shadows to meet him. He cupped his hands together, and gave the hissing call of the night-jar. The signal was answered by a series of similar calls. "The birds are late in leaving the Island this season," he whispered, grinning. "They are all in position now, Captain."

Chapter 15

John surveyed the cove with satisfaction. It was silent and empty, and there was nothing to suggest to the Frenchmen (if they came) that an ambush had been prepared for them. He turned back towards the cave, dropped down into the shaft, and lit his lantern in its shelter: "Come and take a look at our scene of action," he invited Shadrick. The quarryman squeezed his powerful frame through the shaft: "There must be steps beneath this rubble," he commented dourly. "Else they could never have carried the water up." John moved towards the inner chamber, and swung the lantern beam onto the row of chests. The man stared at them in silence. "A rum do," he muttered angrily, and turned back to examine the pillars with professional interest, "and this is a rum place. Mighty cold too."

"We will leave a lantern burning here to light our way down the shaft, and wait outside," replied John. "If they come, we shall have plenty of time to conceal ourselves. We'll do better in our stockinged feet too." Shadrick lowered his lantern to study the uneven, slimy stones: "Ay, that we would, and I'd best be back behind that buttress by the water, the pillars won't conceal my bulk!"

They left the lantern in a position which lighted the chamber end of the shaft, and climbed out into the fresh night air. John parted the bushes, and looked down on the empty cove bathed in pale light. The moon had risen, but its brightness was veiled by scuds of feathered cloud. There was no movement on the water, and no sound except the surge of the sea. Shadrick touched him on the shoulder: "You make yourself comfortable, Captain," indicating the rock ledge beyond the shaft, "I'll keep watch."

When he judged that two hours or more must have passed, John crept forward to relieve Shadrick. The moonlight was much brighter now, but the cove was still empty: the only signs of activity upon the water were the twinkling lights of merchantmen making their way up Channel. Surely the tide must turn soon, John thought, and then the useless vigil would be over. He studied the shore line carefully, concentrating his eyes upon the shining arcs of wet sand left as each wave retreated. Were those arcs still creeping higher up the beach? He tried to judge their position in relationship to some huge blocks of quarried stone left from a recent shipment, steeling his mind to the task to shut out the numbing cold.

A faint splash jerked his attention away from the beach — the brig, her masts bare, had stolen in on the last of the flood tide to anchor in the bay.

John signalled to Shadrick. The big man peered through the bushes and gave a deep sigh of relief: "Began to think we'd come on a wild goose chase," he muttered.

They stared down at the ship and saw that a rowing boat was being lowered, men climbed down into it and took their place at the oars. A muffled order reached their ears, and the boat pulled for the shore. As it reached the shallow water, two men with muskets, leapt out to cover the landing. Two men, in the cocked hats and dark cloaks of naval officers, stepped ashore and stood looking up at the steep cliffs, while the boat was being pulled up above the water line. Two men stayed to guard the boat; the six others, all with muskets slung over their shoulders and four carrying long-handled tools, joined their officers. The commander issued instructions, pointing to the Bow and Arrow Castle and the church, and two men set off as directed.

"Two lookouts, two to guard the boat and six coming up." John whispered to Shadrick. "We'd better get below."

In the cave they stripped off their coats and thrust them out of sight in the inner chamber. "Keep your shoes on till the last moment, or your feet will go numb," John ordered, bending down to loosen his laces. Shadrick nodded, and took up his station against the wall near the water. John chose a pillar close to the inner chambers and extinguished the lantern. As they waited in the paralysing darkness, the smell of the dank air seemed nauseating, and the dripping of the water menacingly loud; but presently their sight became accustomed to the blankness and they could faintly discern a grey light coming from the shaft.

From his hiding place between the block of stone on the beach, Crabber watched the main party begin the ascent of the cliff. When he judged that their attention would be fully engaged in negotiating the steep path, he gave an owl's hoot. Matthew was waiting for the signal. A skilfully thrown stone landed at the foot of the cliff path taken by the churchyard lookout. The slight clatter brought the two guards to their feet, their attention fixed on the deeply shadowed area of rock and undergrowth at the base of the cliff.

Swiftly, their bare feet soundless on the sand, Crabber and Willy Flann stole up behind the luckless men. Willy swung the heavy kevel down on the first man's head. The blow smashed the skull to pulp, crumpling the body to the ground. As the second man turned to fire, Crabber leapt upon him. His long fletching knife flashed in the moonlight and buried itself beneath the left shoulder. The two Islanders rolled the bodies into the shadow of the boat's keel, and picked up the muskets. The second man's hat had fallen off and rolled away. Crabber retrieved it, put it on and marched smartly over to the quarry-stones to retrieve his coat and shoes. On his return, Willy paced across, and when the owl's hoot sounded again causing the French commander to look back towards the beach, he saw his two guards kneeling, their muskets at the ready, on either side of his boat.

Charles Mason had been shaken with inward laughter as he watched the changing of the guard from the eyrie, some twenty feet above the cave, on which Crabber had placed him. It was a narrow ledge of rock formed by the wall of the old castle, and was invisible to anyone looking up from below. Crabber had chosen it because the gentleman's qualities as an in-fighter were an unknown factor, but as he was armed with serviceable looking pistols, he should be able to render valuable assistance to the others as a marksman.

The carefully planned and perfectly timed elimination of the boat guards had filled Charles with admiration for the two

141

Islanders as guerrilla fighters; but it was their cool impersonation of the dead men that had most impressed him, and he now waited in tense expectation to see what the next move in the game would be.

Matthew, having fulfilled his part in the plan for the removal of the boat guards, left his hiding place as soon as the main party were well above him: "I'm going after that devil up at the Castle," he whispered to Mark. "You keep an eye on the main lot." He moved stealthily across the path, and began to make his way upwards through the rough undergrowth that covered the mass of fallen rock beneath the Castle.

The French commander reached the part of the cliff where the landslide had covered his original track to the cave shaft and paused. From here the track divided now, one path leading to the castle, the other a rough roadway, twisting its way past the churchyard wall. The appearance of the cliff face had entirely changed since the night when he had deposited the chests in the cave. He stared at the mass of broken rock above him, trying to remember the exact location of the cave in relation to the church and castle.

Eventually he decided to try the path leading to the church, and the party moved forward again. A few minutes later he reached the steps in the churchyard wall, and stopped abruptly! "These steps!" he exclaimed sharply. "I do not remember them, and see how the brambles have been cut back around them! Light the lanterns."

The commander searched the ground thoroughly — the track was a mass of ruts and footprints, but directly opposite the steps there were signs that someone had pushed through the undergrowth. "Mon dieu!" he ejaculated, turning to his lieutenant: "What is this? Why should anyone want to push their way through such an entanglement? Rouget! Duchard! Cut down these bushes! You others, cover them!"

Two men set to work with axes, and soon uncovered the open space in front of the rock wall. The commander moved forward shining the beam of his lantern over the area, within a few moments it revealed the shaft. "We have found it." he exclaimed, grimly. "But so have others, it would seem!" He

142

drew his pistol and knelt down to examine the shaft: "That cursed cliff fall has covered the steps with rubble," he grumbled, "but I think there is room to get through. Poiret, come with me! The rest of you, stand guard!"

To John and Shadrick the waiting had seemed interminable. Their eyes had grown accustomed to the darkness, but the cold dank air was beginning to paralyse their muscles; even constant flexing of their arms and legs did not seem to stave off the creeping numbness that threatened to overcome them. So it was with genuine relief that they heard the sounds of the Frenchmen hacking at the bushes, and then the officer's voice above them.

A faint light filtered into the cave, and then the scrape and clatter of loose stones warned them of the Frenchman's approach. A lantern's beam swept the chamber and then remained fixed on the cavity in the far wall. More scraping sounds and a second beam of light informed John that another man had descended the shaft.

"Peste! But it's cold down here!" A young, ringing voice echoed strangely in the dank air.

The first man spoke impatiently: "Don't waste time staring around! Come over here, and move these stones!" He was standing beside the cavity, some four feet from the pillar concealing John. He held the lantern aloft in his left hand, it showed him to be short and thickset with a scar running down his cheek. The barrel of his pistol glimmered in the soft light.

The younger man began to lift away the heavy stones to enlarge the cavity, and while their attention was fully engaged on this task, Shadrick crept forward between the pillars. His stockinged feet made no sound on the rock floor, he reached the outer wall and eased his way along it, until he was directly behind the labouring Frenchman. It was heavy work for the boy and he paused to wipe the sweat from his forehead. As he did so the shadows reflected in the water caught his attention. The shadow of the nearest pillar showed a gun protruding from it.

"Sacre Mère!" The cry was strangled in his throat as Shadrick's heavy kevel struck him between the shoulders, sending him crashing to the rock floor. The commander turned to fire at Shadrick, but John leapt forward and brought the barrel of his pistol down on the man's forearm with all the strength he could muster. There was a deafening report as the shot exploded into the floor, scattering a shower of rock fragments, followed by a resounding crash as the loose stones filling the cavity collapsed into the inner chamber.

The commander had reeled against the wall, gasping with pain and cradling his broken forearm above the elbow; but as the force of the explosion sent John staggering back against the pillar, he grasped his second pistol in his left hand and raised it to fire at John. Shadrick flung his kevel at the pistol, and sent it spinning from the Frenchman's hand. The heavy tool landed against his shattered forearm; with a scream of agony he collapsed in an inert heap.

The sound of the explosion in the cave was the signal Charles Mason was waiting for. He was lying on his stomach, his left arm pillowed by his greatcoat, his second pistol loaded by his side. He leant out over the ledge to see one of the guards about to descend into the shaft. He took careful aim and the man rolled over without a sound.

His second shot was not so successful. He aimed at a man who was reloading his musket, but evidently the flintlock must have jammed, for as Charles fired, he bent down to pick up a piece of rock to use as a tool. The bullet whistled over his shoulder — with a cry of rage, the man threw down his useless weapon, picked up a mattock, and dived into the undergrowth. Charles drew back on to the ledge to reload his pistols.

Dingle's chosen position by the churchyard wall had proved to be all too uncomfortably close to the French party when they halted at the steps. As soon as they moved off towards the shaft, he crept along the churchyard wall and entered the graveyard by the main gate. Using the headstones for cover, he crawled forward until he was within about eight feet of the unsuspecting lookout. He waited patiently for the signal from the cave, and then leaned round the headstone and shot the man dead.

When he had reloaded his pistol, he made his way from grave to grave on his hands and knees until he reached the shelter of the wall. He moved along it until he found a place where the capping stone was missing, and from this commanding position he was able to cover the path leading from the shaft. He was rewarded by the sight of a Frenchman stealing cautiously out of the bushes. Suddenly the man pounced, a long knife flashing in his hand. Dingle fired, and the man reeled over, clutching his leg. Isaac rose out of the undergrowth nearby, and shattered his skull with one effortless blow.

Matthew found his task much more difficult than he had anticipated, for the lookout at the castle was most vigilant. He was forced to work his way round the northern bluff of the cove, and then creep back through the quarry workings to avoid being seen. He had just reached the outcrop of rock below the south face of the castle when the shooting began. The lookout's attention seemed to be riveted on the area by the church, and this gave Matthew his chance to close in, for he knew his ancient musket to be extremely unreliable. He moved cautiously forward, and knelt behind a rock to light his fuse. Try as he would, he could not ignite it. Swearing to himself, he peered over the rock, the Frenchman was taking careful aim with his musket at the Virginian gentleman reloading his pistols on the ledge some way below them. Seizing his useless weapon by the barrel, Matthew swung it like a club and struck the man at the back of the neck, his body crumpled up and disappeared over the cliff — but he had already fired.

By the time Matthew reached the shaft, the Stone brothers had brought up the wounded French officer, and John and Dingle had helped Charles Mason down from the ledge. The ball had embedded itself below his left collar bone, but John had staunched the bleeding by using his shirt as a thick pad and binding the wound tightly. Charles declared that no great harm was done, and that if John wanted the Frenchman alive for the authorities, he had better be taken to the house first. To this, John felt bound to agree, for the man was in acute pain and had lost a lot of blood. He instructed the Stone

145

brothers to carry him to the house, and to return immediately for Mr Mason.

"We certainly did need your stretcher, Dingle," he commended the staid groom. "It was well thought of." . . . "Is everybody else all right? Crabber and Willy are still on the beach, I presume. Here comes Matthew! Where is Mark?" — "Matthew!" he called, as the carter approached: "Have you seen Mark?"

"Not for some time," replied the older man, anxiously. "I left him to guard the path."

"Perhaps he is on the beach with Crabber?" suggested Dingle.

"We'd best go down and find out. Bring those two lanterns! He may have been hurt."

"If anything has happened to the boy, that bastard Boisson will answer for it," said Matthew fiercely, as they set off down the path. He shook his fist at the *Marie-Louise* riding serenely at anchor in the bay. "A lot he's done to help his fellows, anyway."

John laughed: "They weren't expecting an ambush, so he may think all is well, but it will be interesting to see what he does when we haul that boat up on the beach."

"Save his own skin, is what he'll do," said Matthew, sourly. "You mark my words!"

There was no sign of Mark on the path, and neither Crabber nor Willy had seen him.

"One Frenchie did come down though." There was growing anxiety in Crabber's voice: "But Willy finished him off!"

"Search the cliff." John ordered. "Spread out, and work your way up slowly. Damn these clouds," he added in annoyance, glancing up at the shrouded moon, "building up now, just when we need all the light we can get. Give me a lantern, Dingle!"

Weary and dispirited, they began an exhaustive search amongst the rough undergrowth and fallen rock of the lower cliff. They found him at last, lying amongst some loose scree below the landslide. He was on his back, his head turned sideways, his eyes wide open, as though staring in amazement at the deepening pool of blood spurting from his chest. Beside him was a mattock. The Frenchmen had prepared their tools with care — the axe

146

blade had been sharpened to a fine cutting edge, and when used as a weapon of defence, it had slashed a great open wound across Mark's chest.

Crabber knelt beside his brother-in-law distraught with grief. A chill breeze had sprung up and dispersed the clouds, and now the full moon shed a relentless light upon the stark outlines of the rocks. Above the gentle surge of the sea, they suddenly heard the grating rattle of halyards running through the blocks, and the creak of lifting sails.

"What did I tell you!" muttered Matthew, sourly. "She's going!"

Crabber looked up in fury, and stared at the *Marie-Louise* stealing away to safety. Suddenly, he rose from his knees and raised a clenched fist to heaven: "A curse on you, Boisson, you son of the devil! Die slow! — Die hard! — And may your soul rot in hell!"

Chapter 16

From the window of the morning room, Elspeth had watched
John and Dingle making their way to the grove of elms. It
was only when their figures had receded into the shadows near
Betsy's cottage that she moved away to sink into an upholstered
chair, overcome by sudden faintness.

After a few minutes, she gathered her forces together and
rang for candles, but instead of the faithful Skinner, a neatly
dressed manservant entered the room. She stared at him in
surprise, wondering which of the Islanders had come to help
Mary, and why he had been sent to wait upon her. It was only
when he spoke that she recognised the seaman she had been
nursing for the past three days: "What are you doing, Hudson,"
she enquired? "I told you to rest in bed."

"Beg pardon, ma'am, but I couldn't stay there no longer,
not with the Captain going off on an attack, so Wiggatt found
me these clothes. I thought I could make myself useful to you,
m'am. I often used to lend a hand in the sick-bay."

The word "sick-bay" brought Elspeth struggling to her feet.
"Sick-bay! Of course we must make preparations in case anyone
is wounded." She limped to the door, thankful to find that with
activity, the sick feeling in the pit of her stomach seemed to
fade away.

She was still busily engaged in the stillroom when Hudson
came to tell her that two of the Islanders had brought in a
badly wounded French officer and were carrying him up to the
improvised sickroom. By the time she had negotiated the stairs,
Hudson had got the man decently between sheets. At the sight
of his lacerated arm, she gave an involuntary gasp, and then
set to work to clean the wound before setting his arm. She
was just tightening the bandages, when Mary entered, looking
quite distracted: "Come quickly, Miss Elspeth, it's the colonial
gentleman now, and he do look poorly!"

The jolting Charles had endured while being lifted up the steep cliff path must have caused him agonies of pain, for his face was ashen except for the grey shadow about his mouth. He opened his eyes when Elspeth bent over him and muttered: "Forgive me — so much trouble for you."

She held a flask to his lips, murmuring: "Don't think of it. You will soon be better." As the life-giving spirit surged through him the greyness about his mouth receded and the laughter returned to his eyes: "Not too soon, I hope!" he said, smiling up at her. She loved him from that very moment.

He was carried up to the spare chamber next to the morning room where Skinner, who deemed it most unsuitable for her mistress to attend to such matters, divested him of his breeches and boots with the aid of Mary. For the sake of peace, Elspeth acquiesced in this arrangement and limped along the passage to look in on the French officer who was showing alarming signs of high fever. She did what she could to relieve him, but the condition of his shattered forearm was beyond her medical skill, and she had little doubt that the limb would have to be amputated.

She returned to Charles's room to find that he had sunk into unconsciousness while being got between the sheets.

"It's as well he has, Miss Elspeth," said Skinner, "for his wound has broken out bleeding again. I will fetch up some boiling water to you."

A startled exclamation escaped Elspeth as she untied the improvised bandages and saw fragments of bone protruding through the skin above a deep, jagged wound that was bleeding sluggishly. Her hands were shaking, but she steeled herself to her task and gently swabbed the wound. When she had staunched the bleeding, she dressed it with basilicum powder, applied fresh pads, pressed the broken ends of the collar bone into position and bound the whole up comfortably. "That should ease him a little," she said, straightening the pillow beneath the unconscious figure, "when he comes round I will give him a cordial, but Dingle must ride over to the mainland for a surgeon as soon as he returns. Whatever can have delayed them at the cove?"

"I'm sure I don't know, Miss Elspeth: but Stone told me that when they went back for Mr Mason, Mr John and the other men had gone down to the beach." Skinner drew up an upholstered chair beside the bed: "You sit here quietly, Miss Elspeth, or you will be quite done up. I will see to everything below stairs and give Dingle your orders."

Elspeth was only too ready to fall in with this plan because she did not wish to leave her patient. She leant back against the soft damask with a sigh of relief, and studied the features of the unconscious man before her. If not precisely handsome, his face was undoubtedly attractive, she thought — even with the lids closed, hiding the laughter that lurked in the depths of his eyes, the good humour showed itself in the lines about his mouth and the wide forehead betokened high intelligence.

She fell to wondering what his life had been and whether his quixotic nature often embroiled him in similar adventures; though most probably, she told herself bitterly, they usually concerned beautiful women — women with the appeal of sensuous, desirable bodies, not a cripple like herself. It was not in her nature to indulge in self-pity, but she was suddenly overwhelmed by a passionate longing to be whole and attractive as other women were, to possess the gift of physical charm.

As though in answer to her thoughts, the man in the bed stirred restlessly, plucking at the sheets with his right hand and muttering incoherently. She leant forward to straighten the sheets and found her hand gripped in a firm clasp. For a moment he was still, but when she tried to withdraw her hand his grip became a vice, and the raving began again. She stretched out her other hand to place a cold compress on his forehead and presently he was quiet again. She told herself fiercely that it meant nothing — the fevered often tried to grasp those nursing them for security, but she did not try to withdraw her hand again; instead, she leant back in her chair, relaxed, and presently she fell asleep.

Skinner, quietly entering the room an hour later, to bring her the news of Mark's death, forbore to wake her. Her young mistress's strength would be taxed to the utmost, she thought, with two sick men in the house and Mary prostrate with grief. She closed the door again silently, her grim old face a study of conflicting emotions, and tiptoed away to deal with Mary's hysterics herself.

Perhaps it was as well for Mary that the week following the ambush flew by in a whirl of domestic activity, for Mark had been the youngest of her brothers and her favourite; but after her initial outburst of hysterical weeping at the sight of his body being carried into the stableyard, she buried her grief in a ceaseless round of work, of which there was plenty with the two wounded men in the house and the endless comings and goings of officials.

Each evening the kitchen was the social hub of the Island, as the Portlanders, delighted at the outcome of the ambush, poured in with commiserations and offers of help. The story of the night's adventure lost nothing in retelling, Crabber and Matthew became the heroes of the hour, and the sacrifice of the youngest member of their family a cause for veneration. A situation which considerably eased Mary's sorrowing heart.

Extra hands had been welcome and Martha, Matthew's wife, a comfortable woman of ample proportions, came to support Mary in the kitchen; and Betty Attwoll, a cousin, undertook the duties of housemaid.

Personal service for the Daintons had materialised from a different quarter. It was dawn before John returned from the cove after supervising the wearisome business of the removal of the dead Frenchmen to the church, and the collection of their tools and weapons as evidence of their intentions. He was cold and exhausted, and the knowledge that he must write a report for Dingle to carry to the Crown Steward before seeking the comfort of his bed, did nothing to cheer his spirits.

He was thankful to find a bright fire blazing in his bookroom and a cold repast laid out on the side table. He poured himself a generous measure of brandy and settled to his tedious task. He had only covered the first sheet when the door was opened by a neatly dressed individual bearing a jug of steaming coffee. It was a moment before John recognised his former master carpenter, for in place of a seaman's greasy pigtail, the man's grizzled hair was cut severely short and he was dressed as a superior manservant: "Good God, Hudson! I hardly recognised you! I am glad to see you are better. Where did you get those clothes?"

"Wiggatt suggested I should wear them, sir. He said they belong to the valet of a former owner of the house."

"Oh, to the absconders!" John exclaimed. "Yes, I believe they left most of their baggage here. I used some of the owner's clothes the first time I visited the Island. It could not be a better disguise for you, Hudson. I intend to give it out on the Island that you are a master joiner — there are no skilled carpenters here, so I shall need you when the building of my new house begins. If anyone questions you, you must say you worked on my father's estate; but in the meantime, in those clothes, any official from the mainland will no doubt think you are my personal servant."

"Be your master joiner!" Hudson exclaimed, his face alight. "But, Captain, I haven't yet explained . . . "

"I know that. I shall want to hear your story as soon as I am through with this immediate business — but you served under me for eight years, and in that time your name was never entered in the log book except for exemplary conduct after the capture of that French squadron off Sicily."

"Ay, that was a good fight, that was! I wanted to come with you this evening, Captain, but Miss Elspeth wouldn't hear of it."

"Certainly not! It would have only added to our difficulties if you had been wounded. Is your back healing?"

"Ay, sir, whatever Miss Elspeth used, it relieved me wonderful — so I can make myself useful to her in the sick-bay now."

Elspeth found Hudson's services invaluable in the days that followed. The man was quiet and capable, but he very seldom spoke and Elspeth, noting the look of haggard suffering on his face, guessed that he was still in a state of shock. She longed to know his story, but felt restrained from asking probing questions by the presence of Skinner who insisted on being in the room when she dressed his back each morning. Perhaps it was as well, she thought, that there was so much to do in the sickrooms, for knowing that he was being useful might help him to find an accepted place in a kitchen community deeply involved in its own emotional crisis.

He slept alone in the small room above the dairy to which he had been carried unconscious from the cove, but he took his meals in the kitchen with the Wiggatts and their relations, as did Skinner and Dingle, for the Girt House, although commodious, did not boast a servants hall. But Elspeth's retainers had their own living quarters to retire to, the sewing room on the first floor being Skinner's strictly guarded sanctum, while Dingle's domain was the comfortable cottage which had been built for him adjoining the stables.

In the event it was the sensitive, self-effacing groom who heard the seaman's story first. A week after he had been brought to the Girt House Hudson was crossing the yard to the servants' privy, when he saw Dingle in the workshop endeavouring to mend a broken gig shaft. He stopped in the doorway, uncertain whether he would be welcomed, but irresistibly drawn to the smell of fresh wood shavings: "If I could be of any help?"

Dingle was as sensitively attuned to the feelings of those around him as he was to the reactions of his horses which he loved. He glanced up and understood the unspoken longing in the seaman's face. "You certainly could. I'm handy enough with leather, but I'm no craftsman in wood. Never had any call to be until we came to this Island, but now what I can't fix myself has to be done in Weymouth."

Because of his sickroom duties, it was late in the evening when Hudson finished the new shaft. Dingle picked up the lantern and led the way across the yard: "Come in to my place for a while. I've just broached a new barrel." He opened the door into a comfortable living-room, where a couple of Windsor chairs stood invitingly before a bright fire.

Hudson stopped on the threshold in surprise: "You do yourself well! This is homely!"

"Miss Elspeth saw to the furnishing herself," Dingle replied. He set the lantern on the table and busied himself drawing two tankards of ale from a barrel in the corner. Then he fetched a

153

cheese and a loaf of bread from the cupboard: "Help yourself," he invited the seaman.

Hudson cut a thick slice of bread and held it under his nose appreciatively: "Fresh bread," he murmured, "'til I was washed up here, I hadn't tasted that for eighteen months or so, not since I left the *Barchester* I hadn't."

"The *Barchester*. Was that the ship the Captain commanded?"

"Ay, and she were naught but a hell-hole 'til the Captain came to us." He blew the froth off the ale and took a long, reflective draught: "She was in a bad state, the *Barchester* was. She was old, you see, and there was so much stinking water in her bilges it slowed her up. The men were in poor shape too, a quarter of her crew suffering from scurvy and many others lousy. We'd been six months at sea under an elderly, useless Captain — he was ill too, died four days before we reached Gibraltar, so I suppose there was some excuse for him. But there was none for his First Lieutenant — a brute if ever I saw one, and as the morale got worse the punishments got harsher. It was a bad time that was, not that I'd ever known a *good* time; not in all the ten years I'd served, I hadn't!"

"When we learnt that a boy of only twenty-two, a favourite of that starched up old Byng, was being given command, it didn't seem very likely that our lot would improve. But then how could we have guessed that we were going to get the Golden Boy of the Sea — as the Captain came to be called."

"I well remember him being piped aboard. A tall, fair-faced, quietly spoken youth — but there was something about his manner that made you feel he would always be obeyed without question. I looked at the First Lieutenant and saw that he had had an unpleasant shock realising that the days of his power were numbered."

"The Captain shook hands with the officers and inspected the crew. Then he turned to the First Lieutenant: 'Well, Mr Percival, I have inspected the ship's company. Now I will inspect the whole ship.' For a moment there was a stunned silence and I wondered if I'd heard aright? There hadn't been an inspection of the ship for months and things were a shambles below the gun deck. I could see Mr Percival was fuming!"

"Well inspect the whole ship he did — right through the orlop and into every hold. He even tasted the men's food being prepared in the galley," a broad grin suddenly transformed Hudson's haggard features: "They said his face was as good as a play when he did so! Then he returned to the quarter deck and issued some startling orders. Mine were to set up wind sails immediately and erect awnings on the upper deck so that the men in the sick-bay could be brought up into the fresh air."

"It was an extraordinary day. A complete inventory of the conditions of the ship's stores and provisions was compiled and all the men's clothing inspected and the contents of the slop chest listed. Then in the evening the Captain had himself rowed over to the Admiral's flagship."

"The next day we sailed, but not until a boat had taken ashore the First Lieutenant, the Purser, the cook and two petty officers and returned with their replacements, and an amazing quantity of personal effects belonging to the Captain including half a dozen bullocks, twelve pigs and twenty nets of oranges and lemons."

"There was a marvellous smell of freshly baked bread and newly killed meat coming from the galley the next morning, but it wasn't until the ship's company was assembled at eleven o'clock that we got the first inkling of the dramatic change that had taken place in our lives, for all the casks of stinking pork, the rotten fish, rat-eaten cheeses and sacks of mouldy flour were piled on the deck in front of him. We just stood and stared at the Captain, but there ain't one of us will ever forget what he said. 'It is against Admiralty orders to buy food other than that provided by the Victualling Department with Government money, so I have re-provisioned the ship out of my prize money. Therefore, if you want to continue to eat well we shall have to take prizes and to take prizes you will have to be both fit and efficient. To be fit you must be clean, so I am making for a certain inlet I know on the island of Minorca. We shall camp there while you clean yourselves and the ship, and to start to get fit, every man will learn to swim. First Lieutenant, you will see that all this revolting foodstuff is thrown overboard.'"

"To say that we were stunned doesn't really describe our feelings, for it's the dream of every sailor to win prize money, and to eat wholesome food into the bargain! But there was the other side of the coin to be considered too. Clearly the Captain meant what he said and few of us on board could swim, and there were many others who didn't care overmuch for being clean either."

"We were becalmed the next evening so I had a party on deck turning my wind sails by hand. Suddenly the Midshipman on watch went running off to the Captain's quarters and came back with the Captain who was stark naked except for a towel round his waist. I pricked up my ears wondering whatever could have happened to bring the Captain from his bath, and him looking as eager as a schoolboy about to see a prize fight. The First Lieutenant points starboard and says: 'There are the dolphins, sir. I counted four of them.'"

"'They are close! Just when we're becalmed too! What a piece of luck! You are in charge of the ship, Robert.'"

"And with that the Captain leaps onto the rail, stands poised there a moment and then dives into the sea. Talk about being thunderstruck, you could have felled me with a feather! I ran to the side and there he was swimming out towards the creatures, and in a minute or so they were all around him leaping and diving, and him laughing and catching hold of their fins. I just stood there gaping! I'd never seen anything like it in all my born days, though, mind you, every sailor has heard tales of how these creatures play with men, but seeing it with your own eyes is a different thing."

"Word went round quick enough, and soon the starboard rail and cannon ports were crowded with men laughing and talking as if it was a fair day. A queer thing it was — a sort of light-heartedness spread through the ship, and with it a feeling that under the command of this laughing boy and his chosen officers life might hold something more than just misery and hardship."

"I can understand that," said Dingle, rising to replenish the tankards, "but how did the Captain deal with the grumblers?"

"Summarily," replied Hudson, chuckling: "The Mediterranean is a fickle sea, one day there is a gentle breeze and clear, deep blue water; the next there's a gale blowing that will rip every sail off your masts and worse, and the changes come so sudden like."

"One such storm blew up two nights later — by dawn the worst was over, but there was still a heavy swell. The fore topgallant mast had gone so I was busy on deck, and had sent for a new topgallant sail. One of the malcontents, a man called Dixon, brought it up and I wasn't surprised to see he was drunk, because the late cook had been his particular crony and had left him a bottle of grog. The fool tripped over a rope, hit his head on the rail and went overboard. I suppose he'd knocked himself out for he sank like a stone. When he went down the second time I thought he was a goner, but suddenly a dark streak came up from the depths and the man's body was hurled right out of the water. Dixon didn't sink again, the shining black shape below kept twisting and turning, planing and diving, propelling the corpse-like figure to the ship's side."

"The Lieutenant was ordering a boat to be lowered, but the Captain, who'd been on deck throughout the storm, cut him short: 'They'd never pick him up in this swell, and I think he's dead already, but our friend will never accept defeat so I'll get the body. You get a rope out to me, Robert.'"

"Have you ever seen the Captain in the water, Mr Dingle? He's a ruddy marvel, he is — and that dolphin weren't much help to him either, for as soon as he'd got hold of Dixon's body, the creature was leaping in and out of the water grinning all over its face, they do grin I assure you, and covering the Captain with spray, but eventually he got a rope round Dixon's waist and we hauled them aboard. Dixon was still breathing, so the Surgeon got to work on him."

"'Do you think he'll live?' asked the Captain."

"'Yes, sir. He'll survive. He must have knocked himself unconscious as he went overboard, added to which he's drunk.'"

"'Drunk! Are you sure, Surgeon?'"

"'Yes, sir.'"

157

"'Then when he's sober and has recovered from the shock, he will be flogged. I will not have drunkenness on duty. It not only endangers the life of the drunkard, but also the lives of those who may have to rescue him. One dozen lashes, First Lieutenant, and tell the cook to bring my breakfast immediately.'"

"Well, we never had no more trouble from malcontents. Justice is justice, when all's said and done." Hudson glanced at the carriage clock on the table: "I must go and look in on my patients. I take it very kindly you asked me in here. It's been very pleasant remembering those good times with the Captain ..." He paused, uncertain what to say next, the haggard suffering returning to his face.

One false move, thought Dingle to himself, and he'll shy off from confiding his troubles like a half-broken colt. He chose his words carefully: "It's been very pleasant for me, too. It gets lonely sitting here by myself of an evening, for I'm a kimberlin here like you. Come again and tell me the rest of your story."

Hudson's face lightened at the hint of companionship: "I'd like to do that. It's the nights that get me down. If I get off to sleep, I wake in a cold sweat fighting to free myself and hearing that boy screaming ... but I must go now."

158

Chapter 17

It was several days before Hudson was able to visit Dingle again, because he was fully occupied with his sickroom duties. After the amputation of his arm, the French officer had drifted off into a coma for two days. When he recovered consciousness he was still in a high fever and extremely restless, so Elspeth ordered Hudson to remain in his room at night.

A comfortable, upholstered chair had been placed by the fire, but even in the short periods when the Frenchman was quiet Hudson was unable to rest. When he was not re-living the horrifying event that had led to his desertion, he was desperately mulling over the problem of his future.

The seaman had been overjoyed when John Dainton had said that he wished to employ him as a carpenter. For a short time he had looked forward to a secure and happy future, but the frequent visits of the Crown Steward and other officials from the mainland worried him intensely, for he realised that if his identity was discovered the Daintons would be plunged into scandal. Even if he managed to remain undetected for the next few weeks could he rely on the silence of the Islanders for ever? The thought of leaving the security of the Girt House plunged him into wretchedness, and where he could go to escape the clutches of the Press Gang or inquisitive magistrates he could not imagine?

After two long nights of misery, Hudson decided to consult Dingle at the earliest opportunity, because he felt sure that the faithful groom could be relied on to put the safety of his mistress above any concern for an erstwhile deserter. And if, as it seemed only too likely, Dingle thought he was endangering the Daintons by remaining in their service, he would probably be able to help him to leave the Island.

159

His opportunity came the next evening when Skinner, noting his haggard appearance at dinner, offered to sit with the Frenchman until midnight. As soon as he had finished his necessary ministrations, Hudson hurried across the yard to Dingle's cottage. He accepted the offer of a tankard of ale and plunged into his story: "You asked me to tell you why I deserted. Well, I'll be brief because there's something I want to consult you about. I was eight years with the Captain in the *Barchester*, then in April '56 the ship was holed in an engagement. We limped back to Gibraltar for major repairs and arrived there a week before Admiral Byng came out from England. He was very short of men, so we were all transferred to different ships. I was sent to the *Intrepid* but she was so badly damaged at the battle of Minorca that she had to be towed back to Gibraltar, so within two weeks I was transferred again, and this time I found myself back in hell once more."

"I won't go into it all now, but my troubles began when I got wrong with the Lieutenant of our division for suggesting I should put up wind sails like we had in the *Barchester*. He could see no reason for cluttering the deck just to relieve the foul smells below, and told me to mind my own business. I did, too, because the men were flogged for the smallest offence and I'd no intention of getting my back striped if I could help it. However, after that he was always on the lookout for something to haul me over the coals for, and made my life a misery."

"I just endured it as best I could until six months ago when we put in to Plymouth to take on more men. They sent a Press Gang ashore and a miserable lot of ruffians they rounded up — but amongst them was a young boy of fourteen who had been apprenticed to a carpenter. A delicate youth he was and terrified of heights, but he had a marvellous gift for carving. Not that any of the officers bothered their heads about that, he was just an ordinary seaman forced to climb the rigging daily until he fell from the foremast yard and broke his leg."

"The Surgeon was the one humane officer aboard, he set the boy's leg most skilfully and ordered me to make a pair of crutches for him. That's how I got to know Jem and when he was well enough the Surgeon arranged for him to work as one of my assistants. I suppose it was our trade that drew us together, but I came to feel for that boy like a father and taught him all I knew."

"Thanks to the Surgeon's care, Jem's leg healed wonderfully and two weeks ago he was walking with only a slight limp. Then an epidemic of fever ran through the ship, Jem escaped it, though as things turned out, it would have been better for him if he had taken the fever!" Hudson stopped speaking and stared into the fire, his hands clenched on the arms of his chair. When he spoke again his voice was very low, but vibrant with hatred.

"We were in mid-Channel then and Jem and I were on deck mending a broken spar. The wind was rising and when the fresh watch came on duty the Lieutenant ordered the topgallant sails to be reefed. I told you the fever was rife, well, one man fell from the foremast rigging and was dead before he hit the deck close by where Jem and me were working. It fair shook the boy up, he was bent over the dead man sobbing, when that brute of a Lieutenant comes along and orders him up in his stead. The look of horror on the boy's face made me see red, but I kept my temper under control and offered to go up myself: 'Young Marsh's leg ain't right yet.' I said."

"But I saw the look of malevolent spite on the Lieutenant's face and knew that we were both done for. I'd have struck him then, if Jem hadn't seen what was in my mind and clutched me round the knees, crying: 'Don't Jack, don't! I'll go — it would be terrible, what they'd do to you!'"

'Yes, you'll go, and he'll be flogged for questioning orders. Start him, Boatswain.'

"He climbed valiantly but he couldn't swing that stiff leg across the topgallant yard — I think I'll hear him screaming till the day I die myself."

Silence fell in the cheerful little room, for Dingle could think of nothing adequate to say. He went to the cupboard and brought out a bottle of brandy, and poured a stiff measure for them both. Hudson drank the spirit slowly, and then straightened his shoulders, wincing as he did so: "I was flogged as we came into Weymouth Bay — thirty lashes, and was taken to the sick-bay.

161

That evening I determined to desert, I'd heard tell that the Captain was living on Portland, so there seemed a faint chance I might get ashore and find him. I got one of the fellows on duty to get my carving and went out to the heads just before daylight. The rest you know — but Mr Dingle there's something I must ask you. Do you think the Islanders would tell on me and so get the Captain into trouble?"

"I can assure you they won't do that. You see if it hadn't been for the Captain, young Crabber would have been hanged in Weymouth six months ago." Dingle refilled the glasses and told the astonished seaman how John Dainton had saved Crabber from the Preventives ending: "My advice to you is to stay here and try and forget the past eighteen months, besides the Captain and Miss Elspeth need you."

He could not have said anything which could have delighted the seaman more, and in the days that followed Hudson came to feel that it was the truth, for the Frenchman was dangerously ill and only Elspeth's skilled nursing saved him; she firmly refused to allow him to be moved to the mainland, and tartly told the visiting officials, impatiently waiting to question him, that unless it was left to her discretion as to when he was fit enough to be interrogated, she could not guarantee that he would live to give evidence at all.

The amputation of the Frenchman's arm had been a simple, if brutal matter, but the bullet in Charles's shoulder was deeply lodged, and its removal called for a degree of fortitude on the part of the patient that strained Elspeth's nerves past the bounds of courtesy. She considered the surgeon's probings to be unnecessarily prolonged and rough, so when having bound up the highly inflamed wound the man suggested bleeding his patient, she was provoked into a comprehensive criticism of his slowness, roughness and dubious medical skill, ending with the dismissal of his services. Astounded, the indignant little man set about collecting his instruments, while Elspeth, suddenly overcome with her own temerity, left the room in search of a cordial for herself, as well as her patient.

She returned to find Charles lying with his eyes closed, a deathly pallor about his countenance which made her regret her hasty dismissal of the surgeon. Suppose he were to die? Feeling much akin to a murderess, she poured out the cordial with trembling hands and held it to his lips. His eyes flew open and read the anxiety in her face: "Don't worry! I shall do very well now that you've rid us of that plaguey sawbones. Thank heaven you did not let the old shark bleed me — I must have lost pints already."

"I am sure I must have seemed shockingly rude, but he was so rough I could not contain myself. When I came in and saw you lying so still, I felt like a murderess."

"Nonsense! More like my saviour, and it was worth all that probing to hear your spirited condemnation of his methods. How did you acquire all your medical knowledge?"

"From a friend of my father, a noted herbalist. My mother encouraged me by giving me charge of her stillroom. It was one thing I could do, you see."

"Not the only thing." The warmth in Charles's voice seemed almost like a caress. "Your musical talent amazes me."

Elspeth coloured delightfully: "For that compliment I must thank my masters," she responded, speaking lightly to cover her pleasure at such praise, "and my father, too, I suppose, for placing me under them. Though I will own they had an assiduous pupil — the time never seemed to drag when I was practising. Now I must go to the Frenchman and you must rest."

She limped away leaving Charles to meditate on the unfairness of life, and to contrast the sweetness of her expression with the petulant sulkiness of the spoilt beauty he had worshipped so passionately in the green days of his youth. The miserable memories of his first marriage crowded in upon him, making him so feverishly restless that the pain in his shoulder became unendurable. He gritted his teeth and forced himself to lie still.

The sound of music drifted up from below. Elspeth, having tended her patients to the best of her ability, had gone instinctively to her pianoforte to resolve the chaos of her thoughts. The phrases of the Bach prelude rose in their limpid purity speaking of things eternal. Charles concentrated his mind upon the music and presently he slept.

Ten days elapsed before Elspeth pronounced the Frenchman to be well enough to be moved to the mainland for questioning; but only five passed before Charles ordered Hudson, who had proved himself to be an excellent orderly, to dress him, declaring that he could no longer endure lying in bed. He was unable to shrug his heavily bandaged shoulder into his well fitting coat, so he compromised with a silk dressing gown, in which exotic garment Elspeth found him about to negotiate the stairs. He turned a deaf ear to all her protests, but accepted her tactful suggestion that as John was expecting an influx of visitors in the parlour that morning he should confine his activities to her sunny morning room over the porch.

During the days that followed they passed a great deal of time there together, falling into an easy companionship that flowered into close intimacy as they discovered their similar tastes and interests, their shared delight in the absurd.

Affectation was alien to Elspeth; she liked to say what she thought and her direct speech had often put her at loggerheads with her stiff-necked, pompous brother, Henry. With Charles she found she could say whatever came into her head without fear of being censured; he shared her dislike of the pretentious, and often after one of her more pungent statements, she would look up and find his dark eyes alight with laughter and some deeper expression that set every nerve in her body tingling.

She knew herself to be in love, but told herself fiercely that this could only be a golden idyll of the autumn, that would end with his return to Virginia as inevitably as the onset of winter would follow the fall of the leaves. She would not allow herself to hope that it could be otherwise, but abandoned herself to the joys of the present, rising each day in a state of happy expectation that brought a new bloom to her beautiful skin and a radiant glow to her eyes.

Even the weather seemed to conspire to make their days together joyous — a particularly mild spell made Charles long to be outdoors, so Elspeth drove him out in her curricle to inspect the site of the new house at Mutton Cove and to explore the southern end of the Island. Driving over the pastures cropped short by the hardy Island sheep, he would share her delight in the sighting of rare plants, the shy antics of the flocks of "snalters" or the miraculous performances of the diving sea birds.

After such days they would return to dine together by candle-light, for John had left them to attend the court of enquiry being held in secret in Weymouth. So the Island was their private world, a place apart from the realities of life, far from censorious eyes or gossiping tongues — a kingdom of their own surrounded by the surging sea.

One morning he found her in the stillroom making an infusion of fresh herbs. He wandered slowly around the room studying the bunches of drying plants and the pots of ointments and lotions. He stopped in surprise at the shelf marked "POISONS" and began to read aloud the names from the neatly labelled jars: "Deadly Nightshade, Autumn Crocus, Foxglove, Henbane . . . I did not know that you had Borgia blood in your veins, my love!"

Her mind was so concentrated on the mixing of her herbs that she did not immediately perceive that he was teasing her, and looked round with such a comical expression of dismay that he moved impulsively towards her and enfolded her in a crushing embrace.

He released her to hold her at arms length, laughing down at her: "I adore you, delight of my heart. What witch's brew did you prepare for me, for surely this Island is an enchanted place."

"None," she spoke lightly to conceal her clamouring emotions, "I am no Circe! You are free to leave when you will."

"And that must be soon, alas! But I shall leave my heart here."

"Will you return for it?" she ventured shyly, but before he could answer they were interrupted by the entrance of Will, his small person generously covered with mud, clutching a bunch of sorry-looking leaves. He spread them out on the table before Elspeth: "I got them all," he said proudly.

Charles glanced curiously at the limp plants: "What are they for?" he asked Elspeth.

"They are all to make a remedy for a chest infection — Orchid root to be ground into powder, Mallow leaves which I must mince and boil at once." She limped to the door and turned back, her eyes dancing with mischief: "The other is Vervain — its name is derived from Herba Veneris, the ancient ingredient of potions for virility!"

In the late afternoon John returned from the mainland with the welcome news that the enquiry was over and its findings most satisfactory. The French officer had given evidence of an intended invasion and had said that Boisson was in the pay of the French government, so the court assumed that Manvers had been murdered by him or one of his crew. The Islanders were officially cleared of any suspicion of being involved in the murder, John and the ambush party were recommended for their vigilance and a reward of twenty pounds was to be given to Will, but nothing of the matter was to be published in the newspapers for fear of raising public alarm.

Elspeth and Charles were delighted at the news, but although Elspeth listened attentively to all John had to say, he soon realised that her interest was only surface deep and that she was living in a halcyon world of her own. He changed for dinner in an abstracted mood, his satisfaction at the outcome of the enquiry marred by the thought of how desperately upset Elspeth would be when the Virginian left. He loved his sister dearly and would have given much to see her happily married, but he was afraid that such a dashing character as Charles Mason could have no serious intentions regarding a cripple, but was merely whiling away the enforced idleness of his convalescence with an amusing flirtation. But in this assumption John was mistaken for he knew nothing of the Virginian's innate chivalry or the tragedy of his past life.

Elspeth and Charles had discovered a delightful place for picnics near the Cave Hole to the east of the lower lighthouse. The flat pastureland known as the Sturt stretched to the edge of the deeply indented cliffs which, at this point, were only some thirty feet above sea level. In the past quarrying had taken place along the cliffs leaving wide, flat ledges which were easily accessible for Elspeth.

166

They went there on the day after John's return, taking a hamper of cold delicacies with them. Charles was unusually silent, so when she had packed away the remains of the meal, Elspeth got out her sketch book, but he leant forward and gently took it from her, saying: "No work allowed on our last day together."

"Our last day!" Try as she would, Elspeth could not keep her dismay out of her voice.

"It must be. God knows I don't wish to go, but now that the enquiry is over I have no excuse to linger, and my business in Virginia is urgent."

"But your shoulder?"

"My shoulder is healing fast thanks to your skill." He leant forward and clasped her hands in his: "Will you miss me?"

"Terribly!" She did not try to dissemble: "But that's a very unfair question!"

"Not so unfair as to take gross advantage of you by saying that I love you, but I cannot help myself . . . I do love you."

"What is so unfair in telling me what I have longed to hear." An unforgettable smile swept over her face and she raised her eyes invitingly: "You see I love you too."

His lips came down hard on hers, and she responded with a wild surging of her heart. When at last he released her, she leant back against the rock and said shakily: "Charles, dear Charles! I never thought that you could want me."

"Want you! Oh, I want you all right! Need you, more like. I never thought that any woman could — heal me as you have done."

"Heal you?"

"Yes." He stood up and began to pace restlessly to and fro across the ledge, his hands thrust deep into the wide pockets of his coat, a bitter expression on his face: "I've been married before, you see."

"Was she called Juanita?"

He stopped and stared at her in surprise: "Yes, but how did you know?"

"I looked after you the night you were wounded," she spoke very gently, "you were delirious for a while." She paused and then added as though the words were being wrenched out of her: "Was she very beautiful?"

"Very." He stood at the cliff edge, gazing down at the sunlit water below as though it mirrored his thoughts: "I had gone on business to the Florida settlements and had to attend a reception there, it was a plaguey dull affair until I was introduced to Juanita." There were dark patches of seaweed beneath the surface of the water, their trailing fronds like tresses of hair — black hair under a white mantilla framing the perfect oval of her face. The bodice of her white dress tightly laced to reveal the swell of her breasts above a tiny waist, and when she moved it was with the sensuous grace of a gazelle. His mouth hardened at the memory: "Yes, she was very beautiful, desirable in every way I thought — green fool that I was! I married her within a month."

He came back to Elspeth and put his hands on her shoulders: "But believe me, my love, perfection in one's bedfellow soon palls when the nights of physical delight are followed by days of quarrelling and misery. Her abominable temper flared up if she was crossed in any way, or if she was bored, and she had been so spoilt that a day without entertainment was anathema to her. But I had to work and that meant being away from home a good deal — very soon she began to find other escorts."

The pressure on her shoulders was becoming unbearable; she put her hands over his wrists and drew them together against her breast, murmuring: "I bruise very easily, you see."

"My love, forgive me." He bent and kissed her, and then turned abruptly and gazed out to sea. "I won't weary you with the unedifying tale of the next two years, but one night I came home unexpectedly and it was obvious from my servants' confusion that Juanita was entertaining upstairs. How her maid secreted the man away from her room I don't know, but his dress sword was lying on the couch. I was so furiously angry that I stripped her and beat her with it, and then . . . well, I raped her, for want of a better word. She hated me from that moment, and when she found she was with child, life became unendurable."

"She came into labour early and the birth was prolonged and difficult. It was twenty-four hours before the surgeon came to

168

tell me that I had a son but had lost my wife. I can't say that I felt anything but relief — relief and triumph at having a son."

Elspeth longed to share that relief, but the words were belied by the brooding, withdrawn expression on his face. When he spoke again his voice was harsh, but curiously flat.

"My triumph was short-lived. Juanita came of pure Castilian stock, and I myself am dark, as were both my parents; but the child they put into my arms had the ashen hair and light blue eyes of the Nordic races — like his father, the owner of the sword."

Chapter 18

Elspeth dragged herself across the ledge, her infirmity forgotten in her desire to erase the haunted bitterness from Charles's face. She put her arm through his, and leant unsteadily against him. He turned, and with tender understanding of her lack of balance gathered her into his arms: "Elspeth. You're so sweet, so true. Here on this island I've come to life again. I'd vowed I would never again give my heart to any woman, but all that vanished when I met you, and you looked up at me with that lovely smile of yours. But I shall not ask you to marry me now, because it will be years not months, before I can return to you, and in that time you may meet another man who would give you a home in England near your beloved John."

She shook her head: "That will not occur! It is you who will meet others — women who are whole, and perhaps . . . "

He put his hand beneath her chin, forcing her to look up at him: "You foolish babe! I might search the world and not see your like again. Beauty, grace and courage combined in one frail body which it shall be my privilege to cherish."

Trotting homewards past the windmills, she ventured to ask him what became of the child.

"He did not survive infancy. The wet nurse I employed for him contracted smallpox, and the child took it from her. — But that is all behind me now. Elspeth, shall you tell John of our understanding, or should I declare my intentions to him myself?"

"Oh, pray do not! For if he knew that I was going to marry you he might abandon the plans for our new house, and I do not want that. Once John has an establishment of his own here I hope to be able to persuade him to send for his children. He thought it would be best for them to remain at Wanworth with Henry, but I know he misses them dreadfully. Besides," she added distractedly, "he might feel constrained to tell Henry about you."

Charles laughed: "Would that be so terrible?"

"Indeed it would! You do not know Henry!"

So he had gone, and afterwards Elspeth was glad that his departure had been so sudden, it was characteristic of his decisive nature she thought; and like a symphony, their autumn idyll had ended in a marvellous climax on that sunny afternoon near the Cave Hole, leaving her with wonderful memories to linger over during the winter days to come.

John, watching her closely, was surprised at the serenity with which she resumed her normal daily life. He forbore to question her, but when, ten days later a courier arrived from Plymouth with a letter for her, he presumed she must have come to some happy understanding with the likeable Colonial and wondered why she did not confide in him.

Elspeth had two reasons for guarding her secret; the first was her desire to see the building of the new house well under way before telling John that she might go to live in Virginia at some future date; the other was the tiny, nagging fear that Charles might forget her when he returned to fashionable Williamsburg, and although his letter written from Plymouth did much to dispel this doubt, her pride kept her silent.

She soon realised that the first of her fears was unfounded, for John had inherited the Dainton passion for building. The façade and dimensions of the house had already been decided upon, but unlike many of his contemporaries, John was determined that internal comfort should not be wholly sacrificed to elegant external design. In this he was enthusiastically supported by the architect, Mr Thomas Gilbert, who suggested that a study of a new book of designs, just published by Mr Abraham Swan might provide Captain Dainton with ideas for suitable ornamental interiors.

Mr Gilbert was only too anxious to satisfy every whim of his rich clients, for he perceived that the building would provide work for himself, his skilled masons and their attendant labourers for several years to come; as the current work on the new church had been temporarily suspended while a county grant was raised, Mr Gilbert was inclined to regard the Daintons' project as a gift of Providence.

John sent to London for Mr Swan's book, and after it arrived he and Elspeth spent many winter evenings poring over designs for pilasters and panelling, architraves and over-mantels. But one raw February afternoon the book also brought to light a source of friction between them.

"Hudson's dolphin carving would fit that design perfectly." John leant over Elspeth's shoulder and pointed to a drawing of a carved chimney piece: "Where shall we put it? Would you like it in your music room?"

"It would be lovely there. But it ought to go in George's room, I think."

"George's room! Elspeth, you are not thinking that the children will come to live with us, are you?"

"Why not? Surely you mean to send for them soon?"

"I do not." The flat finality of his tone startled Elspeth into exclaiming: "But John, I thought you missed them so much!"

"I do. . . . I have seen so little of them, but after our discovery of the French invasion plan it would be quite wrong for them to come here until the war is over. Besides it would be so lonely for them here, they would have no young companions other than the Island children."

"At least they would have their father, and that is far more important, I think."

"Maybe, but when George went to Eton, Maria would be left alone with me, for I think, indeed I hope that you will be living in America by then."

Elspeth coloured: "Perhaps," . . . she raised her eyes to her brother: "Do you like him?"

"Very much! My dear, I am so happy for you." He bent and lightly brushed her cheek: "Where will you live?"

"In Williamsburg. If . . . John, I have not said anything to you in case he should forget me."

"I do not think he is that sort of a man," he answered slowly. The quietly spoken words lifted the tiny shadow from her heart, and she leant against him gratefully, her face aglow with happiness: "I owe all this to you for bringing me here. I shall hate leaving you, alone, and separated from your children."

"Don't trouble your head about me. Just concentrate your mind on choosing the furnishings for my house before you are whisked away to Williamsburg." He crossed the room to the window bay and stared out at the foaming crests of water whipped up by the February gale: "As soon as the spring returns you would do well to visit the warehouses in Weymouth to choose some silks and other necessities for yourself."

She glanced up in surprise: "But it may be a year or more before Charles can come back to England!"

"Very probably. But when at last he comes, he will not be denied, or delayed, I think."

The vision of being swept off to America did not dismay Elspeth unduly, for less than a year ago she had successfully uprooted herself from her quiet life at Wanworth within the space of one week; but to leave the Island before she had seen John comfortably established in his new home seemed to her a poor return for all his kindness. She longed for the end of winter so that a start could be made on the building, but the weather continued wet and blustery and the only outlet she could find for her restive energy was to begin work on a set of embroidered chair seats.

When at last the days lengthened, the lonely pasture above Mutton Cove became a scene of bustling activity as the Portland masons set enthusiastically to work on the exterior of the house. John spent much of his time there, engrossed in the detailed organisation of the project, for all the materials, other than the stone, had to be brought to the Island by sea.

An able man himself, Mr Gilbert the architect, had at first resented his rich client's assumption of command, dubbing his daily visits to the site, "a confounded nuisance". But it was not long before he had fallen under the spell of John's quiet authority, recognising with respect, his efficiency and kindness. No task however menial, went unnoticed if well done, but no slipshod work was tolerated. Watching the Captain pacing to and fro with his hands behind his back, quarter deck fashion, Mr Gilbert had no difficulty in understanding why he had been revered by his officers and crew — and as the walls of ashlar stone rose above the majestic cliffs, Mr Gilbert became a most devoted First Lieutenant.

Returning from the site one hazy morning in August, John found a postboy in the stableyard. He paid off the youth and hurried indoors for two of the letters were for Elspeth. Recognising Charles's handwriting, John went straight up to the morning room delighted to be the bearer of such a welcome present, for his sister had received no news from Virginia since May.

He greeted her gaily: "The postboy has brought you a bonus! Not one letter from Charles, but two!"

She took the letters eagerly, scanned through the closely written sheets of the first and looked up, her eyes shining: "He is well but very busy; the English Government has ordered taxes to be levied to pay for the expeditions against the French, who have been stirring up the Indians along the western frontier. The rest is . . . nothings."

"Nothings!" John quizzed her wickedly: "Nothings! Poor Charles, all his hopes dashed down, and he must have spent hours composing such an epistle! Surely you mean very mportant things."

She chuckled: "Yes, *very* important things." She broke open the seal of the second letter and stared unbelievingly at the single paragraph it contained. She re-read it several times, and then, unable to trust her voice, held it out to her brother. It was undated and simply headed:—

Williamsburg.

My love,

I write in great haste, for I leave to-night to join Washington at Cumberland. The colony has raised 2,000 troops under his command. We are to form part of Colonel Forbes's force for an attack on Fort Duquesne. It will be rough going as the country is mountainous and heavily wooded, so I cannot tell you how long we shall be away, or when I shall next have the chance to write to you. But believe me, my heart's delight, you have all my love wherever I shall be.

Charles.

John put his arms round Elspeth's drooping shoulders and dropped the letter gently into her lap: "Keep it safe — it is a letter to be proud of."

She nodded, unable to speak.

"Don't fret, my dear, he will come back to you. That he has gone to the war is the price you must pay for loving so fine a character. You could not have expected a man of his integrity and love of adventure to sit idly at home when such an expedition was being mounted."

Elspeth brushed away her tears and smiled mistily up at her brother: "You are right, of course; but I wish he had not had to go." She straightened her shoulders with a sigh, and added in a brave attempt to control her feelings: "John, where is this Fort Duquesne?"

"It is at the point where the Allegheny and Monengahela rivers merge with the Ohio. Does that help you?" he replied, grinning at her.

She chuckled: "Alas, it doesn't! Charles gave me a book on the history of America, but to be truthful, I only read the part about Virginia. I have never been an avid reader of travel books like you,"

"Why should you indeed. You didn't have to spend endless days and nights alone in a cabin at sea. I'm no letter writer, so the only occupation open to me was reading. Briefly, Fort Duquesne is west of the Appalachian mountains and directly south of Lake Erie. The French control their vast inland territory by a string of forts situated between the Lakes and the Ohio. Fort Duquesne cannot be more than 200 miles from Cumberland."

"200 miles!" she faltered. "Through virgin forest and across mountains!"

"It will not take them long in good weather," he replied bracingly, "for presumably they will use the road cut by

175

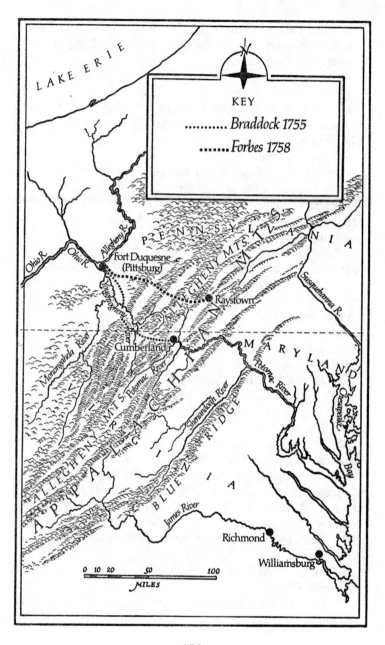

KEY

·········· *Braddock 1755*

······· *Forbes 1758*

LAKE ERIE

PENNSYLVANIA

Ohio R.

Ohio R.

Allegheny R.

Fort Duquesne
(Pittsburg)

ALLEGHENY MTS.

Raystown

Susquehanna R.

Monongahela

Cumberland

MARYLAND

ALLEGHENY MTS.

Potomac River

Potomac River

Chesapeake

APPALACHIAN

Shenandoah River

BLUE RIDGE

Bay

VIRGINIA

James River

Richmond

Williamsburg

0 10 20   50   100

MILES

General Braddock's troops in their attempt on the fort in '55".

With this reassuring information she tried to be content, telling herself that Charles would be safely back in Williamsburg before the winter set in; but in the autumn she received a letter from him that destroyed all such sanguine hopes. Charles wrote that he had reached Cumberland without trouble to find Colonel Washington fuming, because Colonel Forbes, the English commander of the expedition, had allowed himself to be persuaded by some sharp-faced Pennsylvanian contractors that it would be better to cut a new road through virgin forest to the Ohio river, rather than use the road cut by General Braddock's army three years before. Washington had protested at this needless delay and expense, but his advice had been rejected.

Charles covered two sheets in a fluent denunciation of Forbes's folly in not listening to the advice of the only officer of senior rank with previous military experience of the territory, and ended by saying that he did not know when Elspeth would hear from him again as in all probability the summer would have passed before they reached the vicinity of Fort Duquesne.

She did not hear from him again; the only news from America was of a crushing defeat of General Abercrombie's forces at Ticonderoga, near Lake George. The vanguard had been led by the young and popular Lord Howe, who was killed when his party lost their way in the forests and were attacked by the French.

This news depressed Elspeth beyond measure. Charles had spoken of the beauty of the hardwood forests of the Appalachian mountains, bright with azaleas of every hue and the massed white blooms of the dogwood — the symbol of Virginia, in the spring; the maples, red oaks and sweet gums painted vivid scarlet in the autumn. But such beauty was overshadowed in her mind by the chilling remoteness of that vast, little known interior, stretching endlessly westwards from civilisation, and she fell to imagining Charles lost in the forests and being captured, not by the French but by Indians, whose horrific treatment of their prisoners was only too vividly recorded by many early settlers.

177

The pain in her hip had always made sleeping difficult for Elspeth, but now her short periods of rest were punctuated by nightmares. After one particularly disturbing night, she rose early and abandoning her usual routine of partaking chocolate in her morning room, sought refuge from her own company in John's bookroom.

She found her brother seated in the window embrasure, a cup of steaming coffee in one hand, the other thrust into the pocket of his waistcoat. He was staring out at the grey November scene an unusually grim expression about his mouth, but he looked up and smiled as Elspeth limped towards the fire:

"You are down very early this morning. Did you have a bad night?"

"I did. So I decided to have coffee with you instead of chocolate by myself," she paused, noting the significance of his plain buff frock and shining topboots. "That is if you are not off riding immediately?"

He drew up a chair for her and lightly kissed her cheek: "That was my intention, but I will send a message to the stables and order some more coffee for you."

She smiled up at him gratefully, warming to his kindness, but when she poured out to him her fears for Charles's safety he replied, dampingly: "Nonsense! If you are feeling low, come over to the site with me. I want your advice over the archways in the inner hall. A drive in the fresh air would do you far more good than indulging in such fantasies."

The good sense of this remark put her quite out of charity with him, and provoked her into unwisely airing her other grievance: "I should not have time to indulge in fantasies, as you put it, if only you had agreed to send for George and Maria as I suggested."

But on this head he refused to be drawn, and she was left to ponder on the destructive effect of love upon her erstwhile serenity. Even time spent at her beloved pianoforte failed to soothe her troubled nerves. So when Mary entered to say that Betsy Stone had been taken bad with her heart again, she repaired to the stillroom to prepare a stimulant, thankful for something useful to do.

Mary, to whom she presently poured out her troubles, proved to be a far more sympathetic confidante than John: "Lawks 'a mercy, Miss Elspeth, what a terrible thought! It's no wonder you be all muopen like!" She watched Elspeth serenely selecting the digitalis from the poison shelf and added morosely: "Now if only you'd known Mr Mason was going for a soldier, you could've given him some of those poisons of yours — to swallow afore he was tarred and feathered!"

Elspeth's ever-ready appreciation of the ridiculous bubbled over at this macabre suggestion, and when she repeated the gem to John at dinner he shook with laughter. Their shared amusement cleared away the tension between them, but when the servants had finally withdrawn John looked up from studying the port in his glass and said: "Elspeth, Mary didn't say anything to you about Crabber, did she?"

"No, . . . only that if the child she is carrying is a boy, she wants to call it Mark, but Crabber was furiously angry when she suggested it."

"No, I don't think she ought to call it Mark, that would certainly lead to more trouble."

Elspeth stared at him in astonishment. "Why, John, whatever is the matter?"

He did not answer immediately, but selected a nut from the dish before him, cracking it between his strong fingers: "A queer thing happened the day before yesterday," he spoke very slowly, as though choosing his words with care, "I had to go to Weymouth on business. Crabber took me over by boat from Church Ope. We went down to the cove by the path to the south of the churchyard, because they were taking a load of stone down the Castle path. While Crabber was getting the boat ready I noticed that the carters were having to turn north to load at Durdle pier because there had been another small landslide."

"I was delayed in Weymouth, so it was almost dark when we reached the cove again. As always in wintertime, we pulled the boat right up the beach; the evening was mild for the time of year so it was warm work. Without thinking about the landslide, I started up the path only to find that it was blocked about

179

forty feet above the beach. I heard Crabber shouting behind me, but I did not bother to turn back. I started climbing towards my left, hoping to regain the path by the churchyard wall."

"I suppose I had gone about five yards when suddenly the flame of my lantern was extinguished and I was overcome by a deathly cold. I distinctly heard the sound of running feet and then there was a movement of air, as though a heavy instrument had been swung past my shoulder, followed by a horrible croaking sound. I looked round to find Crabber on his knees, crossing himself and muttering in anguished tones. The sounds were quite incomprehensible except for the one word 'Mark'. I realised then that we must be at the exact spot where we found Mark's body."

Elspeth stared at her brother in horrified silence, instinctively longing to refute the tale, but knowing that she must believe all that had been said — John was so reliable, Crabber usually so sensible: "What did you do?" she said at last.

"I suppose the phenomenon could only have lasted a minute or so, although it seemed an age before the cold receded and I was able to re-light the lantern. Crabber's face, as he got off his knees, was an ugly mixture of fear and anger: 'There,' he said, 'its happened to you now, Captain. I tell you, he won't rest in peace until that bastard Boisson is accounted for.'"

"I asked him when it had happened before. 'About a month back,' he replied, 'I shouted to you not to go that way, but you took no notice. I thought it might not happen if I was with you, else I wouldn't have followed. Not for all the gold in Egypt, I wouldn't!'"

John stopped speaking and filled Elspeth's glass with port before refilling his own. Elspeth sipped the ruby liquid slowly, grateful for its steadying effect on her mind; "Do you think Crabber has told anyone else about this — Matthew Wiggatt, for example?"

"I don't know — and it is too delicate a subject to broach directly. If I should chance to see Matthew I will try to find out if Crabber has confided in him. I am sure he has not told Mary anything, so you should do your best to persuade her to choose another name."

In the event it was Elspeth who saw Matthew Wiggatt first. She was busy in her glasshouse when she saw him approaching the kitchen door. Guiltily aware that her own worries might have blinded her to the troubles of those around her, she called him over on the excuse of inspecting her plants.

Matthew had a profound admiration for the Captain's sister. He entered, respectfully doffing his hat, and hastened to explain his presence in her garden by saying that he had killed a pig the previous day and knowing that Crabber and Mary were particularly partial to the chitterlings, he had brought the delicacies over for them. He put down a blood-stained parcel on the shelf and beamed at Elspeth.

The kindliness shining from his homely countenance inspired Elspeth to confide in him at once.

"Ay, ma'am," he replied, "Crabber did speak of it to me, and a mighty rum do it is. Mark will lie quiet in the end I'm sure. The trouble with my young nevvy is that he's too impatient. I tell'd him straight — you can't hurry God. It was a strong curse, but there, when Benny Attwoll cursed that London overseer for unfairly dismissing him from the quarry, it was near on twenty years before the b---, begging your pardon, ma'am, 'beggar' took and died."

Elspeth could not help smiling at this philosophical view of the matter: "You don't suppose Crabber has told Mary about it, do you?" she enquired.

"No, that he hasn't. I made it plain to him he mustn't do that on any account with her being in the family way. It would put her in a rare fantod, it would. She was upset enough over the name for the coming child, for rightly, Crabber won't hear of it being called 'Mark', but we've cleared that caddle by suggesting to her it should be called 'Matthew' after me. So don't you go troubling your kind heart over it, ma'am," he added, so far forgetting his position as to pat her on the shoulder in a fatherly manner: "You've enough worries of your own with your man away at the wars, and besides young Crabber has got plenty to occupy his mind at present, and that problem will keep him from thinking overmuch about Mark!"

Overcome by his consideration, Elspeth blew her nose vigorously, and called Matthew's attention to her plants. She lingered in the glasshouse for some time after he had gone thinking over the homely wisdom of his words. His simple faith made her feel ashamed that she had allowed her fears for Charles's safety to overshadow the problems of those around her. Mark's death had been a tragedy, but it should not be permitted to come between Mary and Crabber now, to spoil Mary's joyous expectation of another child to replace the daughter she had lost. It was this problem, Elspeth supposed, that Matthew's obscure remark about "Crabber having plenty on his mind now" referred to, and she wondered how best she could help the young couple. After prolonged consideration she decided there were only two things she could do — she must try to get Mary to confide in her and she must not inflict her own private worries on the household again.

Armed with this newly-found determination to be calm and cheerful, she left the glasshouse and hurried towards the kitchen; but as she did so she caught sight of John riding into the stable-yard, and her conscience smote her again as she recalled her rash remarks about George and Maria. If it had not been for John she would never have come to the Island to be mistress of this comfortable house — or met Charles. She would still be shut away in that mouldering wing of the Priory, subjected to the humiliating knowledge that her elder brother and his wife considered her presence there a heavy and unattractive burden.

She recalled with misery the grim expression about John's mouth when she had unexpectedly opened the bookroom door, and wondered how she could have been so selfishly preoccupied with her own problems when her brother's were far greater. He had lost his wife, been forced to give up the naval life he loved, and was now separated from his children. Far from the Island being a place of peace for him, he had become deeply involved in shielding a smuggler, solving a murder, frustrating a French invasion plan, housing a deserter and the domestic problems of the Islanders themselves. But at least, Elspeth thought, as far as John was concerned there was something she could do — she could make herself seem the serene and happy companion she had been to him before Charles came into her life.

After dinner that night Elspeth told John about her interview with Matthew: "Perhaps," she ended, "it would be as well if you used the ferry the next time you have to go to Weymouth." It did not occur to her to question John as to the nature of his business in Weymouth — had she done so, her newly found determination to be calm and cheerful would have suffered a severe setback.

Chapter 19

John had gone to Weymouth in response to a letter he had received from the Crown Steward asking to see him on urgent business. To John's surprise it had been brought over by a messenger who, Hudson informed him, was waiting in the kitchen to take back an answer. The letter gave no indication as to the nature of the business the Crown Steward wished to discuss, and John could not imagine what this could be.

He was reluctant to make another journey to Weymouth, for he had been there two days before to order materials for Fleece House, and to see Robert Samways, the sailmaker. The expedition had taken far longer than he had anticipated because it had been impossible to tie up on the Melcombe side of the harbour; for besides two three-masted barques unloading there, the quayside had been crowded with liberty boats taking on stores for four ships of the line anchored in the bay.

Crabber had managed, after a heated argument with the owner of an evil-smelling offal boat, to bring the *Mary* alongside the Ope steps near Robert Samways' sailshop, and rather than waste time jockeying for position across the harbour, John had walked back along the High Street and crossed over to Melcombe by the bridge. His business there completed, he had had to waste a further half hour, because the central spans of the bridge had been raised to allow a coal carrier to pass into the inner harbour. Standing near the Custom House surrounded by the sights and sounds of the naval life he had been forced to relinquish, John had vowed not to visit the harbour again until the squadron had left the bay.

Inwardly cursing the Crown Steward, John had unwillingly penned a brief note for the messenger and ordered Crabber to be ready to sail from Church Ope at noon. However, on this second expedition the Melcombe quayside was comparatively empty, and within an hour of leaving the Girt House John was being ushered into the Crown Steward's comfortable, panelled library.

"Captain Dainton. How good of you to come immediately!" The Crown Steward rose and shook John warmly by the hand: "You will take a glass of marsala with me? Did you sail over or come by the ferry?"

"I sailed over, and luckily was able to tie up at once — both sides of the harbour were damnably crowded when I was over here on Tuesday."

The words were polite, but their implication was not lost upon the elder man. He coughed and said hastily: "Sometimes the harbour is overcrowded especially when there is a squadron in the bay. There is talk of extending and widening the Melcombe quay, and even of building a new bridge further west, opposite St Nicholas's Street." He brought John a glass of marsala, took a chair opposite him by the fire and diplomatically changed the subject: "And how is Miss Dainton?"

"My sister is well, thank you."

"Has she had any news of Charles Mason? He wrote to me before leaving Williamsburg, and Miss Dainton told me that he had joined Washington in Cumberland. Apparently Washington did not agree with Colonel Forbes's plans for the advance on Fort Duquesne?"

"So Charles wrote in his letter, but Elspeth has not heard from him again."

"It must be most worrying for her — and the news of our defeat at Ticonderoga must have further distressed her. One cannot help feeling that the campaign has been sadly mismanaged and of course, losing Howe . . ." The Crown Steward once started on the subject, seemed unable to stop and entered on a lengthy discourse on the conduct of the war.

John listened in growing amazement and annoyance. Surely he had not been summoned from the Island merely to discuss the war in America, unless, the thought suddenly occurred to him, the Crown Steward had received news of Charles's death; but if so, why did he not come into the open and say so? He emptied his glass and shifted impatiently in his chair, effectively ending his host's monologue.

"Your glass is empty! Let me refill it. What do you think of this marsala?"

"It is excellent, but I must not stay too long, as I should like to be back at Church Ope before it is dark. You said you had some urgent business you wanted to discuss."

"Yes, yes, of course — the business." The elder man refilled the glasses and seemed to brace himself for an unpleasant duty: "The trouble is I fear I shall not be able to explain this to you without making myself appear an officious meddler, but after much hesitation I decided I must speak to you."

"Three days ago Captain Hargreaves, who commands the squadron in the bay, gave a dinner on board the *Newcastle* for various officials in the district — the magistrates, including Willerby, myself and about a dozen others. Hargreaves is evidently a man of comfortable means, the wine was of a rare vintage and there was a quantity of silver on the table. But what caught Willerby's attention was a wooden server — a circular tray with an ornamented rim, cunningly fitted to hold salt cellars etc. It had a central handle carved in the shape of a leaping dolphin — a beautiful piece of work."

"Willerby asked Hargreaves if it had come from the Orient, but Hargreaves said: 'No, it had been made by the ship's carpenter, but unfortunately we lost the fellow. He had been flogged for insubordination and was sent to the sick bay. According to the men there, he went out to the heads at first light and was never seen again. As a matter of fact, the incident happened here as we were sailing out of the Bay. We presumed the fellow fell overboard and was drowned: but there was one queer thing about it, he had just completed another fine piece of carving — a panel for an overmantel, and he took this out to the heads with him, so he may have hoped to swim ashore with it. I suppose no such panel has ever been found, or that a master carver called Hudson has set up work in the town?'"

"Nobody present had heard of such a man, but that officious little terrier, Willerby, promised to set up enquiries — post notices offering a reward for information and that sort of thing.

I suggested that the area around Portsmouth would be a more likely place for the panel to have come ashore, but Willerby, who knows nothing about tides, pooh-poohed the idea and made me agree to make enquiries on the Island. However, I shall not do so. You see, Captain Dainton, because of my unique position on the Island I cannot help hearing certain things, — and have come to my own conclusion about the matter — a conclusion which I pray, will not occur to anyone else."

For a full minute there was silence in the comfortable room, and then John looked up with his disarming smile: "I must be growing old. I was forever drumming into my junior officers the dictum that a successful action depends upon attention to detail. It was most careless of me not to have changed Hudson's name."

A sigh, as though of relief, escaped the Crown Steward. He rose briskly, and refilled the glasses. John thanked him and said: "Hudson served under me for eight years. He is a man of exemplary character, and his story is one of sickening injustice. One of the most unpleasant aspects of the navy is that life on the lower deck is often made hell for the men by bad officers. But what made you so sure that I had rescued Hudson?"

"I knew that a man of that name was working on your new house. Gilbert told me so . . . I beg you won't think that my time on Portland is spent prying into your affairs, but you must be well aware that as a major source of employment on the Island, the building of your house is the chief topic of interest to everyone living there. You know what Gilbert is like, he is so enthusiastic about the project that he can talk of nothing else. I asked him, in the course of a casual conversation, how he was managing for carpenters as none of the Islanders are skilled in that trade, and he told me that you had sent for a man from your father's estate in Sussex — 'a master in wood' was how Gilbert described him."

"I thought nothing of this until the man's name was mentioned on board the *Newcastle*, and then another piece of information flitted into my mind — something Collins had said to me soon after the French arms incident. 'Early that morning I had taken a search party to the cove as my sergeant had reported seeing footprints in the church tower, but they turned out to be Captain Dainton's. We found him sitting on the churchyard wall watching a squadron sail out of the bay, and he told me he had been in the tower the previous day. Young Will Wollage was there too, clipping the grass, and neither of them had noticed anything unusual'."

"Coincidence not evidence, you may say, but there and then the certainty of what you had done formed in my mind and my immediate reaction was to ensure that nobody would set enquiries afoot on the Island except myself."

He stopped speaking and leant forward to refill the glasses once more, casting an appreciative glance at his unflurried guest as he did so. John sat at ease in his chair, one booted leg across the other, his face betraying nothing but polite interest in the evidence being unfolded against him.

"Time," continued the Crown Steward, "time to think the matter over carefully, was what I needed; because I began to feel that the fantastic notions racing through my brain could only be due to an excess of excellent port. Unfortunately," he added dryly, "they still remained with me in the cold light of the following morning."

John laughed: "I did not think successful lawyers indulged in fantasies. Pray, where did your imagination lead you?"

"To the cave where the French arms were stored. I did wonder at the time what had induced Will Wollage to confide his dangerous secret to you. The answer was now clear . . . he hid the fugitive there while Collins searched the cove. Furthermore when I visited your house to interview the wounded Frenchman I noticed that you had acquired a new manservant, he was dark like the Portlanders but he did not speak like one of them."

John looked up from contemplating the dregs of wine in his empty glass: "Very interesting speculation," he said lazily, "but what are you going to do about it?"

"Ah, that is the crux of the matter," replied the Crown Steward. "For it seems that I am faced with a conflict of duty."

"Conflict of duty!" John interrupted sharply, all traces of nonchalance gone: "You can teach me nothing about that! Conflict of duty has changed me from a respectable naval captain into a common lawbreaker; and as for conflicting loyalties, they tear one apart until one is in danger of becoming a witless wreck! I was convinced that my first loyalty was to the man who had befriended and promoted me, and who was being unjustly blamed for the loss of Minorca; but when I found Hudson half-drowned on the beach and saw his lacerated back, I began to question the rightness of my action."

"I had 220 men under my command in the *Barchester*, and when I left her I can honestly say that she was a happy ship. Life on the lower deck is seldom pleasant, but men can tolerate hardship if they can be given a sense of purpose and if efficiency and good work is praised. I was able to wield them into a superb fighting unit and they were rewarded by taking prizes. By resigning my command to defend the Admiral, I resigned many of them to a life of unabated misery once more. How can that be counted right?"

"I understand your feelings," said the lawyer sympathetically. "In my profession one is often faced with similar self-questioning. But from what Miss Dainton has told me of her life in Sussex, *she* has certainly benefited from your decision, as indeed have many of the Portlanders now employed by you; and that is the reason why I intend to do nothing further in the matter of your carpenter. If he were apprehended, you might be forced to leave the country, and to my mind, the whole population of the Island would be the poorer for your going."

"You are very good; but I hope it will not come to that."

"I hope not too, but you would be unwise to ignore such a possibility: for the one enemy you have made on the Island is the one man most likely to hear that enquiries are afoot for a deserter. I am referring to Heap, the sexton, and I know he would like to do you harm."

"Because I deprived him of Will's services, you mean. But why should he be the most likely person to discover that there is a hunt on for Hudson?"

"He comes over to Wyke Regis every Saturday to see the curate about the services for the following day. I cannot prevent Willerby from making enquiries in Wyke — and Heap keeps a woman there — a harmless enough creature, but very given to gossip."

"That is certainly a matter of some concern," said John thoughtfully: "Perhaps, my best course would be to talk to Crabber Wiggatt. He might be able to find out if Heap is suspicious of Hudson in any way. It is not an uncommon name, after all."

"One solution might be to send the man away immediately — but I suppose that would be against your principles?"

"Principles!" John enunciated bitterly: "Principles are damnable! I have come to the galling conclusion that they should only be held by men of no imagination — men who can never see the other side of the coin. The devil of it is that there *is* another side to this coin — I have Elspeth's welfare to consider. But I shall never give Hudson up." He glanced out of the window, noting the fading daylight and rose to take his leave. "I must go now, or we shall miss the tide. I cannot thank you enough for warning me of this impending trouble; or tell you what it means to me to be joined in it by someone of such understanding as yourself."

The *Mary* was moored at the George Steps near the seaward end of the quay, with Crabber sitting in the stern gloomily surveying the state of the tide. He could not imagine what was delaying his master and he had no fancy for tacking to and fro against a flowing tide in a failing breeze, when the ebb could carry them effortlessly out to the Island in about ten minutes. But when at last, John descended the steps, he forbore to make any comment on the adverse state of the tide, for, (as he explained to Mary later,) a simpleton could have seen as how the Captain looked right werret like. Instead he cast off in silence and applied himself diligently to the uncongenial task of beating out into the bay.

It was not until a long series of tacks had brought them near to the anchored squadron that John broke the silence: "The *Newcastle*," he said, pointing to the foremost of the four ships of the line, "that's the ship that Hudson deserted from, and I have just learnt that they are making enquiries about him, or

190

to be more exact, that the magistrate, Mr Willerby, is making enquiries for them."

"That bigoted little bastard!" exclaimed Crabber explosively. "What does *he* want to go poking that pock-marked nose of his into things that don't concern him — he ain't in the navy! He'd best not try making his enquiries on the Island, or maybe he wouldn't leave it with a whole skin!"

In spite of himself John could not help laughing: "Then it's as well for Willerby, that the Crown Steward has undertaken to handle all enquiries on the Island himself, and his will be — er — discreet."

"Ay, he's a downy one, the Crown Steward," said Crabber, and then added, as the thought occurred to him: "But how did he nobble onto Hudson?"

John recounted the gist of his recent interview while Crabber listened in growing dismay: "It's a bad business, there's no mistaking that, Captain! For if it's to be horned all over, the one most likely to hear of it is Uriah Heap, and he'd like to do you harm."

"Because I've removed Will from him, I suppose," said John.

"That, and the reward."

"The reward?"

"Ay, the government reward that was made to Will. You don't think the boy would have been allowed to keep it, if he'd still been with Uriah, do you? Not likely! That money would be safe in Uriah's coffers now — or spent on that wily little piece of his in Wyke!"

This confirmation of the sexton's double life momentarily diverted John: "Extraordinary! I can't imagine that old miser spending his money on trinkets!"

"Not trinkets, but a solid investment in property! You got me wrong, Captain. Joanna Brigstock ain't no lightskirt, she's a widow. Nat Brigstock kept the inn, The Fisherman's Arms, and Uriah used to put up there. When Nat died Joanna was homeless, so Uriah installed her in a cottage in Shrubbery Lane — no doubt thinking he could do as he liked with her there. But the joke of it is, he can't! Joanna was too clever for him! She made such a song and dance about her reputation, and his as sexton, that knowing she was a real favourite amongst all the old gossips of Wyke, he was hoist with his own petard, as they say — and has to come back on the last ferry every Saturday night, . . . Boom over, Captain."

Crabber's long series of skilful tacks had brought them to a point south-east of Ope Cove, he eased in the mainsail and the *Mary* glided into the cove on the flowing current.

By the time they had pulled the boat up the beach it was almost dark. Crabber handed John a lantern saying: "What about Uncle Matthew? Can I talk this business over with him?"

"Of course — and anyone else you think trustworthy. I will speak to Hudson, but I don't want Miss Elspeth worried with it yet. I shall just tell her I was delayed on business."

He turned and hurried up the cliff path, his thoughts so concentrated on the problem of Hudson and how it might effect Elspeth, that he was oblivious to Crabber's shouted warning about the landslide. Balked by the fallen scree, he started climbing to the left and so crossed the place where Mark was killed; and at that moment, as he later confided to Elspeth, the flame of his lantern was suddenly extinguished.

Chapter 20

Crabber lost no time in setting out for Weston to inform his uncle of the dramatic occurrences of the afternoon. He strode past the windmills, oblivious to the cheery greeting of the miller, for his mind was deeply occupied with conflicting emotions. On the one hand he was looking forward with smug satisfaction to telling Matthew that now the Captain (whose confirmation would be indisputable) had experienced the terrifying manifestation on the cliff. Not that Matthew or any of his cronies had doubted Crabber's tale, but as all the Islanders were fervent believers in the power of spirits, everyone had carefully avoided that particular spot and so no one had been able to corroborate his story.

On the other hand he realised the disastrous implications of the news that enquiries were being set about for Hudson. He was well aware that Heap hated the Captain and would be delighted to do him harm — he had openly said as much in the taproom of The Portland Arms. If the Captain left the Island Crabber could not imagine how he could support Mary and two children on the meagre income he could earn honestly by fishing, and as the smuggling trade was at a standstill, a return to their former poverty-stricken existence seemed inevitable.

Something must be done to silence Heap — but what? Unconsciously his stride quickened as several violent, but impractical solutions passed through his mind, but these he regretfully rejected, realising a more subtle approach was needed. By the time he reached the Wiggatt's cottage he was no nearer to solving the problem, but his temper had risen considerably. He jerked up the latch and burst into the room.

His uncle and aunt were seated either side of a cosy fire of cow clotts — the flat platters of dung that Martha had collected and dried during the previous summer. Matthew

193

glanced up at his angry young relative and laid aside his pipe: "*Now* what's fretting you, nevvy?" he asked resignedly.

Crabber plunged into his tale, pacing restlessly up and down the tiny room as he did so. Matthew's face darkened as he listened, for the story touched a chord of ancient memory, arousing that deep instinctive awareness of anything that threatened the freedom of the Island. It was an integral part of every Portlander's heritage derived from their first ancestors, the Baleares people, famed in legend as "the stone slingers".

"Bastards!" he muttered. "Bleeding bastards! Making enquiries are they? Well, they'll not come hounding that wretched man here! Why, if they fetch him off here to flog him to death, they'll be daring to send the press gangs next, and that's one evil we don't suffer from on the Island."

"Flog him to death!" interspersed Martha in horrified tones.

"Ay, he's a deserter, ain't he? So he'd be flogged through the fleet as they call it, and very few survive that!"

"But how are we going to prevent it?" said Crabber desperately. "Uriah would dearly love to do the Captain harm. And there's no doubt but the Captain would be in trouble for harbouring the man."

"Ay, that he would," agreed Matthew, "and it's not only your job to be considered, nevvy. There's over fifty of us working on the house at Mutton Cove, and thirty more building that smart carriage drive from Weston." He reached for his tobacco jar and re-lit his pipe, an operation that seemed to absorb his whole attention: "It'll need a deal of thought," he said at last.

"A deal of thought!" exclaimed Crabber derisively: "Why I daresay we might fret our gizzards green *thinking*, but that won't help us — its action we need."

"Ay, but not over-hasty action that one of us might swing for," his uncle retorted.

Somewhat abashed Crabber sat down on the stone wall-bench knocking the cloth off Martha's birdcage which hung from a hook above it, causing its startled occupant to protest in a series of nervous twitters. The goldfinch was Martha's pride and joy and she hurried over to calm it: "Gawkhammer!"

194

she admonished her nephew. "Making my bird all joppety-joppety with your clumsiness. If neither you nor Matthew can think of what to do, you'd best be off to see Pipit Pierce — he's got a good head on his shoulders and you'd probably find him at The Lugger now."

The two men were in no way averse to this suggestion, and left the cottage with remarkable promptitude; for when Martha was annoyed her tongue could sting like a whiplash, and as Matthew confided when the door was safely shut behind them, there was no sense in sitting about to be abused.

They found Pipit Pierce in a corner of the taproom enjoying a jug of the home brewed ale for which the ancient inn was famous. He was a dark, wiry little man, a foot shorter than most of his fellow-Islanders but respected by all of them for two outstanding abilities — he was a master carver in stone and the most powerful swimmer on the Island. He was over fifty years of age and highly intelligent with a retentive memory for stories and traditions handed down from older generations; his pride in these traditions, particularly those concerning the rights and privileges of the freeholders made him an esteemed member of the Court Leet.

He greeted the Wiggatts in the low, harmonious voice which as a young apprentice, had earned him the nickname of Pipit, and enquired if his son, Sparrow, who worked as Matthew's ape boy (in charge of the rear horses of a team) was behaving himself.

"Sparrow's a good boy. He ain't in trouble but the rest of us are, as Crabber will tell you," replied Matthew, determined not to let the recounting of the disastrous news interrupt his enjoyment of the foaming ale that had been set before him.

Martha's suggestion of consulting Pipit had been a shrewd one, for, as always, he reacted strongly to any possible infringement of Island rights; and as he was currently employed in carving an elaborate representation of the Dainton arms to be incorporated in the handsome pediment at Fleece House, he had no wish to see the Captain leave Portland. Besides, as a master craftsman himself, he could appreciate Hudson's skill in wood, and took a secret pride in the knowledge that both the stone and wood carving at Fleece House would bear comparison with that of the great Vanbrugh mansion at Eastbury.

The trouble was that although Pipit could see the necessity for securing the sexton's silence he could not see any way of bringing it about. All that was decided was the names of those who should be asked to join the conspiracy.

For Crabber there was one satisfactory outcome to the evening —Pipit's reaction to the tale of the manifestation on the cliff was all that he could have desired. The little man had crossed himself hastily and exclaimed: "That dratted Frenchman has a lot to answer for! Mark my words, there'll be no peace on this Island until that score is settled!"

A week later they met again in Southwell. They had abandoned the cheerful comfort of The Lugger, for the squalid secrecy of The Ragged Louse and the fetid atmosphere did nothing to improve their spirits. There were six of them seated round a dirty table studying a handbill which Richard Comben, the lighthouse keeper, had seized in Weymouth. Comben was the only Portlander who dared to frequent the dockside taverns of the town when naval ships were in the bay, for his Trinity House pass gave him immunity from the Press Gang.

"Pipit told me to go over and see if I could find one," Comben said, pointing to the handbill. "It were'nt very difficult, for there were several about. But I took that from The Boot, because I've known Uriah go in there."

"There's none on the Island," Shadrick Stone reported: "But how to stop Uriah leaving it baffles me."

They fell into dejected silence which was only broken by the arrival of Pipit Pierce, who stepped briskly into the room saying: "I know I'm a bit behindhand, but I've been down at the ferry with Joe Gorman. I've worked out a possible scheme and wanted to find out if he'd agree to it. Well, he did — though he wasn't that keen on it. So all we need now are several of us who are strong swimmers, some furniture, a horse and cart and a stormy night."

They stared at him open-mouthed, with the exception of Crabber whose seaman's knowledge gave him an inkling of what was intended: "What about the tide?" he asked sceptically, "You'll need that to be right too, won't you?"

Pipit considered this; "Yes," he agreed. "it'll need to be flooding in, so that we can fetch the body out of the Fleet and bring it back here to be buried. That way, there won't be any awkward questions asked."

"You mean you're going to tip him out of the boat!" exclaimed Isaac Stone gleefully.

"Certainly not — this is an accident, not a murder! Everyone in the boat will have to swim for it."

The colour drained out of Willy Flann's face as he glanced round the group and realised with horror what his part in the drama was likely to be. He instantly regretted his reputation as a fine swimmer: "You realise it's December," he gulped. "The water will be mighty cold."

"I know, that's why we'll need the horse and two strong men on the sandspit. I think we've got a good chance of survival, but Uriah'll succumb for a certainty."

"And more than likely Joe will too," put in Matthew: "I'm not surprised he hadn't much stomach for the scheme."

"I've promised Joe I'll bring him off safely, and you can trust me to do it," replied Pipit. "I know it's risky, but can any of you think of a better plan?"

"It might work," said Crabber slowly, "but we don't need a stormy night, just a dark one and two horses would be better than one."

Pipit called for more ale and they settled down to work out the details of the plan. Several hours later when they were about to leave the inn, Pipit handed Crabber the handbill saying: "You'd better show this to the Captain, but mind you, not a word to him about our plan. It would be just like a kimberlin to throw a rub in the way of what's been done for his own sake!"

Crabber laughed: "I daresay you're right and he would think of some objection, though I never think of him as a kimberlin now."

The handbill only served to increase John's worries. He had taken what steps he could to protect Hudson by warning him

197

not to leave the plateau, and by painstakingly coaching him in the details of his imaginary past at Wanworth in case he should be questioned. He had also felt it necessary to take Mr Gilbert into his confidence. The architect (already primed by the Crown Steward) assured him of his discretion in the matter, and promised to tell him if any strangers appeared at the building site making enquiries about those employed there.

John's most difficult decision had been how much or how little to tell Elspeth. His natural inclination had been to tell her everything, for he knew he could rely upon her to support him whatever he did. But before he had an opportunity to do so, he had come across her sitting at her pianoforte, her hands clasped in her lap, an expression of such intense suffering on her face that he had moved impulsively towards her and put his arms round her shaking shoulders.

He could guess the cause of her misery for the postboy had brought a thick package to the house that morning. He had watched Elspeth search eagerly through the pile of bills, but there had been no letter from Charles amongst them, and she had turned away and limped out of the room. Holding her close to him, he had decided it would be too cruel to add to her burdens by telling her of the fresh troubles that were gathering about their heads.

Crabber had exercised no such restraint with regard to Mary's feelings, and had discussed the plans for Uriah's elimination at great length. Mary's subsequent conviction that she was about to become a widow as well as a mother did stop him telling her about the manifestation on the cliff; and he spent an uncomfortable few days trying to make light of the dangers involved in capsizing the ferry boat. Since he was only too well aware that the project was extremely hazardous, his efforts did little to appease her fears, and on the following Saturday afternoon she bade him a tearful farewell, firmly believing that she would never see him again.

Pipit Pierce had spent the intervening days perfecting his plans. He had purchased several items of cheap furniture in Weymouth and one handsome oak chest which had taken his fancy. With considerable forethought he filled this with several blankets and a change of clothing for himself and the other swimmers; and, when the Weymouth carrier delivered it to the Passage House on Saturday afternoon, he instructed Joe Gorman to put some of his own clothes in it before ferrying it across to the sandspit.

Joe was understandably anxious about the whole project, and would have been glad of any excuse for abandoning it, but the weather was perfect, a thin mist hung over the Island and only a light breeze disturbed the surface of the passage. Reluctantly Joe set the boat in motion for a covered cart drawn by two horses was approaching from the southern side. On landing Pipit assured himself that nothing had been forgotten, and issued his last instructions to Matthew and the Stone brothers who were attaching one end of a long coil of rope to the cable post. Crabber and Willy Flann lifted the coil onto the ferry and paid it out as Joe guided them back to the northern shore to await the arrival of the sexton.

The Passage House had never been noted for its comfort, but on that damp December evening it seemed more cheerless than usual. They tried to while away the time by playing cards, but the tension ruffled their tempers and they gave up the game in anger. The smouldering fire gave out very little heat, but when Crabber went down on his knees to blow it up, he only succeeded in filling the room with smoke.

"Oh, give over!" exclaimed Willy, coughing. "My throat's that parched already."

"That fire's never been no girt sheakes," agreed Joe gloomily. "Rum's what you need, and so do I, for I'm clammy as a cockle snail. I've got a drop under the floor here."

He bent down to prise up one of the stone slabs, but Pipit pushed him roughly back into his chair: "Fool!" he said curtly. "You won't have a chance of survival unless you're sober. Listen, there's your dog barking!"

Crabber sprang up and opened the door: "You're late, . . ." he began angrily, but the words died on his lips as he stared at the woman in the porch in consternation.

"You need to mend your manners, young man!" Joanna Brigstock wagged an admonishing finger at him and stepped into the room: "Why, whatever is the matter?" she cried, for rage and chagrin was plainly visible on all their faces.

"The time's the matter," exclaimed Crabber seizing her arm. "We've been here two hours or more waiting for Uriah. Where is he?"

"In bed with the ague, and you take your hands off me," she replied tartly, eying Crabber with dislike. "It's Joe I've come to see; to tell him Uriah won't be fit to come over to the Island for a week. He looked right poorly when he arrived this morning, but he would insist on going into Weymouth. Shaking like a leaf he was, when he got back on the fish cart. I told him he'd been a fool to go, but he said it had been 'worth his while' and then collapsed in a heap at my feet!"

"I'm sorry to hear it, Mrs Brigstock," said Pipit diplomatically. Determined to conciliate the affronted widow, he embarked on a long explanation about Willy and Crabber helping him with the load of furniture, ending: "And we much appreciate your coming out at night, so that we need wait no longer."

Much gratified by his understanding, Mrs Brigstock showed alarming signs of settling down for a good gossip, but Crabber's manifest impatience made her change her mind and she took her leave with an acid reference to young people having no respect for their elders these days.

The door had hardly closed behind her before Crabber and Willy gave vent to their fury and frustration, but they were cut short by Pipit: "Stubble it!" he ordered. "Sooner or later we're sure to sink the b---. But let's hope we succeed next Saturday, for what I want to know is what did Uriah find out in Weymouth that was 'wortl his while'."

The implications of his words effectively stopped their grumbling, and they set about dismantling their carefully made preparations in sullen silence; with the exception of Joe, who was exasperatingly cheerful as he ferried them over to the sandspit with reckless speed, for he was only too anxious to be rid of the Portlanders.

When he returned to the Passage House Joe bolted the door carefully, extracted a bottle of rum from his secret hoard and celebrated his release from the immediate prospect of a horrible death, by drinking himself into a stupor.

Chapter 21

With the approach of Christmas Elspeth found her determination to be cheerful sorely tried. There was still no news from Charles, and she missed George and Maria so much that it was only with great difficulty that she restrained herself from quarrelling with John on this vexed subject again. She had not done so, because on each occasion that she had longed to release her feelings in this way, she had caught a withdrawn and brooding expression on her brother's face and had sensed that he, too, was under considerable strain.

The kitchen community was not very cheerful either. Twice in the past week she had found Mary in floods of tears, while Hudson looked positively haunted, though this she could understand, because John had told her that the *Newcastle* was anchored in Weymouth Bay.

Everything, she thought gloomily, seemed to be conspiring to add to the general air of despondency hanging over the house including the weather, which on this particular Saturday morning, could only be described as sullen. A chill wind penetrated the casement of her morning room, the deep ruts in the road outside the house were filled with pools of murky water left by the overnight rain, and the sea stretched away to merge with the lowering sky in an undefined expanse of greyness.

Elspeth shivered, she did not care for driving out in such weather but her Christmas gifts must be delivered this morning for tomorrow would be Christmas Eve. She limped resolutely towards the bell rope, but before she reached it there was a light tap on the door and Skinner entered the room: "Could you come to Mary, Miss Elspeth? She started her labour early this morning, and is in great pain."

By late afternoon Mary's child had still not been delivered and she was suffering from bouts of delirium. Elspeth wished that she had followed her own inclination and sent for the accoucheur from Melcombe, but when she had suggested this to Crabber at mid-day he had vehemently refused to let her do so, saying that his aunt, Martha Wiggatt, was an experienced midwife and would be able to do all that was necessary.

Afraid that she had unwittingly offended against some Island custom, Elspeth had retired to the stillroom to prepare a cooling draught for Mary. When she returned she found that Mary's fever had increased and she cried out continually for Crabber, who, Martha abruptly informed her, had left the house to help her husband and Pipit Pierce with a load of furniture.

Something in Martha's manner warned Elspeth not to probe further, but as she watched Mary toss restlessly on the bed between her spasms of pain she began to fear for the safety of both mother and child and dared not leave the sickroom when dinner was announced by Skinner, who was supervising Betsy Attwoll's culinary efforts in the kitchen. Braving Martha's anger, Elspeth asked Skinner to find out if Crabber had returned yet as he was urgently needed at Mary's side. A few minutes later Elspeth heard her brother's voice at the door, with a sigh of relief she hurried out to meet him.

"Elspeth, my dear, you must come down to dinner. You have had nothing to eat all day and will be quite knocked up."

"I cannot leave now. Mary is seriously ill and is rapidly growing weaker. I have just given her some boiled hyssop syrup to try to bring on the birth; if the child is not born soon it will be too late to save either of them. Has Crabber come back yet?"

"I did not know he had gone out. Where did he go?"

"To help Matthew and Pipit Pierce with a load of furniture, or so Martha says, but I do not believe a word of it. John, something extraordinary is going on, for Mary keeps crying out for Crabber and muttering some nonsense about him being drowned at the ferry with Willy Flann."

"Drowned at the ferry! Is she delirious?"

"Yes, but because there is something on her mind, and Martha will tell me nothing. Other names come into her raving too, Isaac and Shadrick — they are the Stone brothers, aren't they? And Heap the sexton."

"The sexton!?"

The inflexion in his voice made Elspeth catch his arm: "John. You *do* know what is happening! You must tell me about it!"

He shook his head. "I wish I did know. I have heard some news which concerns Heap, but how it could be connected with this rigmarole about furniture and the ferry, I cannot imagine. However I will go down there now and find out."

"Not now, it is dark!" she protested, but at that moment Martha came to the door: "Miss Elspeth, can you help me? The child is coming at last!"

John rode down the hill to Fortuneswell as fast as the treacherous conditions would allow. He could not imagine what the Islanders could be doing at the ferry, but one thing had struck him immediately Elspeth had mentioned the names of those involved. With the exception of Pipit Pierce, who, he recalled, had been ill at the time, all of them had been with him at the French ambush at Mutton Cove. He knew that they had all sworn to be revenged on Boisson, but surely the Frenchman could not be landing smuggled goods at the ferry, or could he? If so, what sort of trap could they have set for him there, and how did Heap fit into such a scheme?

Was Heap himself the key to the mystery? John knew that all the Portlanders disliked him, but why should they set a trap for him at the dangerous Smallmouth passage instead of waylaying him somewhere on the Island, where any one of them could have disposed of the man without needing the help of half a dozen of his fellows? And why should they suddenly want to dispose of him; if the sexton had discovered Hudson's identity and planned to reveal it to the authorities, John could understand that the Islanders might resent this, but surely they could not think that any official action would be taken against them?

Could their minds be working like this because, if so, the risks they were running now stemmed initially from his own action in rescuing Hudson, and Hudson's story was an indirect consequence of his own loyalty to the Admiral. All this brought the rightness of his damnable principles into question again

John thought bitterly, but as he guided his mount onto the sandy track past the 'mare' he was jerked out of his self-persecution by the sound of distant shouting. He spurred the horse into a gallop for ahead of him wavering beams of light shone faintly through the enveloping darkness.

The sand muffled the sound of the animal's hooves and John was amongst the Portlanders before they were aware of anyone approaching, for the scene at the water's edge was only lit by the feeble glow of two lanterns, one swinging from the cable-post the other from the canopy of a covered cart.

The tide was flooding in from the Roads, deepening and widening the passage as it gathered momentum from the surging water piled up in Weymouth Bay by the overnight storm. Joe Gorman was lying in a crumpled heap near the cable-post from which a length of rope dangled ending in a noose encircling his body. Matthew was shouting encouragement to his horses who were straining at their collars to pull ashore the upturned ferry boat. The head of the boat was already grinding on the sand, but the stern was swinging in the strong current, and clinging to it, striving desperately to find a foothold in the swirling water, was Willy Flann.

As Matthew lashed his beasts to greater effort, John rode forward to help Isaac Stone who had waded knee-deep into the shifting shallows and was heaving with all his bull-like strength upon a second rope running from the cable-post. Crabber was a powerful swimmer but the icy water was numbing his limbs and he could no longer do battle with the relentless current. Bearing all his weight down against the saddle, John drove his frightened horse into the water and turned it on a parallel course with the shore. As the eddying current pulled the rope taut across the animal's chest swinging Crabber against its flanks, John reached down from the saddle and grasped the noose about his waist. Crabber flung up his arm and seized hold of the flowing mane and the horse plunged back to the safety of the sandspit.

John saw with relief that Joe and Willy had been revived and were busy stripping off their soaking clothes by the cart, but of Pipit Pierce, Shadrick Stone or the sexton there was no sign: "Where's your brother?" he shouted to Isaac.

"Over the dune, helping Pipit," the quarryman replied pointing westwards and starting to run in that direction himself.

Between the sandspit and the Chesil Beach the waters of the Fleet formed a shallow lake; as John galloped past Isaac the clouds parted and the young moon cast a pale light across the rippling water revealing struggling figures on its seaward edge. Without hesitation John urged his horse into the water again for he knew there was no strong current to contend with here. The horse splashed through the shallows, but although it was soon forced to swim, the flooding water carried it effortlessly towards the beach where John could see two men pulling an inert body onto the shingle. Shadrick turned at the sound of hooves crunching on the shingle: "Captain!" he gasped, his jaw dropping in surprise. He paused and then asked hoarsely: "The others — are they safe?"

"Yes, they're safe," replied John, dismounting. "But Heap is dead, I suppose."

Shadrick was stunned into silence, but Pipit Pierce who had been searching through the pockets of the corpse, rose holding out a sodden paper: "Ay, he's dead," he said grimly, "and it's lucky the rest of us aren't too, with the tide flooding in and capsizing the boat." He paused and looked John squarely in the face. "An accident, that's what it was, but you'd best take this, Captain, and burn it . . . your man will be safe amongst us now."

An hour later John reached the Girt House and went straight in search of Elspeth: "John," she cried, "I am so thankful to see you. Did you find Crabber? Is he safe?"

"Yes, he's safe and will be here shortly. I will tell you everything later. Is Mary all right?"

"The child, a healthy girl, was born shortly after you left, but Mary is very weak and cannot rest for anxiety. I told her that you had gone to find Crabber, so could you come yourself to tell her that all is well?"

The girl in the bed opened her eyes and clutched John's arm wildly: "He's dead isn't he?" The weak voice verged on the edge of hysteria. "I know he's dead and my little mite is fatherless!"

"Nonsense," he replied, smiling down at the scarlet scrap of humanity cradled in her arm, "Crabber is very much alive, and is hastening back to see his beautiful daughter."

So the Wiggatts' Christmas was a joyous one, and although Elspeth could not share their lightness of heart, she did feel truly thankful that John and Hudson had been relieved of the greater part of their anxieties. But the New Year brought the postboy at last, with a thick package from America containing the wonderful news that the campaign was over. Charles wrote that after innumerable delays, and the setback of a reconnoitring party of English troops being cut up with the loss of 300 men, the Virginians had entered Fort Duquesne on 25 November, to find it a smoking ruin — the French having set fire to it before retreating the previous day.

The success had induced the Indians to sue for peace, and a conference, which he would have to attend, was to be held in Pennsylvania in the spring. In the meantime, as the army was engaged in rebuilding the fort, the only Christmas gift he could obtain for her was of Indian work. Elspeth lifted the exquisitely-made slippers of softest doeskin from their wrapping, and laughed shakily to herself as she recalled Mary's forebodings about tar and feathers.

Her peace of mind restored, Elspeth forbore to tax John with the vexatious question of the children, and when in the spring it became known that the Duc de Choiseul, the energetic prime minister of France, was building a fleet of flat-bottomed boats in preparation for an invasion, she felt thankful she had not done so.

The threat of invasion intensified during those summer months of 1759. Intelligence reports brought news of fifty thousand French troops being massed along the Channel coast and the militia was called out; but for Elspeth the summer days were happy ones for the major building work of the house was finished in June, and her time was fully occupied in the delightful task of choosing the furniture and decorations, and considering schemes for the laying out of the garden.

She was too busy to think about the consequences of an attack on Portland, but John, mindful of those hidden French guns at the cove, was only too well aware of the strategic importance of the Island. He said nothing to Elspeth, and as it was glorious summer weather, she did not think it unusual that he should spend much of his time sailing round the southern half of the Island with Crabber. She did not guess that he was studying all possible landing places and discussing their defence with the Governor and the Crown Steward.

The attic floor of the new house had been made into an observatory, and in July John set up a large telescope there. Scanning the Channel from this commanding position, John was glad that his children were safely at Wanworth and fervently wished that Charles Mason would return to claim his sister before the sails of the French fleet were sighted.

The telescope became a source of endless fascination for Crabber, but John guessed that it was not only patriotic fervour that caused Crabber to spend long hours in the observatory — the French sails the young boatman was really interested in sighting were those of a certain black-hulled brig — the *Marie-Louise*.

Chapter 22

"Cor! That's primer, that is!"

Dingle looked up from giving a final polish to one of the brass side-lamps of Elspeth's new curricle, which Will was studying with open-mouthed admiration: "As handsome an equipage for an invalid lady as you could find anywhere," he agreed, running an expert eye over the immaculate vehicle drawn by a matched pair of grey ponies. He turned his attention to Will and added grimly: "And mind you behave yourself if you're to ride on the rumble. Keep your back straight and fold your arms, as I've taught you! Where's your hat?"

Will reluctantly produced an unworn, but dust-laden black hat from his wicker basket; "I hate wearing a hat!"

"Maybe you do, but you aren't driving out with me improperly dressed." Dingle dusted the offending article vigorously, and handed it back: "Put it on, and mind you find these herbs Miss Elspeth wants — things aren't too well with her, so I want her to enjoy her drive this morning."

"I'll do my best. Do you think that Mr Mason's ever coming back?"

"It's not for me to say, or you either." But the severity of his tone had no effect on the irrepressible Will.

"Well, I hope he ain't deserted Miss Elspeth. He's been gone near on three years, and there weren't no invasion to stop him coming back last winter. Gone to New York, Mrs Wiggatt tells me. I 'spose there's hundreds of good lookers there!"

These sentiments so exactly echoed his own that Dingle was unable to think of a suitably damping reply, but at that moment Elspeth appeared on the steps of the portico, and with a terse admonition to Will to "Hold their heads!" he hurried forward to lift his mistress into the carriage.

It was a glorious September morning, but Elspeth was in low spirits. Yesterday had been her twenty-sixth birthday, and she feared she was rapidly fading into an old maid for Charles showed no signs of returning to England. After attending the Peace Conference in Pennsylvania he had undertaken a variety of missions as a legal representative of the Virginia Assembly, and was obviously carving a successful career for himself.

Elspeth was haunted by the fear that he had come to feel that a crippled wife would prove a hindrance to his career. There was nothing in his letters to support this depressing thought — nothing except that she had not heard from him for three months, and he had always remembered her birthday before.

John's present had been the new curricle, which had been built to his special design by Mr Miles, the coachbuilder in Dorchester. It was low-slung, with a broad, detachable step to enable Dingle to lift her into it. To show how much she appreciated this generous gift, Elspeth had decided to drive over to Church Ope taking Will to collect plants from the cliffs. Now that they were comfortably settled in the new house she found time hung heavily on her hands, but fresh ingredients for her herbal remedies were always needed.

She stopped the curricle in the shade of the old castle, but Will, instead of running to the ponies's heads, sat staring at a dilapidated ketch at anchor in the bay, her peeling paint and grimy sails proclaiming her humble status as an ore carrier.

"That's a queer set-up!" he exclaimed, with all the Portlander's instinctive mistrust of strangers: "They're putting someone ashore."

"Some mealy-mouthed stone merchant too mean to hire a horse to ride up the hill, I suppose," said Dingle, disgustedly. "I'd best go down and find out which quarry the man wants. You get busy with those plants, Will."

Will reluctantly picked up his basket and set off on his appointed task. Dingle helped Elspeth to a comfortable rock seat and then made his way over the headland. Elspeth leant back against the warm rock, thinking how happily Dingle had adapted himself to the Portland way of life. Since his marriage to Betty Attwoll, nine months ago, he had even come to think like an Islander, regarding all strangers as intruders. It would be impossible to ask him to uproot himself again and accompany her to America, though it now seemed only too likely that the question would never arise.

She sighed and gazed out at the sparkling water of the bay. The battered little ketch was swinging serenely at her mooring, but the rowing boat had disappeared from sight behind the bluff of the cliff. If only it was Charles they were rowing ashore she thought? And then chided herself for being so foolish, for the ketch was far too frail a craft to have crossed the ocean.

Unaccountable tears stung her eyelids; she brushed them away and determined to go home. What could Dingle and Will be loitering for?

"Dare I hope you weep for me, my love?"

She looked round unbelievingly at the sound of that beloved voice.

He was standing a little above her, regarding her with the enigmatic smile that she remembered so well.

"Charles! Charles! My darling, is it really you!"

She attempted to rise, but he leapt down to the ledge and lifted her into his arms, holding her close. She put her arms round his neck and raised her face invitingly, all her radiance restored. He brought his mouth hard down against hers, and so they remained a long while.

Later when they were seated together on a sun-warmed ledge she asked wonderingly: "Charles, how did you come here? Surely not in that battered old boat?"

"Battered old boat be damned! I landed at Plymouth on Tuesday and was determined to arrive here some time on Wednesday. She was the only craft available for hire, so I promised her master fifty guineas if he could make the passage in twenty-four hours, but we were becalmed." He read the confusion in her face and added, teasingly: "Oh, little faithless one, you thought I had forgotten your birthday!"

He drew a small leather box out of his pocket and closed her fingers over it. When she opened it the sun's rays flashed against the facets of the deep-blue sapphire, colouring the surrounding diamonds in a blaze of iridescent light.

Elspeth lifted shining eyes to Charles: "What can I say, except thank you! For you already know that I love you and belong to you alone."

"And I adore you, delight of my heart. How soon can you marry me?"

"Whenever you wish, . . . But where shall we be married? The new church is not finished yet?"

"In the ruined church of course. I should like to be married here at the Cove — the scene of the adventure that brought us together." He grinned boyishly at her: "You must just pray it won't rain, my love!"

"Indeed I will — fervently! Splashing up the aisle through pools of water is not my idea of romance — but I do not know if the old church is still licenced for marriages."

"No matter, I'll buy a special licence in London." He took both her hands in a firm clasp: "I must leave you next week, but my business in London will only detain me for a few days. The *Hampton* sails from Greenwich at the end of the month; she is a comfortable ship and I know her master quite well. If you agree, he will come into Weymouth Bay and pick us up."

"I shall be ready." She laughed shakily: "John was right. He said that when you came you would want no delay."

"John is very discerning. He sees all and says little. Shall we go and tell him our news?"

Trotting homewards across the plateau, Charles's eyes were immediately drawn to the imposing stone house flanked by two wings, standing on the far cliffs. "By Jove, Elspeth, the house looks splendid! I'm determined to explore every nook and cranny of it, from the attics to the cellars."

Elspeth chuckled: "You'd best not tell John you want to see the 'attics.' He has made the whole of the upper floor into an observatory, complete with a telescope, and spends hours of his time up there."

"As well you warned me. I don't wish to prejudice my chances of gaining his consent to our marriage."

"Stupid!" she said lovingly. "Of course, he will be delighted that I am going to marry you. The only person likely to object is Henry, so I am not going to write and tell him anything about it until after we have sailed. We don't want him posting down here, casting a damper over everything. . . . Do you like our gates?"

The deeply rutted cart track that led from Weston to Mutton Cove was now a well-made carriage drive leading to tall, delicately scrolled iron gates set in a high, dry-stone wall. These were flung open at their approach, within them the drive widened ending in a broad sweep of gravel fronting a house of ashlar stone built in the classical manner. As the curricle drew up before the fine Ionic entrance porch, the door opened and John came down the steps to greet them his face alight with pleasure.

Dinner that night was a joyous affair, Mary having risen to the occasion by serving a variety of delectable dishes to mark the household's approval of the match. Elspeth chattered happily about all the arrangements that must be made, but John was not surprised to notice faint lines of exhaustion about her eyes, for she had insisted on showing Charles all over the house herself, even climbing the curved stone staircase to the observatory. It had been a delightful afternoon, for Charles had been immensely enthusiastic over all that had been done, and indeed, the product of Elspeth's imagination and John's practicality was a house of character, charm and comfort, in which no detail from the wig cupboards to the new-fangled water closets had been overlooked.

So when asked to endorse a scheme for sailing over to Weymouth the next day to show Charles some of the interesting buildings in the town, John said, with marked lack of enthusiasm: "It might not be possible — the wind has risen considerably this evening."

His tone caused Charles to look up from pouring himself a second glass of port, and a quick glance of understanding passed between the two men.

Charles rose and went to Elspeth's chair: "Then that settles the matter. I've already suffered a surfeit of choppy seas this past six weeks and should much prefer to spend the morning riding out with John to inspect the lighthouses and the quarries. And you, my love, will rest, or you will be quite done up before entering the married state, let alone embarking on a long and arduous voyage immediately afterwards."

John's prediction regarding the weather was right, for the next morning a sharp wind was blowing as the two men cantered across the Great West field towards the lighthouses. The Brethren of Trinity House had ordered the two lighthouses to be built in 1716 to try and reduce the number of wrecks in this dangerous area of the English Channel. They were sited north and south of each other to help navigators to avoid the notorious Portland Race and the Shambles, a bank of sand four miles south-east of the Bill.

The keeper, Richard Comben, was delighted to see visitors approaching, for the southern end of the Island was uninhabited and apart from a few shepherds he seldom had the chance of a friendly gossip to relieve the tedium of his work. Coal fires provided the lights and carrying the fuel up the twisting, spiral stairs was an arduous and never-ending labour.

However the news that Mr Mason had at last returned to claim the Captain's sister had reached the lighthouse, and Comben offered his congratulations to Charles, saying, somewhat disconcertingly, that he had often watched him and Miss Elspeth picnicking near the Sturt: "Out on the east cliff you used to sit, sir. I took note it was Miss Elspeth's curricle 'cos there aren't many folks come out this way nowadays."

He mounted the spiral stairs rapidly as he spoke, so Charles, following breathlessly behind, was spared the necessity of answering.

At last they reached the top and came out onto the rickety balcony that encircled the building. From here the view extended halfway across the Channel, and Comben pointed out to Charles the position of the Shambles and explained the tidal movements of the turbulent waters of the Race. It was necessary to shout to hear one another against the rising wind, and the spume from the waves breaking over the rocks reached them on the balcony.

Comben turned to go inside, saying: "If the wind backs South or South-West, there'll be a mighty lot of water in the Bay to-night. You ought to take Mr Mason to see the Blow Hole later, Captain. He should hear the voices clear then."

"What did he mean by voices at the Blow Hole?" Charles asked John as they rode back towards Southwell.

"The Blow Hole is a deep natural shaft. In rough weather the spray comes right up the shaft. The noise is tremendous — a peculiar, eerie sound. The Islanders believe it is the souls of the drowned crying out to the living."

"They sound as superstitious as the Indians."

"They are." A smile hovered about the corners of John's mouth: "Didn't you notice the bay trees planted either side of the iron gates, and at the entrance porch?"

"I did, and wondered why you had put them there?"

"They are to keep away evil spirits."

This startling pronouncement momentarily disconcerted Charles: "You can't believe that!?"

"I don't," replied John, amused at the other's concern: "But the Islanders do, and as no good purpose could be achieved by ignoring such customs I obtained some. The planting of them was attended by a general display of goodwill, not, I think, untinged with relief."

"I can see why you are revered here," said Charles thoughtfully.

"I don't know about that," replied John. "But Elspeth and I recognised that these people have many admirable qualities. They are hard-working, intelligent and law-abiding, and by making the best use of the natural resources of this peninsula they have created a standard of life far superior to that of their fellows on the mainland. Our object was to live in harmony with them."

In the late afternoon they set out to visit the Blow Hole. On their way across the garden, they met Crabber returning from an inspection of his boat, which he had winched to safety on a sheltered ledge earlier in the day.

"Mr Mason wishes to go to the Blow Hole," explained John. "You'd best come with us, and tell him something of its history."

Nothing loth, for the phenomenon exercised an unending fascination for him, Crabber nodded and held open the gate leading onto the broad cliff path. The three men fought their way towards the Bill in silence, all their energy being directed in remaining upright against the force of the wind. Dark clouds had gathered over the West Bay, and scuds of rain hit their faces horizontally, stinging like so many malevolent wasps, so that they were glad to reach the slight shelter afforded by the concave depression.

The shape of the depression reminded Charles of a dewpond, but the earth around the shaft was bare, the grass having been killed by the rising spray. The three men knelt and gazed down at the raging water far below.

The noise was indescribable, for above the booming thunder of the sea siphoned through a narrow cleft, came a curious high-pitched wailing sound unlike anything that Charles had ever heard. The booming thunder was continuous, but the wailing was intermittent, striking against the ear-drums in unexpected savagery.

Suddenly Crabber leapt back, his face ashen, and his eyeballs dilating wildly: "It's Mark!" he cried. "Mark, calling there!"

"Nonsense!" replied John crisply. "Mark was killed, not drowned."

"No matter," Crabber muttered. "You know as well as I do, Captain, he still waits to be avenged!" And with this cryptic utterance he strode off in the direction of his uncle's house in Weston.

"That eerie wailing was the voice he heard, I suppose," said Charles, staring after the retreating figure of the boatman.

"Yes, though it is usually ascribed to the crying of the drowned," replied John phlegmatically. "I'm soaked to the skin! If you've seen enough, I suggest we get back to the house while we can still stand against the wind."

It was almost six o'clock when they reached the house to find that Elspeth, having ordered the dinner to be put back one hour, had gone to change her dress. They stripped off their soaking outer garments and retired to their bedchambers to relax in steaming hip baths before blazing fires. An hour later

216

John tapped on his guest's door to enquire if he was ready, and together they descended the curving stone staircase to the library, but to their surprise, Elspeth was not there.

She joined them some ten minutes later, saying: "Whatever happened at the Blow Hole? There has been such an upset in the kitchen! Crabber has not come home, but Martha has come over from Weston with an extraordinary story about Crabber hearing Mark calling, and he and Matthew have gone off to The Lugger. Luckily Martha has offered to stay here to help Mary, who is quite distracted — but I cannot think we shall have a very good dinner."

"How tiresome!" John sounded unusually irritable. He told her what had occurred, ending: "The trouble is the boy can't get Mark's death out of his mind . . . However I don't suppose anything will come of it. The wailing sounded much as usual to me."

The dinner, if it did not comply with Elspeth's rigorously high culinary standards, was excellent enough, and as the noise of the rising wind did not penetrate the solid stone walls the three soon forgot the troubles in the kitchen and the wildness of the night.

Elspeth was looking radiant; she had chosen to wear a gown of deep-blue velvet which matched the glowing sapphire in her ring. The soft candlelight burnished her red-gold hair and enhanced the beauty of her flawless skin. She sat opposite her brother at the circular, mahogany table listening to the male talk of military campaigns with serene contentment. It had been her dearest wish that Charles and her brother should like one another, and to see them so obviously enjoying each other's company, brought her supreme happiness. She decided to retire early and leave them to re-live their battles over the port.

They fell in with this scheme readily enough, for they were deeply engrossed in discussing that ever-fruitful topic, bitterly engraved on the hearts of all serving officers — the gross interference of incompetent government officials who knew nothing of the situation in the field. It was many hours later, when the third bottle of port was empty, that they reluctantly decided it was time to collect their night-candles from the table in the hall.

It seemed to Charles that he had hardly laid his head upon the pillows before he was wakened by an urgent knocking, that was repeated at his host's door. He hurried across the landing to find John hastily pulling on his clothes in the pale, grey light.

"There's a ship in trouble off First Beach. Do you want to come out with me?"

"Of course! Give me two minutes."

In the stableyard Dingle had three horses saddled; in silence they made their way across the Great West field and galloped over the Sturt to find a crowd of men already assembled on the cliff.

The wind had veered to the south during the previous evening, piling up a huge accumulation of water in the West Bay, and now with the turn of the tide, a tremendous sea was flooding round the Bill. The dull, grey sky was streaked with long, rolling banks of dark cloud, giving sinister warning of heavy squalls of rain.

It was one such squall, John thought, that must have been the undoing of the stricken brig plunging and rolling in the troughs of the savage waves off the tiny inlet known as First Beach. Her foremast had gone leaving her shrouds trailing in a tangled mass, and even as they dismounted, a huge wave poured over her cascading along her deck; but before it had reached her stern the approaching squall burst upon her from her starboard quarter, heeling her over until her deck was almost vertical, snapping her mainmast with a crack like muffled gunfire. The rain descended in sheets, obliterating the brig from view and soaking the watchers on the cliff.

"Are all hands lost?" shouted Charles to a young man hurrying past him carrying a coil of rope and a grappling iron.

"Oh, ay," he replied indifferently, climbing down over the rocks to the stony beach lined with men waiting to seize what plunder they could when the doomed ship broke up.

But one man was living — as the squall passed they saw the brig perilously close to the arm of rock runing out from the base of the cliff. She was still afloat, wallowing in a deep trough, and lashed to the stump of her mainmast they could see the figure of a man.

The figure moved, gesticulating wildly to the watchers on the beach. The men there had formed themselves into a human chain, bound together with rope, and the two leaders, who John recognised as Crabber and Shadrick Stone, were making their way out onto the wave-washed ledge, using their grappling hooks to steady themselves against the force of the upthrown spray. The figure on the brig strove to unloosen his lashings, slashing desperately at the tight, salted coils. At last he freed himself, and bound by one single coil round his waist, staggered across the deck expecting a rope to be thrown. But the men on the ledge remained immobile, watching his struggle with cynical unconcern. The man fell to his knees, imploring them for help, his despairing cries borne on the wind to those gathered on the cliff.

Charles leapt forward impulsively, shouting: "Why don't they do something? We must get down there!"

John started to follow him, but as the brig plunged through the crest of an incoming wave her stern rose revealing her name — *Marie-Louise*. He caught Charles's arm, restraining him. "There is nothing we can do. This is their affair — it's Boisson!"

Water poured over the deck engulfing the kneeling man and smashing him up against the bulwarks, only to be jerked back like a lifeless puppet as the water receded.

A huge wave towered above the starboard bow driving the *Marie-Louise* to her end against the submerged ledge with a hideous rending of strong oak. The cascading torrent splintered the stump of the mast releasing the coiled rope; it flew outwards, hurling the inert body into the foaming sea to be crushed between the ruptured planking and the rocks.

Only then did the Islanders spring to activity, the foremost men, immersed in ice-cold spray, working waist-deep in the swirling water to rescue the precious timbers needed for their houses.

As the group of elderly men on the cliff dispersed to assist in carrying away the plunder, John found Matthew at his elbow:

"This is a good hour for all of us, Captain. Mark's death avenged, and Mr Mason safely returned to claim Miss Elspeth."

Charles took the old carter's extended hand and shook it warmly. "I suppose Crabber will always believe it was Mark's voice he heard at the Blow Hole . . . I must say it was uncanny!"

"Ay," agreed Matthew, turning to survey the salvage work with obvious satisfaction. "The wheels of God grind slowly but they grind exceeding small."

*   *   *   *   *   *   *   *   *   *   *   *   *   *

SOURCES

Admiralty Files. A.D.M. 2/76, 2/157, 2/518, 3/64. (Public Record Office).

Dorset Recipes from Manuscripts. (D60/74 Dorset County Record Office).

Mrs C. Durston, List of Portland Wild Flowers.

Exhibition of 18th Century Conversation Pieces. (Loan Exhibition, Fermoy Art Gallery 1976).

Harvey's Guide to Weymouth 1800. (Weymouth Public Library).

Map of Dorset (1789). (Weymouth Public Library).

Map of Dorset (1825). (Weymouth Public Library).

Map of Portland. (Webb) (1800). (Public Record Office).

Map of Portland. ((Wyld) Sansom Documents. (Dorset County Record Office).

Sansom Documents. (Dorset County Record Office).

Sansom Documents. (Bodleian Library, Oxford).

Rev. Edward Stukeley, Diary, extract for 23 August, 1723. (Bodleian Library, Oxford).

John Upham, Watercolours. 1821. (Weymouth and Portland Borough Council).

BIBLIOGRAPHY

Janet Arnold, *Patterns of Fashion* (Patterns taken from original specimens), Vol. 1 (1977).

C. Aspinall-Oglander, *Admiral's Wife* (Life and Letters of Mrs Edward Boscawen) (1940).

William Barnes, *A Glossary of the Dorset Dialect with a Grammar* (1886).

J. H. Betty, *Island and Royal Manor of Portland* (1970).

Maureen Boddy, *Dorset Shipwrecks 877-1974* (Dorset Magazine).

Iris Brooke, *History of English Costume* (1949).

Lord Brougham, *Statesmen of the Times of George III* (Vol. 1, 1839).

J. S. Buckingham, *A Summer Trip to Weymouth and Dorchester including an Excursion to Portland* (1842).

Elizabeth Burton, *The Georgians at Home* (1967).

E. J. Climenson (editor), *Diary of Mrs Lybbe Powys, 1756-1808* (1899).

G. de Courtais, *Women's Headdress and Hair Styles* (1973).

Peter Cunningham (editor), *The Letters of Horace Walpole 1756-1762* (Vol. 3 1856).

C. W. and P. Cunnington, *Handbook of English Costume in the 18th Century* (1972).

P. Cunnington, *Costume of Household Servants* (1974).

Dictionary of National Biography.

T. C. Edwards and B. Richardson (editors), *They Saw it Happen* (1958).

Dorset Archaeological Society—various volumes.

David Erskine (editor), *Augustus Hervey's Journal* (1953).

J. T. Flexner, *Washington. The Indispensable Man* (1976).

M. D. George, *London Life in the 18th Century* (1965).

E. Gillett (editor), *Elizabeth Ham by Herself, 1783-1820* (1945).

Ronald Good, *The Old Roads of Dorset* (1966).

J. A. Gotch, *The Growth of the English House* (1909).

A Guide to the Museum of Local History, Weymouth (1975).

J. Hutchins, *A History of Dorset* (First edition, 1774).

J. Hutchins, *A History of Dorset* (Third edition, 1863).

Inventory of Historical Monuments in Dorset (Vol. 2 S.E. Part 2, 1970).

Derek Jarrett, *England in the Age of Hogarth* (1976).

Sir Charles Lyell, F.R.S., *A Second Visit to the United States* (1849).

Hugh McCausland, *The English Carriage* (1948).

A. T. Mahan, *The Influence of Sea Power upon History* (1889).

R. B. Nye and J. E. Morpurgo, *A History of the United States* (Vol. 1, 1965).

George Osborn, *Exploring Ancient Dorset* (1976).

E. W. Otter (editor), *A Southwell Maid's Diary* (1930).

A. Parreaux, *Daily Life in the Reign of George III* (1969).

R. Pierce, *Methodism in Portland* (1898).

William Pitt, Earl of Chatham, *Correspondence*, edited by the executors of his son John, Earl of Chatham, from the original mss in their possession, 1838. Vol. 1.

Dudley Pope, *At 12 Mr Byng was Shot* (1962).

A. Raistrick (editor), *The Hackett Diary—A Tour through the Counties of England and Scotland, 1796* (1967).

Eric Ricketts, *The Buildings of Old Weymouth* (Parts I and II, 1975, 1976).

Marion Sichel, *Costume Reference—18th Century* (1977).

J. Smeaton, *The Building of the Eddystone Lighthouse* (Second edition, 1793).

J. Stevens Cox (editor), *Dorset Dishes of the 17th Century* (1967).

J. Stevens Cox (editor), *Dorset Folk Remedies of the 17th and 18th Centuries* (1970).

Lazlo Tarr, *History of the Carriage* (1969).

Virginia (American Guide Series, Oxford University Press, New York, 1952).

J. J. Walklet, *A Window on Williamsburg* (1966).

J. W. Warren, *Island and Royal Manor of Portland* (1939).

E. Wilson, *A History of Shoe Fashions* (1969).

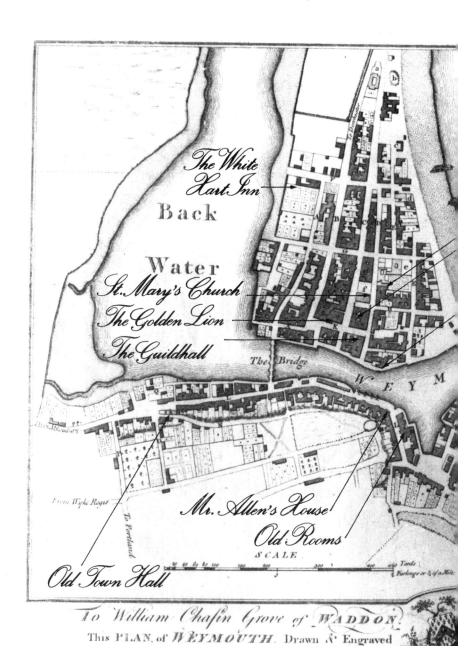

The White
Hart Inn

B a c k

W a t e r

St. Mary's Church

The Golden Lion

The Guildhall

The Bridge

W E Y M

From Wyke Regis

To Portland

Mr. Allen's House

Old Rooms

SCALE

Old Town Hall

To William Chafin Grove of WADDON.

This PLAN, of WEYMOUTH. Drawn & Engraved